ALL HALLOWS' EVIL

SARAH E. GLENN
EDITOR

Mystery and Horror, LLC
Tarpon Springs, FL

All Hallows' Evil
Copyright © 2013 by Mystery and Horror, LLC
First Trade Paperback Edition

All stories in this anthology have been printed with the
permission of the authors.

All rights reserved.

This is a work of fiction. Any resemblance to any actual
person living or dead, or to any known location is the
coincidental invention of the author's creative mind. This
includes historical events and persons who may have been
recreated in a fictional work.

ISBN-13: 978-0989007627
(Mystery and Horror, LLC)
ISBN-10: 0989007626

Printed in USA by Mystery and Horror, LLC
(www.mysteryandhorrorllc.com)

Dedication

This book is dedicated to the Staff and Volunteers of Magna Cum Murder who spend every Halloween weekend working to advance the mystery genre. Your hard work is appreciated by those who love mysteries.

ALL

HALLOWS'

EVIL

SARAH E. GLENN
EDITOR

Mystery and Horror, LLC
Tarpon Springs, FL

TABLE OF CONTENTS

Norman's Skeletons

By Gloria Alden

"It was a dark and stormy night." That beginning of the Bulwer Lytton book kept running through Angie's mind. It made sense since it was a dark and stormy night and Halloween, too. Not that she was superstitious. Angie considered herself a practical person not given to flights of fancy. Still, traveling on a back road with few houses and only trees lining the road, it seemed spooky. Especially since their bare branches bending and swaying looked like skeleton hands reaching for her car. She hoped Uncle Norman and Aunt Twyla's house would be coming up soon. Aunt Twyla had called asking her to come this weekend. She wanted the nieces and nephews to come for one last visit before they moved away. It had been years since Angie visited them.

"I'd like you all to look over things we're not taking with us and see if you'd like anything before everything is auctioned off," Aunt Twyla said.

The call surprised Angie since she'd only recently returned to Vermont. She called her brother to see if he was going, but he told her he wasn't. He didn't want any of their junk, and his wife hated that creepy place.

"Would you like me to get something for Petey? Like one of Uncle Leonard's stuffed animals? A raccoon maybe?" she'd asked.

She laughed when he gave her an emphatic 'no', and said she was only kidding. She didn't want any of Uncle Norman's stuffed critters from his taxidermy hobby nor his skeletons, either.

Her GPS spoke up, startling her after a long silence. "Turn left in .5 miles," the voice said. Angie glanced at the dashboard noting the mileage. Without a moon or lighting, it might be hard finding Uncle Norman and Aunt Twyla's driveway.

She breathed a sigh of relief when she spotted their rusted and dented mailbox. The last two letters from their name were missing, making it 'Skelet' instead of 'Skeleton'. She was always thankful it was her mother who was Uncle Norman's sibling and not her father. She'd have hated having that last name. She remembered her parents watching *The Red Skelton Show*. Of course his name wasn't spelled the same. Her dad used to tease her mom asking if she was related to him. But her mom said one skeleton in the family was enough. She wasn't sure what her mom meant, but now she wondered if it was Uncle Norman and not the TV star. He not only stuffed dead animals he found or shot in hunting season plus a few pets, but he collected animal skeletons, too. He had a museum of his collection in their old basement which would have been creepy even without his dead animals.

The driveway to the house was long with overgrown bushes on both sides. Just before she reached the farmhouse, a girl with blond hair in a blue dress jumped out in front of her car. Angie slammed on the brakes, avoiding hitting the girl. Her heart beat a rapid drum beat. *Is that Lolly? Aunt Twyla said only Marty Jr. and Elvis would be here. Did she come after all?* She lowered her window and leaned out.

"Lolly! What are you doing? You scared me to death. Not a good move jumping in front of a car, you know."

The girl stared as if in a trance, then turned and disappeared into the woods.

"Wait," Angie called out. "Don't run away." But the girl didn't return. *It must not have been Lolly, but she looks like I remember her. Of course that's been years. She'd be older now. I wonder who the girl is.*

She felt relieved to see the farmhouse when she emerged from the woods.

Good, she thought, *the lights are on inside and out. Maybe someone will know who the girl is.* Angie saw two cars parked in the driveway. *Marty Jr. and Elvis must be here,* she thought. *It would have been nice to see Lolly again. We had such fun when we stayed at Uncle Norman and Aunt Twyla's farm as kids. I wonder what she's doing now.*

She parked her car behind the others and pulled her suitcase out of the back. Before she could ring the doorbell, the door opened and Aunt Twyla greeted her with a big hug. Angie found her face pressed into Aunt Twyla's ample bosom.

"Little Angie. How good to see you after all these years. Come in and tell us all about what you've been doing. Are you hungry? Dinner's almost ready. Nothing fancy like you probably had out in California. Just plain farm food," Aunt Twyla rambled on as she took Angie's arm to lead her down the hall. "Leave the suitcase. I'll have one of the boys take it upstairs."

"It's good to see you again, too, Aunt Twyla," Angie said when her aunt paused. "How's Uncle Norman tonight?"

"Oh, not so good. As I told you on the phone, he's in a wheelchair and can't talk. He can let me know when he wants something, though." She laughed.

"Hey, boys! Look who's here," she announced as she led Angie into the sitting room.

Angie took a quick glance around the room. Nothing seemed to have changed since she was last here. Same furniture, same wallpaper, same fireplace with a fire in it tonight since it was a bit chilly. The only difference was Uncle Norman in a wheelchair. He looked much smaller and shriveled now. One side of his face drooped. She smiled at him and said, "Hello, Uncle Norman. It's nice of you to have me here to visit."

He looked at her and made a garbling unintelligible sound.

She kept her smile in place. "I have lots to tell you about what I've been doing." *But probably not about the divorce, the lost job and the house, too,* she thought.

"You two must be my cousins, Marty Jr. and Elvis. It's been so many years, I'm not sure who is who," she said.

Both had dark hair and dark eyes. The man on the couch with a trim haircut, neat chinos, a button down oxford shirt, and one foot crossed over the opposite knee spoke first.

"I'm Marty. Skip the junior." He nodded at the other man. "That's Elvis, the famous singer."

3

Angie sensed a goading undercurrent in Marty's voice. *Sibling rivalry?*

"It's good to see both of you again." She shook Elvis's hand when he struggled out of the recliner to offer his hand. Unlike his brother, he wore jeans frayed at the knees and a faded Rolling Stones T-shirt. His dark hair could use a haircut, Angie thought. "Are you really a singer?"

He nodded. "Some" was all he said before sitting back down.

Angie sat down on a chair between the two men, facing Uncle Norman. Aunt Twyla hovered in the background behind him.

"How's Lolly?" she asked looking back and forth between the two men.

She heard Aunt Twyla suck in her breath, and the boys looked away.

"Lolly disappeared many years ago," Aunt Twyla said quietly. "You didn't know?"

Angie shook her head her eyes wide with shock. "No, I didn't. No one told me. What do you mean she disappeared? When? Where?"

"It was almost fifteen years ago. She was a freshman at the University of Vermont. She didn't want to fly to Florida on Spring Break where her parents were. She had a job and couldn't get much time off. When she called and asked if she could come for a visit, we said yes, of course, but she never came."

"And she was never found?" Angie looked around at all of them. Uncle Norman stared at the floor and the others bowed their heads as if not wanting to answer.

"No," Elvis spoke up. "We haven't stopped hoping she'll be found, though. Dead or alive, we need closure."

Tears welled up in Angie's eyes. "I'm so sorry," she said fighting the tears. "No one ever told me," she repeated.

Aunt Twyla shrugged. "I told your parents. They said they'd let you know, but maybe they didn't want to upset you. You were taking some tough courses at the time, I seem to remember. I think you were having boyfriend problems, too."

Yes, I was, Angie thought, *and I never should have married him, either.*

4

"How are Uncle Martin and Aunt Sally doing?" Angie asked Marty.

"Mom and Dad moved back to Brattleboro to stay year-round now." Marty said. "Mom hasn't stopped hoping and looking. She's obsessed with Lolly's disappearance. She feels guilty because they stayed in Florida longer that winter."

"She keeps Lolly's bedroom ready and waiting just as she left it." Elvis said.

"Did the police ever find out anything?" she asked.

"Her car was found on a back road about twenty miles from here," Marty put in. "But any fingerprints were wiped clean. Elvis was a suspect for a while."

"Why?" Angie looked at Elvis, but he didn't answer.

"I was out of town and had a good alibi. Elvis was around, but he was stoned and can't remember anything about where he was that night." The disgust in Marty's voice was obvious.

The vision of the girl she almost hit popped into Angie's mind. How could she have forgotten? Without pausing to think, she blurted out. "I almost hit a girl near the house. She jumped out of the trees in front of my car." She paused as they stared at her with mouths slightly open except for Uncle Norman, who continued to stare at the floor.

"She had blond hair and was wearing a blue dress. I thought it was Lolly for a moment and then realized Lolly would be older now, and why would she run into the woods?"

Aunt Twyla shook her head emphatically. "No, that couldn't be Lolly even though we all wish it was. If Lolly were in the neighborhood she'd come to the house."

"Unless she has something to hide," Marty said.

"What do you mean by that?" Elvis glared at him.

Marty shrugged. "Maybe she got involved with some druggies and got hooked. Maybe it was one of those so called friends of yours you used to hang around with."

"Not Lolly. She wasn't into the drug scene, and I never introduced her to any of that group."

"I wonder who the girl I saw was," Angie said.

"Are you sure you didn't imagine it?" Marty asked.

Angie shook her head. "It wasn't my imagination."

"Well, it is Halloween, and they say it's the night ghosts roam about. Maybe you saw a ghost." His laugh showed he didn't believe it and was poking fun at her.

Angie glanced at Aunt Twyla and saw a frightened look on her face as she twisted her hands in her lap. *She's upset. Poor old dear. Well, it's making me nervous, too.* Angie thought. *If it wasn't a real person could I have seen a ghost? I wonder if she's seen the ghost before – if it's really a ghost.*

Taking pity on her, Angie changed the subject. "So Aunt Twyla, just where are you and Uncle Norman moving?

Aunt Twyla visibly relaxed. "We're going to the Happy Days Retirement Community in Rutland."

"Won't you miss your friends moving so far away?"

"Not many left anymore. We picked Happy Days because Norman's cousin, Eleanor, is up there. You remember her, don't you?"

Angie nodded her head and pictured the over endowed woman with a huge pile of bleached blond hair on top of her head. She wore tight clothes showing every bulge in her body.

"Well, she's up there and loves it. She said there's lots going on there all the time. They play bingo, have dances and everything." She sighed. "I need a little fun in my life."

"It sounds like you'll enjoy it," Angie said before turning to her cousins. "Where do you two live now?"

"We don't live together," Marty said. "I live in Boston. I'm an investment banker and have an apartment in a good area."

And you're an egotistical braggart, Angie thought. She turned to Elvis and smiled. "And where are you living these days?"

"He never left our town," Marty said.

Angie ignored him and kept looking at Elvis. She could see him clenching his jaw.

Finally he spoke. "I still live in Brattleboro, but I have my own apartment."

She waited for him to go on. When he didn't she turned to Aunt Twyla. "If you'll show me where my room is, I'll take my suitcase upstairs."

"Oh, you must be hungry. Dinner's almost ready. Elvis, take Angie's suitcase upstairs. She'll have the room next to yours, the blue room."

Angie said, "I can carry it up, Aunt Twyla. I remember the room."

But Elvis was already up and had her suitcase. She followed him up the steps. When he opened the door to her room and flipped on the light switch, he turned around and made a little bow. "At your service, ma'am," he said with a twinkle in his eyes.

She grinned at him. "Do you want a tip?"

"Not necessary, ma'am." He nodded and smiled.

What a difference a smile made to his face. Angie found she liked him much better than his arrogant brother. "You're nothing like your brother, are you?"

He sobered and his eyes became shuttered. "No."

She glanced beyond him to make sure Marty hadn't come up and said in a low voice. "I like you a lot better. He's rather egotistical, isn't he?"

A smile returned to Elvis's face. "That's putting it mildly."

"So now that you don't have your brother answering for you, what do you do?"

Elvis bit his bottom lip as he looked at her. Finally, he said, "I am a musician. I play a guitar in a blues band – The Brattleboro Blues Boys. I also have a music shop – All about Blues - and sell and repair instruments as well as give lessons. My apartment is over the music shop." As if picking up on the next question she wanted to ask, he said, "I live alone. I was engaged for a while. We planned on getting married once the music store took off, but she found someone who had more to offer."

Angie glanced toward the hall and stairs.

Elvis made a little face showing his disgust. "Yeah, my brother. She discovered he had more financial security. They had a fancy wedding, and she's enjoying life without working and buying just about anything catching her fancy."

"Oh, Elvis. I'm sorry." She touched his arm.

7

"Don't be sorry for me. Once I saw what was important to her, I realized I'd escaped an unhappy marriage." He smiled down at her. "And what's new with you? Why did you move back to Middlebury – that's where you are, isn't it?"

"Kind of the same thing. I got involved with the wrong kind of guy, only I married him. Now I'm thinking you were the lucky one getting out before it was too late."

"Your parents don't live there anymore, do they?"

She shook her head. "No, they're in Florida, but I still have a good friend, Becky, there. I've always stayed in contact with her, so when my life in California fell apart, she talked me into returning to Middlebury. She got me a job in the library. I found a small apartment. I thought maybe there'd be something here to help furnish it. It's rather bare right now."

He grinned at her. "Are you thinking of some of Uncle Norman's stuffed animals?"

"Oh, God, no!" She shuddered. "His stuffed animals are like what you see in museums and not too bad, but could you imagine having them in your home? Say an owl on a bedroom dresser staring at you when you woke up?"

He laughed. "I was thinking more on the lines of that big black bear."

"No. Where would you put it?" She snorted out a laugh.

"In my music store. It would be an attention-getter."

She grinned. "Would you have it holding a guitar?"

"Dinner's ready," Aunt Twyla called up the stairs.

They smiled at each other then headed down. For the first time in a long time, Angie felt happy.

Aunt Twyla had them hold hands and say grace around the large round table before she went to the kitchen for the food. Uncle Norman sat with head down and hands on the arms of his wheel chair, so the circle wasn't quite complete.

"Let me help you, Aunt Twyla." Elvis headed to the kitchen with her.

"So what were you two laughing about upstairs?" Marty asked her.

"Oh, this and that. Catching up and remembering some of the fun we had here growing up," she prevaricated.

8

He looked a little skeptical, but didn't say anything more as Aunt Twyla and Elvis started bringing in the food; a pot roast with potatoes, carrots and onions, plus a bowl of green beans, a large salad and a basket full of fresh baked bread. Inhaling the warm smell of the meat and vegetables, Angie heard her stomach growl. Aunt Twyla took their orders for drinks, and returned with coffee while Elvis followed with pitchers of iced tea and water.

Aunt Twyla fixed Uncle Norman's plate and cut up his meat. He ate slowly and rarely looked up until Marty asked, "So what are you going to do with Uncle Norman's collection of animals and skeletons, Aunt Twyla?"

Angie looked at her wondering about that, too. Aunt Twyla hesitated and glanced at her husband. He stared at her waiting for her answer. Finally, she took a breath, looked away from him and smiled at the others. "I thought I'd ask if one of the many Vermont State Parks would want the animals and skeletons. Most of them have nature museums."

Angie looked at Uncle Norman to see what he thought, but he'd returned to eating his meal. She wondered how much he understood, but since he seemed to understand when the question was asked, probably more than most thought he did.

"Tomorrow, we'll go through the house so you can look things over to see what you might want," Aunt Twyla said. "Of course, there'll be some things I'll want to take, but I'll tell you what those things are. Our new place at Happy Days only has a sitting room, a bit of a kitchen, two small bedrooms and one bathroom, so not much can go."

Looking at his wife, Uncle Norman garbled something unintelligible.

She patted his hand and said, "No, there won't be any room for the animals and skeletons."

He shook his head and scowled and again sent out a stream of sounds making no sense.

"Well, maybe one small one," she replied.

He kept scowling and shaking his head. Obviously, she hadn't told him what he wanted to hear.

"Don't worry about it, dear. Everything will work out."

He stared at her until she looked him in the eye and gave a little nod, then he calmed down and went back to eating.

9

Angie wondered what it was he wanted. It seemed as if Aunt Twyla understood him even though nothing he said made sense. She glanced at her cousins. Marty looked at her and rolled his eyes. She ignored that and looked at Elvis. He'd returned to his meal looking thoughtful.

Angie and Elvis helped Aunt Twyla clear the table and do dishes while Uncle Norman wheeled himself back to the sitting room. Marty excused himself to go to his room to use his laptop to take care of business.

"Did you understand what Uncle Norman wanted?" Angie asked.

Aunt Twyla said, "Not totally, but he's having a hard time with the move. After all, he's lived here all his life. He was born in the room upstairs where my son was born, the one that died soon after birth. The only child I had."

Angie vaguely remembered hearing she'd had a baby that died. "What did you name him?"

"Preston, after my daddy," she said.

"That's my middle name." Elvis looked surprised. "It's not a common name."

"Your parents felt sorry for me so when you were born a few weeks later, they gave you the middle name. They figured if I were to have another son, I could still name him Preston."

They visited in the sitting room after dishes were done until Uncle Norman left for his room. Aunt Twyla got up. "I'm going to help Norman into bed. I'm a bit tired so I'm calling it a night, too. Feel free to stay up as long as you want and talk, it won't bother us."

Marty was still upstairs so Angie and Elvis chatted about the times they'd stayed here as children.

"I always hated coming," Angie admitted. "It seemed so spooky, but my parents insisted, and once I got here Aunt Twyla made me feel welcome, but Uncle Norman was a little scary, I always thought."

"Was it the basement with his collection?" Elvis smiled at her.

10

She shuddered. "At first, but then I got used to it and actually found it interesting until what Marty did that time."

Elvis cocked his head. "Which time in particular? He was always playing pranks on us, as I remember."

"He wasn't a very nice older brother to you, was he?"

"You have no idea," Elvis said with no hint of a smile in his eyes or voice. "He picked on Lolly a lot, too. I tried to stop him, but being two years younger and smaller, I was no match for him."

"Didn't you tell your parents?"

"I gave up on that. He always had some excuse making Lolly and me look like crybabies. So what was the trick he played on you that scared you so much?"

"He put one of Uncle Norman's stuffed snakes in my bed under the covers." She shuddered even thinking of it.

Elvis frowned. "It could have traumatized you for life."

"I'm still terrified of snakes."

"It's no wonder. Are you going to go to the basement tomorrow when we tour the house?"

"I don't think so," she said. "I can't think of anything down there I'd want."

"It might help you to get over your fears to face them – without Marty around," he said.

"Can you imagine Marty not taking an opportunity to still pull some prank on me or you? I seem to remember him hiding behind that big bear and growling when you came down the stairs. I can still hear you screaming." She grinned at him.

Elvis laughed. "It's funny now, but it sure wasn't then."

He sobered and thought about it and then looked at Angie. "Why don't we go down now and look at that basement?"

She looked at him with mouth open and eyes wide. "Now? You've got to be kidding, Elvis."

"Is it Halloween that has you spooked, or the basement?" His look challenged her.

"Maybe a little of each." She thought of the girl, who'd run in front of her car. *Was it the ghost of Lolly?* No, it was some girl running away from something. She hoped she was safe now.

He watched her and waited, saying nothing.

11

Finally, she decided to excise old fears hovering like ghosts in her mind. "Okay, but we need to go quietly so we don't disturb Aunt Twyla or Uncle Norman, and heaven help us if Marty gets wind of what we're going to do," she said.

He grinned, stood up, and held out his hand. She put her hand in his and they walked silently to the basement door in the entryway attached to the kitchen. Elvis opened the door and felt around for a light switch and flooded the basement with light and shadows. He started down the steps with Angie close behind him, almost stepping on his heels. As she breathed in the damp and moldy smells of the basement, it brought back familiar memories.

At the bottom they stood side by side looking around. There was the huge black bear standing on its hind legs. *A totally awesome creature,* Angie thought. *I wonder where Uncle Norman found it.* She was sure she'd been told once, but couldn't remember now.

Together they wandered around looking at the collection of stuffed animals and skeletons whispering comments to each other. Angie realized she didn't feel spooked or threatened by Uncle Norman's collection, not even the large snake when they came across it, not that she wanted to touch it.

"Look at the skeleton of what is probably an eagle," she whispered to Elvis as she saw it hanging from the rafters. "Isn't there a law against killing one?"

He nodded. "Maybe he found it dead. It's awesome, when you think about it," he whispered. "I'm still thinking about that bear. I can picture it in a corner of my shop."

She grinned at him. "Holding a guitar or banjo, right?"

"Playing kid games?" Marty said from the steps.

Elvis and Angie looked at each other before turning around.

"Just wanted to see if everything looks as we remembered it," Elvis said.

Marty looked around and made a face. "Totally gross. All of it. I wonder what's behind that curtain. Do you think it's where Uncle Norman keeps a safe with his money?"

He walked over to pull back the curtain and drew in a sharp breath.

12

Angie came up and peeked around him and let out a small cry. "Oh, my God, Elvis. There's a skeleton, and she's wearing the same blue dress as the girl who ran in front of my car." She started to whimper.

Elvis put his arm around her, but couldn't take his eyes off the skeleton of a girl hanging from a hook by a wire attached to the top of her head. Wispy bits of blond hair seemed to be glued to spots on the skull.

"Lolly," he said and swallowed.

"Yes," they heard from the steps.

They turned and saw Aunt Twyla.

"You had to come down here and snoop." She shook her head sadly. "I was going to get rid of her before everyone came, but it slipped my mind until Angie mentioned the ghost. I was waiting for everyone to go to bed. I didn't expect you to come down tonight."

"I think you owe us an explanation, Aunt Twyla." Elvis's eyes and voice held barely suppressed anger. "It is Lolly, isn't it? She did show up here."

Aunt Twyla nodded. "It was an accident. I didn't mean for her to die." She swallowed and looked away composing herself before going on. "I'd gone for groceries so I could fix a good meal for her. When I came home, I saw her car here. When I didn't see her downstairs, I thought she'd gone up to the room she always stayed in." She looked at Angie. "The room you always stay in, too. So I went up to see if she had everything she needed, but she wasn't there. I heard sounds from our room, so I went and opened the door." Here she paused and swallowed as tears started to stream down her face. "Norman and Lolly were together. I think he was forcing himself on her, but he always denied it. Anyway, I grabbed one of the large candlesticks on the fireplace mantle in our room and went to hit him on the head. I was that angry. He heard or sensed me coming, rolled over as I was bringing the candlestick down and I hit Lolly instead." She started sobbing and couldn't continue.

Elvis and Angie listened in horror and waited until she composed herself. "I killed a niece I loved and to this day wish it had been Norman instead."

13

Speaking through gritted teeth Elvis said, "Did you check to see if she was dead? Did you call an ambulance or anything?"

Angie could feel the pain, grief and anger emanating from him as he stood beside her.

Aunt Twyla took a few convulsive breaths and said, "Of course, I checked. She was dead."

"And you never called the police or let any of us know about her?" Elvis's voice was rising.

"I didn't know what to do." She looked at him as the tears still coursed down her face. "I was going to call the police even though I knew I'd go to prison, but Norman talked me out of it. He said he knew it was an accident, and he deserved to be the one who died. I shouldn't be the one to go to prison. Norman convinced me we should cover it up. He said I'd be spending many years in prison because no one would believe I was innocent. My fingerprints were on the candlestick. He told me he'd divorce me so I'd never have a home to come back to when I was released."

In spite of her story, Angie felt sorry for Aunt Twyla. It seemed to her Uncle Norman was the villain here.

"And you let Uncle Norman use her body for his collection?" Elvis's voice seethed.

Angie put her hand on his arm, afraid he'd tear into Aunt Twyla. She wouldn't blame him if he did, but knew he'd regret it later.

Aunt Twyla shook her head emphatically. "No. No. No." She started crying again. "He said he'd give her a decent burial up on the hill where some ancestors were buried over a hundred years ago. I didn't go to watch. Other than a few sentences, I didn't talk to him for years and years after that."

"When did you find out what he'd done?" Angie asked quietly.

"Not until right before his stroke. I went down to the basement to get something and noticed he'd put up a curtain. Like you, I checked and saw what you saw. I was as horrified as you were. I went upstairs and we had a horrible fight. I screamed and threw things and told him I was going to the police. He shouted and said he'd saved my life and that was all the thanks he'd got from me." She took a deep breath. "And then he

14

collapsed, and I've been taking care of him ever since because I didn't know what else to do."

Aunt Twyla sank down onto the steps and bowed her head. "I'm so sorry. I'm so sorry," she kept repeating.

Angie looked up at Elvis as he stood with eyes closed. She put her arm around him and he looked down at her. "All these years of waiting and wondering and hoping," he said in a low voice, his eyes full of tears.

"You did say you wanted closure," she reminded him softly.

He nodded and swallowed. "Yes." He glanced over at Aunt Twyla who seemed to have shrunk in size. "You know I don't blame her as much as Uncle Norman. Lolly wouldn't have willingly been with him. I know that. She found him totally creepy. He was molesting her and I only wish he hadn't moved before Aunt Twyla brought that candlestick down. It makes me ashamed to be a Skeleton."

"Your dad isn't like him and neither is my mother," Angie said.

"You're not a Skeleton," Aunt Angie spoke up.

They both looked at her.

"You're my child, Elvis. I got pregnant thinking the boy would marry me. We'd been dating for a while and were in love. But he got scared thinking of marriage and joined the Army to get away. We were both only eighteen. Norman always had a crush on me and was willing to marry me, even though he knew I was with child by another. He didn't want to raise you, though. He didn't want any reminder of the guy I really loved so he made arrangements with his brother and sister-in-law, your parents, to adopt you. I've kept track of your father over the years, Elvis, and he's a man you can be proud of."

Marty laughed. "So you're not my brother. No wonder we're nothing alike."

Angie looked up at Elvis. "What are you going to do?"

He shook his head. "I don't know, but I do have to tell my parents, and as far as I'm concerned, they're my parents and Lolly was my sister. I'll let them decide, but one thing I know: Lolly is going to have a proper burial."

Angie noticed he didn't say he thought of Marty as his brother.

A garbled shout came from the top of the stairs and Norman appeared at the top of the steps in his wheelchair. With a strong push on the wheels, he plunged forward and he and the wheelchair tumbled down the steps and crashed into Aunt Twyla, who couldn't move in time.

Elvis and Angie ran to them. Elvis pulled the wheelchair off Aunt Twyla. Uncle Norman lay off to one side twisted and motionless with eyes wide and staring. Elvis knelt down beside Aunt Twyla and felt for a pulse.

"She's still alive," he said. "Marty call 911. Aunt Twyla, we're calling for help. Hang on."

She opened her eyes and stared into his and, with effort, said, "I've always loved my little boy. I never forgot him." She closed her eyes.

The doorbell chimed when Angie walked into All about Blues and looked around. She smiled when she saw the tall black bear standing in the corner holding a banjo. Elvis came out of the back room and his face lit up when he saw her.

"Angie! You finally came to see my shop." He walked over to her grinning.

"Yeah. I thought maybe it was best to let things settle down. Love your guard bear," she said smiling at him. "I thought it was about time I came to see how my favorite cousin is doing."

"Not your blood cousin, remember." The look in his eyes passed a message that made her heart quicken.

She nodded. "Yes, I know."

Gloria Alden taught third grade for twenty years. She loved teaching, but wanted to have more time for writing, and much of her retirement years have been spent that way. Her published short stories include "Cheating on Your Wife Can Get You Killed," winner of the 2011 Love is Murder contest and published in Crimespree Magazine; *"Mincemeat is for Murder" appearing in* Bethlehem Writers Roundtable, *"The Professor's Books" in the* Fish Tales *anthology; "The Lure of the Rainbow" in* Fish Nets, *the newest Guppy anthology, and "Once Upon a*

Gnome" in Mystery and Horror, LLC's Strangely Funny. *Her Catherine Jewell mystery novels are* The Blue Rose *and* Daylilies for Emily's Garden. *She also has a middle-grade book,* The Sherlock Holmes Detective Club *based on a writing activity her students did at Hiram Elementary School. In addition to writing, she's passionate about books and they are rapidly taking over her home. She lives on a small farm in Southington, Ohio with two ponies, some cats, five hens and her collie, Maggie. She blogs on Thursdays with* Writers Who Kill *and once a month with the* Fish Tales Anthology Blog.

The Carver

By Erin Farwell

The face began to take shape, but the walls were too thick for the shadows to fall properly. Chris Andrews picked up a small chisel. With smooth, even strokes he scraped the interior of the pumpkin until he was satisfied. Selecting an awl, he enhanced the fine lines around the mouth and the hag's scowl came to life.

Turning the pumpkin, he began adding details to the eyes.

"Chris, we need to talk."

Ignoring the interruption, he traded the awl for a medium-tip linoleum carving tool to create depth of the slice without cutting through the wall of the pumpkin.

"I know what you found out, or what you think you did, but it's not what it seems."

"Sure it isn't." Trading the carving tool for a small saw, he added thin slits near the eyes. The light would show here, next to the shadows, creating the effect that the hag's eyes followed you as you walked by. Here was the true artistry, something that Patrick couldn't appreciate and didn't have the patience to achieve.

"Chris, please. You need to understand."

Finally he turned. "No you need to understand. You stay out of my business and I'll stay out of yours."

Dry corn stalks rattled in the breeze, throwing shadows across the path. The autumn moon shone bright overhead, so bright that Jake didn't need to use the flashlight on his bat-belt as he worked his way through the maze. His mother and Dylan were behind him somewhere, probably kissing. Ugh. Still, it was better than crying, or drinking, which was all his mother seemed to do since his dad had died in the afghan place.

Skipping between the rows of corn, he put those thoughts behind him. He'd been five when his dad had died, practically a baby, and he didn't remember him much. But now he was ten, almost grown up. Still, he was a bit disappointed that he wasn't trick-or-treating with his friends tonight. Ten wasn't too old for Halloween, but Dylan had other ideas. It wasn't all bad. Jake got to wear his Batman costume and Dylan had brought him a whole bag of Snickers bars to eat all by himself, so he'd said okay.

At first he'd thought the corn maze was stupid, but boy had he been wrong. The paths were dark and creepy and it was easy to get lost, even with the other people in the maze. The best was when he was alone, like now, and could pretend there were monsters in the corn and he had to save his mom or they'd eat her up.

He reached a fork in the path, each way leading to a dark unknown. The stalks were too high to see over, but Jake guessed he was close to the finish. He listened, hoping the sound of the other people in the maze would guide him, but all he heard was the rustle of the corn. A shiver of fear slithered down his back. His mom and Dylan should have caught up with him by now. Glancing over his shoulder, he saw only the empty path.

He looked up and found one of the three high platforms that were placed around the edge of the corn maze. His mother told him that people stood up there to watch the maze, making sure no one got lost. The dark silhouette on the platform near him didn't move, not one bit. What if he wasn't a person at all, but a zombie who waited for people to get lost and then came down to eat them? Jake shivered again.

"Hey sport."

Jake jumped. His heart beat so hard he thought it would explode, like he'd read in a comic book once. "Dylan," he said, hoping he didn't sound like a scared little kid.

Dylan nodded at him then turned and called out, "I found him Maggie. He's fine."

A moment later his mom came around the bend in the path. She sighed with relief as she reached for Jake's hand. He'd told her a hundred times that he was too old to hold hands, but this time he took it and held on tight. She smiled down at him.

"Did you find the way out?" she asked.

Jake shook his head. "I think we're close, but I'm not sure which way to go next."

Dylan looked down each path then up at the moon, as if it would guide them. "Well sport, what do you think?"

This was one of the things he liked about Dylan, that when he asked Jake a question, he'd listen to the answer. Jake considered the paths again. "I think if we go to the right, it will take us out."

"Right it is, then."

Once again Jake led the way. The path curved twice and then they were out into the open field that surrounded the maze. "We did it!"

"You did it, sport. We just followed your lead."

Jake felt more proud of himself than he could ever remember.

"Come on Maggie, let's take Jake on the hayride and go make some s'mores."

"Yeah, Mom. The line for the hayride is this way." Jake ran ahead, whooping and hollering, his cape flaping behind him. This was a great Halloween.

The hinges on the door to the old barn squealed in protest when Chris shoved his way inside. All season he'd told Drake Logan to fix the damn thing. How was he supposed to create in conditions like this? Flipping the switch, he let his eyes adjust as the overhead lights flickered to life. The large tank still had pumpkins floating on the surface, like a giant's game of bobbing for apples. Someone had cleaned the work tables, but bits of pumpkin guts and rind still lay on the surface and covered the floor beneath.

Chris sighed. He'd told the minions to give the place a good clean-up. Even though the corn maze would be open for another few weeks, tonight was the culmination of the last month's efforts. Halloween marked the end of the month long "Pumpkin Walk" at Logan's Corn Maze Farm, and this barn had been his workshop. With his team of eight minions, they had carved over 2,000 Jack o' Lanterns that were displayed along the meandering path through the small wooded area near the corn maze. Of course all of the big ones, the great ones, the truly scary ones were created by him.

The problem was that pumpkins rot. Soaking them in water with a little bleach then spraying them with acrylic kept them looking nice longer, but in the end they turned to mush. Chris took a month away from his graphic design studio each October to work in this fickle and impermanent medium. Every year he created the theme of the walk, carved the primary pumpkins and oversaw the creation of the others. He and the minions checked the display every day, carving new pumpkins to replace the ones that had started to sag. For six years he'd worked for Logan's Corn Maze and enjoyed the challenges and reaped the rewards and kudos, which were his due. Everything had been perfect, until this year.

He knew he was depressed--his father had died only two months ago, but that was only part of the problem. There was also Patrick, with his tight t-shirts and tighter jeans who caught the attention of too many women. He also wanted to paint the Jack o' Lanterns, add Spanish moss for hair, hats, stuff like that. But Chris was a purist and there was no place for such fads in his workshop.

Unfortunately, Logan had liked some of Patrick's designs and had hinted that Chris should do more of that kind of work next year, which was never going to happen. He was a master carver, well respected. Besides, if Logan wanted Chris to play nice, he needed to do the same.

Then there was Amy. Restless and beautiful, his wife flitted from career to career like a butterfly to flowers. She'd never hung around the farm, never cared about what he did here, until this fall.

Maybe he needed to walk away from her, from the farm, even his business. Stupid, he knew, and this wasn't what he wanted, not really. What he needed to do was take some time off and think things through. As soon as he closed up the Pumpkin Walk, he'd pack a bag and head to the cabin.

Decision made, Chris picked up the jacket he had left there earlier in the day and started for the door. Amy said she was going out tonight, some party or something, but he wanted to be home when she returned. They needed to talk. The minions would finish up tonight and tomorrow they'd do the final clean up, throwing away all of their hard work.

He'd reached for the light switch when he noticed that his tool box was open. One of the minions must have needed something and couldn't be bothered to close it again. He stomped over to the table and did a quick inventory. Peelers, graters, chisels, awls, small saws, knives, they were all accounted for. No, they weren't. His best knife, the one that had been forged by a blacksmith, was missing.

The walkie-talkie on his belt crackled to life, followed by an indiscernible string of words.

Snatching the thing from his belt, he pushed the button and said, "This is Chris. What the hell do you want?"

"The light in the big Jack o' Lantern in the center of the main display is out."

Chris swore under this breath. "Get one of the minions to fix it."

More static. "Can't reach anyone else."

"I'll take care of it then." At least this was a problem he knew how to fix.

The last of the stragglers worked their way into the Pumpkin Walk, some lingering longer than expected, cutting things close. Then the biggest risk of the night, dragging the sawhorse over the path with the closed sign hanging from it, but no one saw.

Slipping through the darkness, avoiding the motion sensors and lights, was easy. The last of the visitors were almost through the display. A minute later the large clearing emptied of the sightseers. The giant Jack o' Lantern in the center of the display glowed brightly until a wire was cut. Light still shown from the smaller pumpkins, but it didn't matter. Chris would only have eyes for his creation.

The inside of the pumpkin was slick, but not much movement would be required. Crouching low, surrounded by the smell of rotting pumpkin, the wait was only a minute or two before Chris lumbered down the path.

He walked behind the display and leaned into the back of the Jack o' Lantern to fix the light. The look of surprise on his face was almost comical.

"Trick or treat."

The knife slid between his ribs, once, twice. Amazing what you can learn on the Internet.

Chris jerked back, taking the knife with him, stumbling over pumpkins, smashing them underfoot until he finally collapsed. Stepping carefully around the broken bits of pumpkin was difficult, but the goo made it easy to drag Chris' body into place.

Carved faces glowed along the moon-lit path and Jake shivered in the cool night breeze. There had been a sawhorse in front of the Pumpkin Walk and a sign saying it was closed, but Dylan said it was supposed to be open and the Jack o' Lanterns were lit, so they walked around it. They had the path to themselves and even with the bright moon there were lots of dark corners in the woods. Goosebumps ran down his arms. Jake stepped closer to his mom. They both yelled when a pumpkin with a face like a vampire suddenly lit up in front of them.

"Motion activated," Dylan said with a laugh. "They really pulled out all of the stops for this."

Jake grinned. Being scared was okay if there was someone else with you.

"Now I'm afraid to go any farther," his mom said.

"Don't worry. Sport and I are here to protect you."

"Sure Mom, we won't let anything bad happen." Jake loved it that Dylan included him.

Pumpkins lined the path, peeked out from behind trees and flickered like they had real candles in them. "Mom, that one looks just like Mr. Mullins, my first grade teacher."

"Jake, that's not very nice." She studied the pumpkin with a face like a ghoul. "Though I think you're right."

Jake laughed and ran ahead. Around the next bend, the woods were dark and silent. The trees grew thick here; their empty branches almost hid the moon and the perfect Halloween display lay before him. Hundreds of pumpkins glowed in the dark, some had faces; others had scary scenes like haunted houses or ghosts in graveyards. In the middle of them all sat the biggest pumpkin Jake had ever seen. Even unlit, he could tell that it had an evil face with big, pointy teeth. It looked like it was eating a scarecrow.

"Too bad that big one isn't lit. I bet it's the best Jack-o-Lantern in the place," Dylan said, coming to stand next to him. "Maybe they closed the path until they got it fixed."

"It doesn't matter, I have my flashlight." Jake unclipped it from his bat-belt and shone it on the pumpkin. He was right, the face was scary, with big eyes and a warty nose and it was eating a scarecrow.

Jake's mother screamed.

Lieutenant Susan Blake and Detective Gary Benedict stepped over a scarecrow lying across the path as they headed toward the crime scene.

Susan shuddered. "That thing looks like it committed suicide by jumping off that platform."

Gary looked at the straw and clothes scattered over the ground then up at the platform. "No, the body's too far away to have jumped. This thing was pushed or thrown. It was murdered."

In the four months that Susan had been assigned to work with Gary Benedict, she had learned his ways and foibles fairly easily but there were times, like now, when she wasn't sure if he was joking or not.

Gary took another moment to examine the clothes. "Good quality stuff. I'm surprised it was used for a scarecrow."

"Well that explains it then, "Susan said. "He was killed for his money." Her humor was rewarded with a quick smile.

"Perhaps, but we have a more serious matter to deal with." He led the way to the sawhorse that marked the beginning of the crime scene. They identified themselves to the uniformed officers, then ducked under the yellow tape and walked down the path to the primary site.

Jack o' Lanterns leered from behind bushes or atop posts and Susan suppressed a shiver. Halloween had never been her favorite holiday even as a kid and nothing had changed.

"Fill me in on the victim and why the ME is so sure that he knew his killer."

Susan flipped open her notebook, glad she had arrived before him so she was prepared for his questions. "The victim is Chris Andrews, 42. Owned a high-end graphic design studio but takes a month off each year to carve the pumpkins for the farm. He and his wife Amy had been married for nine years, no kids. Mother deceased ten years. Father deceased two months ago, Alzheimer's." A Jack o' Lantern lit up nearly at her feet. Susan stifled a scream even as she tripped into Gary.

Steadying her with one hand under her elbow, he chuckled. "Clever. Motion activated and completely unexpected."

Susan grunted in response. Clever wasn't the first adjective that came to mind. "Anyway," she said, pulling her arm from Gary's grip, "the knife used to kill the victim belonged to him and was unique. He'd had it specially made and kept it with his carving tools in a barn at the edge of the property that they used as a workshop. It isn't something he left lying around or that the patrons would have known about."

"Was it possible that he carried it with him and someone used it against him?"

"No, at least not according to the people he worked with. He kept a small pocket knife on him to use in the display area and the good knife stayed in the barn. No one was allowed to touch it without his permission."

Gary nodded. "That narrows down the possible suspects, which is a relief."

Susan understood. At over three hundred acres, Logan's Corn Maze Farm was an impossible site to contain. There were hundreds of ways on and off the property. If the killer had wanted to leave, he was probably already gone.

They rounded the last bend in the path and came to the site of the murder. The small section of the woods would have been dark and mysterious under normal conditions, but the glare of the crime scene lights shattered the intended atmosphere. A massive pumpkin held center stage. Slanted eyes, bulbous nose and a wide mouth full of sharp teeth, its creator had expanded on these basic elements and somehow infused them with evil intent.

Or maybe it was the body wedged between the teeth that created the effect.

Gary studied the Jack o' Lantern with its human sacrifice for a moment before walking closer. Susan had learned not to speak while her boss gathered his first impressions of a crime scene. Instead, she watched as he walked around the body, staying outside of the perimeter created by the second string of crime scene tape. The ME stood on the other side of the tape and waited for him to finish his circuit. Susan hurried forward, pen and notebook ready.

"Good evening, Dr. Reed. You look lovely this evening."

The ME had come from a party and bits of her Raggedy Anne wig peaked out from under her hair covering. "Don't start with me," she warned. "It took me three months to talk my husband into wearing a Raggedy Andy costume and now he's at the party by himself. From the texts he's sending me, I won't be expecting any treats when he gets home tonight."

"Well, at least he'll be coming home," Gary said, nodding toward the body.

Dr. Reed sighed. "Nothing like death to put life in perspective." She pulled off her gloves and ducked under the tape. "It will take my people a few more hours to finish processing the scene, but I can tell you that he had been dead for a very short time before the body was discovered. Perhaps as little as five minutes or so, which would put time of death between 9:15 and 9:30."

"Who found the body?"

"Maggie Scott, Dylan Harper and Maggie's son Jake," Susan supplied.

"A boy saw this?" Gary sounded pained.

"Yes and from what the responding officers said, the kid is fine. The path was dark, the pumpkin wasn't lit and he had shone his flashlight on the body for just a few seconds before the mother's boyfriend realized what was going on and hustled them all away."

"Okay. Besides finding the body, did they see or hear anything?"

Susan nodded. "The beginning of the Pumpkin Walk was blocked by a sawhorse, but they walked around it and started down the path. According to the owner and the staff, there was no reason for the path to be closed."

"What about the sawhorse? Where did it come from?"

"They use it to block the path during the day when they're 'freshening the exhibit' as they call it." Susan checked her notes then nodded. "They throw away the rotted pumpkins and replace them with fresh ones. The Walk had been open all night until about fifteen minutes before the body was discovered."

Gary nodded. "So whoever did this either knew Chris Andrews was headed this way or somehow lured him here. That person took a big chance, several actually." He sighed as he looked back at the body. "Anything else?"

Susan hesitated a moment. "They didn't notice anything along the Pumpkin Walk, but the boy insists that there was a monster or something on one of the platforms."

"Why did he think that?"

"Apparently the boy was lost in the maze and looked up at the platform to see if anyone was watching him. He said there was someone standing there but that they didn't move. He thinks it was a zombie or something. Anyway, the officers took their statements and cleared them to go home."

"Good." Gary turned back to Dr. Reed. "What else can you tell us?"

She tugged off her hair covering, taking the wig with it. Her dark hair was at odd contrast to the big round circles of blush on her cheeks. "There might have been a scuffle of some kind behind the large pumpkin. Several of the smaller Jack-o-Lanterns were knocked over or smashed. The knife was shoved in at an upward angle, so the killer could have been shorter than the victim, who was 5' 10", or the victim had fallen or was leaning over the killer when he was stabbed. Before you ask, the scene is too chaotic to give you an answer as to which is more likely, but the autopsy should provide more information.

"The victim has mashed pumpkin on the back of his shirt and jeans, which could have happened when he fell or while he was placed in the pumpkin. We know he died less than a yard from where the body is displayed and there are distinct drag marks. Mashed pumpkin is pretty slick, so it wouldn't have taken a lot of strength to drag the victim and place him in the

28

pumpkin's mouth." She looked back over to her staff. "There are a lot of shoe prints around the display, probably from workers and some of the patrons. We have some shoe prints in the smashed pumpkin bits, but most are too smeared to be of any use. We'll keep working on it, though."

"So the killer could be tall or short, male or female?"

"That about sums it up."

"What about blood? Will the killer have gotten some on his clothes?"

"The victim was stabbed in the heart with two quick, vicious jabs. The killer shoved the knife up under the ribs and had a pretty direct shot at the heart. He or she was either very lucky or very prepared and there wouldn't have been any significant splatter."

"Thank you, doctor." Turning to Susan he said, "Let's talk to the owner of this operation."

Gary and Susan found Drake Logan waiting for them in the central concession area. With his jeans, work boots, and flannel shirt, Susan decided he looked the part of the farmer.

After a few words of introduction, Gary asked, "What can you tell us about what happened here tonight?"

Logan sighed. "That's just it. I don't know what to tell you. We had a busy night, always do on Halloween. It seems like the adults like to dress up and have a good scare as much as the kids do." He gave a sad smile. "We have the corn maze, which is where we started, then there's the hayride that takes people out to a field with a bunch of bonfires where they can roast marshmallows and such. There's also the haunted barn, that's mostly for older kids and adults. We added the Pumpkin Walk six years ago. Well, I guess you've seen that already."

Susan smiled. "I wish I could have seen it under better circumstances." This is a big production, with all of the attractions plus the concessions."

"We also have a petting zoo and a bouncy house for the little ones."

"Was the farm always used this way?"

Logan's smile had a bitter edge. "My family's farmed this land for over ninety years. There were good years, bad years and the kinds in between, but we always managed. Then the bottom went out of the corn prices and things started getting difficult. I opened the corn maze and it did well until some others opened up nearby. So we added more stuff, something for all ages, until it's like it is now. People come, they always do, and this has been a good year. Not a great one, but good enough." He sighed. "We used to be a real farm, grow real crops. Now we're mostly a side-show."

"How did Chris Andrews figure into this?" Gary asked.

"He visited the corn maze once and asked me why there weren't any Jack o' Lanterns. Told him we had 'em all over the place but he explained that pumpkins were just pumpkins until they were carved and became Jack o' Lanterns." He smiled at the memory. "We got to talking and the next year he did the first Pumpkin Walk. It's been a big draw."

"Did you get along well with Mr. Andrews?"

Logan considered that for a moment. "He had an artist's temperament and was a perfectionist to boot. A few people couldn't stand to work for him for more than a day; others come back year after year. He was good at what he did and he could teach it to others. That's the key. I don't think he was happy this year, though." He paused a moment. "His dad died a few months ago and I'm not sure how things were between him and his wife. And one of the new workers had some good ideas about changes to the Pumpkin Walk, but Chris was resistant. Yep, there was some tension this year."

"What's going to happen now?" Susan asked.

"We've got plenty of time to figure that out. The Walk was supposed to end tonight anyway. Tomorrow is the clean-up and then the pumpkin crew scatters until next fall."

"So tonight was the last night Chris Andrews would be at the farm."

"Yep, I guess it was."

After a few more questions for Drake Logan, Gary and Susan went in search of Sam Walker. They found him sitting on the back of a hay wagon, smoking a cigarette with shaking hands. As they drew closer, Susan saw that it wasn't just his hands that were shaking, but his whole body twitched in a disjointed dance.

30

"Hi Sam, Mr. Logan said we'd find you over here."

The man jumped as he heard his name then turned away, watching them from the corner of his eyes. His clothes were torn and patched; his jean jacket was well worn, with ragged edges at the sleeves and collar.

He seemed afraid but spoke with defensive aggression. "Why do you want to see me? I mean I didn't have nothing to do with this. I never worked with Chris, just Mr. Logan. I wanted to carve the pumpkins but he said he needed me for more important jobs."

Sam's hands shook so hard that Susan doubted he could hold a knife steady enough to carve the most basic of faces. The slightly sweet odor of marijuana wafted from Sam's coat. She wondered what else he was on.

"But Sam, Mr. Logan told us that you were on top of the platform near the Pumpkin Walk when Mr. Andrews was killed. We'd like to ask you about that," Gary said quietly.

"What do you want to know?"

"Did you see Chris Andrews going into the Pumpkin Walk? Did you see anyone else from the farm go in there?"

Sam scuffed out his cigarette and pulled out a fresh one. His hands shook so hard that he couldn't get it lit.

"Sam," Gary said, reaching for the lighter and holding it steady. Sam got the cigarette lit and drew in a lungful of smoke. "Who did you see go into the maze tonight?"

"No one," he mumbled. "Not during the time you mean. I didn't see anyone."

"And why is that?" Gary asked.

"I wasn't up there then." Sam looked up at Gary and pleaded. "Please don't tell Mr. Logan. I was only gone for a few minutes, okay, maybe twenty, that's all. I watch the part of the maze at the finish and anyone who gets lost there figures it out pretty quick. And there is never any trouble on the Pumpkin Walk. You can't get lost and there are usually lots of people." Sam leaned back against the wagon as if exhausted by the short speech.

"Okay, where were you?"

Sam's eyes darted around the dark field, as if looking for an escape. Susan took pity on him. "Look at me, Sam," she said

31

in a calm voice. She waited until he made eye contact with her before she continued. "We don't care about anything except who killed Mr. Andrews. That's all we're here to investigate."

Sam's foot tapped against the wagon as he pondered her words. After a moment he said, "I got a call on the walkie, I couldn't tell who it was but it was on my channel, the one for the maze."

"Did everyone else hear the message?" Gary asked.

"Well sure, I mean all three of us up on the platforms heard it. Mr. Logan and Mr. Chris are the only ones who have their own channels."

"Okay, so you got a message. How did you know it was for you?"

"Well, whoever it was said my name, said 'Sam' so I knew it was for me. The others guys probably stopped listening then, but you can ask 'em. I'm sure they'll tell you." He pushed his hair away from his sweating face. "Anyway, someone told me that my car had been broken into. So I had to go and check, you know. Make sure nothing was missing."

"Okay Sam, so who called you about your car?"

He looked at her with big eyes. "That's just it, I don't know. I couldn't tell from the voice, but I didn't waste any time worrying about it. I hitched a ride on the hay wagon 'cause it goes near the employee parking field. I checked and my car was fine."

"So, did you come straight back?"

"Yes ma'am," he said without meeting her eyes. "Though I may have taken a cigarette break first."

Susan smiled a moment. "Did you worry about people seeing you leave, or looking up and seeing the platform empty?"

"No, ma'am. Not really. I mean most people don't look up, do they?"

"Okay, Sam. One more question and then we're through."

Their witness looked both hopeful and scared as his jumpy eyes met Gary's.

"When you got back to the platform, did you notice anything different about it?"

Sam and Susan both stared at Gary in surprise.

32

"Different? No, I mean how could it be different? It wasn't moved or anything if that's what you're asking."

"Not that, no." Gary looked at Sam as if willing the stoner's mind to clear, just for a moment. "I mean, did you see anything, bits of pumpkin or straw or anything like that?"

"Oh that." Sam's face brightened. "Well there was some straw up there but I figured it just came off my clothes from being on the hayride, you know? There weren't no pumpkin guts, but I did slip on the ladder and crack my shin. It still hurts."

"I'm sorry to hear that Sam, but thank you for your help." Gary gave a small nod then turned away. Susan followed closely behind.

Patrick Moynihan met them halfway up the hill as they were headed back to the farm entrance. "Mr. Logan said you wanted to speak with me."

He was handsome, Susan would give him that, but it was in the obvious male-model kind of way. His dark hair was thick and artfully styled and he had the body to carry off the tight jeans and t-shirt, but he knew how attractive he was, diminishing the effect.

"Yes we would," Gary said. "Where would you like to talk?"

Patrick nodded to a set of benches under a light pole and the trio walked over and sat down.

"I'd like to ask you a few questions about your relationship with…"

"I'm not having an affair with Amy."

"Excuse me?"

"I said, I'm not having an affair with Amy, Chris' wife. Some people thought I was but it isn't true. We're just friends."

"Okay," Gary said. "Good to know, but what I wanted to ask you about was your relationship with Chris, not his wife."

"Oh." Even the shadows couldn't hide Patrick's blush. "Well, we worked together, we were friends."

"Really?" Gary turned to Susan. "Is that what you heard?"

Feigning surprise, Susan made a point of looking through her notes. "Why no, Detective Benedict. In fact we were told that there were some creative differences between them, a rivalry of sorts. They had different ideas of how the Pumpkin Walk should be designed."

"Oh that," Patrick said. "It wasn't important, just you know, business."

"I don't think Chris saw it that way," Gary said. "In fact, we were told that he was very upset that you went behind his back to show your Jack o' Lantern designs to Mr. Logan."

"Well if he'd used them in the first place, I wouldn't have had to go behind his back, now would I?"

"Did you go behind his back about anything else?" Susan asked. "We heard that Chris Andrews and his wife were having some problems."

"Well that started long before I showed up," Patrick said. His eyes widened with horror when he realized what he said. "Look, I don't mean that she and I, that we…"

"This time I will ask the question." Gary leaned forward as his voice hardened. "Were you and Amy Andrews having an affair?"

Patrick looked away. "I guess we were."

Susan and Gary exchanged glances.

"You guess?" Susan asked.

"Well, yes. We were, but it wasn't serious, not really. I mean she's pretty and all, but kind of old. Besides, I'm leaving for Denver next week. It's not like we're in love or anything."

"Did Chris know?"

Patrick shrugged. "Sometimes I thought he did but other times I wasn't sure. He's been kind of moody and uptight and it was worse the last few days."

"Do you know why?"

"Not really. Sometimes he'll take a break from carving and take a walk around the farm. There are lots of barns and outbuildings here and he'd go exploring, which is stupid. I mean he's been working here for six years; what does he think he's going to see?"

"Did something happen that made you think he'd learned about the affair?"

Nodding, Patrick said, "Two days ago he came back from his walk all upset and with a lot of straw on his clothes. I thought

34

he'd found out where Amy and I were, ah, meeting, but he never said anything to me."

Susan's phone vibrated and she read the text message before handing the phone to Gary, who read it in turn and nodded.

"Patrick," he said, "Will Mrs. Andrews corroborate what you've told us?"

"Huh?"

"Will Mrs. Andrews tell us the same thing you did?"

"I guess. I mean she didn't work with us so she didn't see Chris come back from his walk that day, but she'll tell you about us meeting in the hay barn."

"You say the affair wasn't serious, and maybe it wasn't for you but could it have been for her?"

Patrick looked at Gary with blank eyes.

"Patrick, could Mrs. Andrews been in love with you even if you weren't in love with her?"

"Oh." Patrick thought a moment. "Maybe but I don't think so. I mean she knew I was leaving and it was my last night at the farm."

"Okay. Did you know that her husband owned a very successful graphic design studio and that he'd just inherited over three million dollars from his father? With Chris Andrews out of the way, Amy is a rich woman. Maybe that would be enough for you to ignore the fact that you didn't love her."

"What? Are you crazy? Do you think I killed Chris to have Amy or her money? What kind of a guy do you think I am?"

The detective let the question hang in the air a moment. "Where were you tonight between nine and ten-thirty?"

"Are you kidding me? I was with Amy. Well no, I was supposed to be with Amy. She had told me that she couldn't meet tonight, but later I found a note on my windshield telling me to come to the hay barn. They store the bales there that they use on the rides but once the wagons are loaded, no one goes in the barn for the rest of the night so it's a good place to, you know."

"So you went to the hay barn to meet Amy. Then what happened?"

"She never showed. I'm not supposed to call her in case Chris picks up her phone, so I waited almost an hour. I was getting kind of angry so I called, but her phone went to voicemail. I got tired of waiting so I went to leave but my car had a flat. Must've driven over a nail. Then I couldn't find the jack and everyone I called was busy, so I had to wait longer. Finally Joe Wallace, he works out by the bonfires, he came over and helped me change the tire."

"What time was that?"

"Around ten, ten-thirty, I don't know." He sounded scared.

"Did you ever find out what happened to Amy?"

"No, and I'm worried."

"She's okay," Susan said. "After we found her husband, an officer was sent over to her house. She had just come back from a baby shower."

"Then who sent me the note?"

"Do you still have it?" Gary asked.

"No."

"I have one more question and it may seem odd: did you give away any clothes?"

"Give them away? No. I am missing some things from the car, though. You know, stuff I keep just in case I need a change. It's hard to get all the hay out of your clothes."

Lights glowed around the edge of the corn maze but the rest was in darkness. Susan found it spooky, yet at the same time she wanted to dive in and solve its puzzles. Maybe she'd come back next week and give it a try.

They'd left Patrick a few minutes ago. He wasn't the brightest bulb but he was smart enough to realize that he was in trouble. He had no alibi for the time of death and there was enough circumstantial evidence to arrest him, but Gary wanted to check a few more things first.

Now her boss stood next to the ladder of the platform that Sam had abandoned to check on his car. He knelt down and rubbed his hand over the lower rungs. "Slick" he said. Then he sniffed at his fingers. "Pumpkin. Careful on those first two rungs," he said as he started up the ladder.

Susan let him get near the top before following. She couldn't help but smile when she reached the platform. The near-full moon shown down and she half expected to see a witch on a broom fly past. The breeze was crisp as an apple and smelled of autumn. From here the twists and turns of the maze was revealed. The basic shape was a pyramid with the words "Logan's Corn Maze" intertwined around it. She followed the path with her eyes from the entrance but quickly became confused.

"Are you done?" Gary asked.

She felt herself redden with embarrassment. How could she have forgotten what they were up there to do? Then she wondered, what were they up there to do?

Gary picked something up from the floor of the platform. "Straw" he said. "And the end of a joint."

"No surprise there." She looked toward the Pumpkin Walk. "I can see most of the path, and certainly where the techs are still working, but I'm not sure if I could recognize anyone from this distance."

"There are a set of binoculars hanging here and if you step closer to this side, you'll see the start of the Walk."

"You're right. If it was someone I knew well, I could probably recognize them from here."

"Exactly. It would have to be someone you knew well." He looked at her as if waiting to see if she followed his logic. She didn't. "What else do you see?"

She looked over the edge again. "Well, there's our murdered scarecrow, but other than that, I don't see much."

"You see more than you realize."

Susan stumbled and stifled a curse. She'd lost count of how many times she had tripped on the dirt road. Even with flashlights and the bright moon, it was easy to misjudge the uneven surface of the packed earth. They had started at the barn closest to the corn maze and worked their way out. They had found the pumpkin barn, the hay barn, and a barn full of old equipment. One full of tractors and another filled with apples. She still didn't know what Gary was looking for.

Did Patrick kill Chris for the woman, or the money, or both? Did Amy Andrews hire or trick Patrick into killing Chris for her? She was having an affair but that didn't make her a killer; Patrick either, for that matter. Her mind wandered to the murder of the scarecrow. And she began to understand.

Another barn, smaller than some she'd seen, larger than others, came into view. Stumbling behind Gary she caught herself against a fence post to keep from falling, snagging her jacket on a nail. "Shit."

Gary looked back at her. "Don't you just love farm life?"

"This is why I own a condo."

Reaching the barn, Gary pulled the door part-way open then stopped. He swung it open and closed again then turned to her. "I think this is it."

She looked at the barn, the door, then at Gary. "If you say so."

They stepped inside and he flicked on the overhead lights. Sturdy and neat, it was a sharp contrast to others they had seen. Bales of hay were piled in corners and the air smelled sweet.

Gary studied the closest bale then took out a pocket knife and cut the twine. The bale popped open. Inside a camouflaging layer of hay were plastic bags filled with green leaves. After putting on a pair of gloves, Gary picked up a bag, opened it and sniffed. "Marijuana."

"You weren't supposed to find that."

Susan turned. Drake Logan stood in the doorway, a shotgun pointed between her and Gary.

"No, we weren't." Gary dropped the bag and turned, hands out to his side as a sign of non-violence. "We were supposed to think that Patrick killed Chris."

"I liked Chris, I really did. Patrick, not so much."

"So Chris found out about this place?"

"No, first Chris found some weed growing in the ditches. Great place to plant the stuff. No one looks in ditches. Then he found this place. Still don't know what tipped him off."

"The hinges."

"What?"

"The hinges," Gary said again. "The hinges on the other barn doors squeal when you open the doors, but not these."

"Clever, but clever won't help you."

"We already have several policemen and a forensic team here. Do you really think you can kill us and get away with it?" Susan asked.

"Don't know, but I've already killed once so I'm willing to try again."

"But you can't do it here. You don't want your whole operation discovered in the process."

"You're right. I think we should take a walk."

"No, I'm tired of walking. How about you, Susan?" Gary sat down on a bale of hay and Susan followed his lead. "You can't kill us or even shoot us here without leaving some trace evidence, a blood trail, something, and we aren't leaving, so what are you going to do?"

Logan stared at Gary as if he was crazy. "I'm pointing a loaded rifle at you."

"I know and I don't care."

"What if I point it at her?" Logan turned toward Susan.

"Shoot her, shoot me; you still have the same problem with blood evidence."

Gary sounded so calm Susan wanted to kick him until she saw him reach for his weapon.

"Put the rifle down," he said as he stood pointing the gun at Logan.

"No, if I can't shoot you, you can't shoot me."

"You really don't understand," Gary said before shooting Logan in the thigh.

"So the Logan Corn Maze is actually a million dollar marijuana production and distribution network," Susan said. She and Gary were leaning against a squad car. The ambulance had just left with Drake Logan and Dr. Reed. Several police officers were securing the barn. "Chris Andrews discovered the operation and Logan killed him, but why tonight?"

"It's Halloween." Gary reminded her. "It was the last night that both Chris and Patrick would be here."

"So he stole the clothes from Patrick's car and made the scarecrow. He left the note on Patrick's car then later puts a nail in the tire to strand him at the back of the farm. After that was taken care of, he called Chris and lured him to the Pumpkin Walk."

"And then he called Sam and told him his car had been broken into, getting rid of the one potential witness who could cause a real problem."

"Okay, but why risk the scarecrow?"

"In case anyone looked up. He didn't want people to see an empty platform. Instead a boy looked up and thought he saw a monster."

"And while Sam was gone and after he put the scarecrow in place, he moved the sawhorse. That was a huge risk."

"Not really. If someone had seen him, he would have abandoned his plan and found another time to kill Andrews."

Susan nodded, still following the trail of clues. "So Logan hides behind the pumpkin and kills Chris when he comes to fix the light."

"Actually, Dr. Reed thinks Logan was in the pumpkin."

"Why?"

"I have no idea. Anyway, he kills Chris with the knife he had taken earlier in the day, climbs up the platform and throws the scarecrow off, comes down and acts like nothing happened. Patrick doesn't get back to the maze until after the murder, leaving him without an alibi. Everything goes according to plan."

"Yet he still got caught."

"Yep. Logan got the trick instead of the treat."

Although Erin Farwell has a business and a law degree, she spends her days writing, teaching art classes (metal clay) and taking care of her family, which includes her husband, daughter, three cats, two guinea pigs and two fish. Erin grew up in the small town of Berrien Springs, Michigan and lived in Chicago for many years before moving to Roswell, Georgia, just north of Atlanta. She loves to travel and has been fortunate enough to visit many states as well as go to Paris, France, Salzburg, Austria, Munich, Germany and Venice, Italy. She's also been to parts of Belgium and Slovenia. She and her husband climbed together to the top of Kilimanjaro in Kenya and traveled to China to adopt their daughter. Her first mystery novel, Shadowlands, *was published in 2012. http://www.erinfarwell.com*

Dead and Buried Treasure
By Barb Goffman

"Hey, all you single ladies," the DJ called. "It's time to catch the bouquet. Come on out to the dance floor."

My best friend, Katie, nudged my arm. Her large diamond ring sparkled in the waning sunlight pouring through the oceanfront resort's glass walls. The beautiful, late-summer day was slipping into night with wisps of pinks and reds chasing each other across the sky. "Go on, Lizzie. Now's your chance."

Katie probably sounded happy, encouraging even, to anyone within earshot. But I could hear the slight irritation in her tone, how she emphasized *go on*, how she pushed me a little too hard.

Katie and all my other friends—*all* of them, counting today's bride—were already married. And not only had they married, but they married up: established doctors, lawyers, and businessmen with big houses and island vacations and things I could only dream of. Katie's wedding, a month after college graduation, had been so extravagant, it was mentioned in the *Miami Herald*. In the three years since then, she'd spent her days decorating her house, working out, and going to the beach. Living the dream, she called it. She'd also been trying to find me a guy. But I was a chubby brunette living near South Beach, Florida, a trendy section of Miami. A size eight. Guys weren't exactly lining up at my door. Katie was losing patience.

I tottered out to the dance floor, feeling my black cocktail dress ride a little higher than it probably should. I let it. Maybe I'd catch someone's eye, as well as the bouquet. There wasn't much competition for the flowers. You could count the number of single women at this wedding on one hand. Just me, a few of

41

the groom's friends, and the bride's fat cousin. Well, fatter than me, anyway.

My friend Meghan turned around to toss her bouquet. *Please let me catch it. Please, please, please.*

"Get ready," Meghan called.

If I didn't find a guy soon, my friends would drop me. I could already feel it starting. The girls' nights they forgot to invite me to. The inside jokes that everyone got but me. The unanswered texts. They usually liked to socialize in couples these days, and I was the odd woman out, the awkward chubster who'd made her first real friends in college after she joined a sorority. Of course, they'd had to accept me then. I was a legacy.

But they didn't have to keep me now.

"One," Meghan said.

Oh, God, if my friends dropped me, I didn't know what I'd do. I'd be left alone with my tiny apartment, a go-nowhere research job, and no chance of a real future. Majoring in sociology hadn't been the smartest idea, nor had graduating during this horrible economy, but I could only stay in college so long.

"Two," Meghan said.

I plastered a smile on my face and nervously ran my hand through my chocolate-brown hair, pushing it back behind my right ear. I should have dyed it long ago. Maybe that would have made a difference. All my friends were blond. And tall. And stacked. That's what guys liked. I couldn't do tall or stacked, not without killer heels and a couple Wonderbras. But I'd always thought my wavy brown hair would help me stand out. That had been a mistake. The only guys I'd ever attracted were nerds. Nice guys. Sweet guys. But, as Katie always pointed out, they also were "no-potential losers."

"Three!"

The bouquet went flying, a symbol of my hopes and dreams. I knew it was silly. Catching the bouquet wouldn't mean I'd find a husband. But I was twenty-five and desperate. I elbowed the fat cousin out of the way, made a small leap, and felt adrenaline surge through me as my fingers curled around the bouquet stem. I teetered, windmilling my arms to keep my balance. Then I stood up tall and proud. I'd snagged it! I dipped

42

my nose in the pink roses and hydrangea to breathe in the sweet smell of victory.

As I looked around the room amid the applause, I saw Katie mouth, "Finally."

For a second, I could have sworn I heard my grandma whispering in my ear. *You don't need a man to be happy. And you don't need your snotty friends either. You're great just as you are.* Grandma began saying things like that after she came to visit last year, but she was wrong. Throughout my childhood I'd been friendless, a quiet introvert, terrible at small talk. I couldn't go through that again. So I needed to find a husband—a rich one, preferably—to pass Katie's test. For my future. For my happiness.

So I would finally fit in for good.

I looked down at the flowers, so pink and pretty and full of potential.

Please, God, let this work. Please.

A half hour later, I was sitting at our table, trying to think of something interesting to say, when the waiters began serving the cake. It was pink, Meghan's favorite color, with buttercream icing. I tasted a small forkful. Mmm. The strawberry cake was soaked with champagne. I reached for another bite.

"Really, Lizzie?" Katie said. "Do you need that cake?"

I looked up. Some of the husbands at our table were digging in, but all of my girl friends had pushed their plates away untouched. I set down my fork and did the same, ashamed.

"If I weren't working, I'd eat it," our waiter said as he set down the last plate on our table. "I hear it's delicious."

He was about my age, maybe a little older, with light brown hair curling a bit below his ears. His eyes were green and bright. He smiled at me and leaned down, whispering "one slice won't kill you," before he headed back toward the kitchen.

"Don't even think about it, Lizzie," Katie said.

I twisted toward her. "What?"

"I see that dopey look on your face. He's a waiter, for God's sake." Katie then turned away to continue the conversation she'd been having about the best time to visit Paris. Something else I could only dream of.

I excused myself to go to the restroom. It was empty when I got there, thankfully. I sat at the cool marble counter and touched up my makeup, then pulled out my phone and called up the romance I was reading. Katie would be quite unhappy to know I was hiding in the bathroom, but I couldn't help it. Being alone was such a relief.

After about twenty minutes, I figured I had to rejoin the party, so I returned to my table. Everyone was off dancing. The cake plates had been cleared. I sat alone, admiring the pink-and-purple rose centerpiece and my hard-won bouquet, kicking myself for not finding a date. Attending this wedding with someone, anyone, would have been better than coming alone.

"Don't like the music?" Our waiter had materialized by my side, refilling my wine glass.

"Oh, I'm not much of a dancer." Lie. I liked to dance, though I wasn't great at it. But better to lie than admit I was dateless. Although I guess that point was obvious.

The waiter perched on the chair beside me. Up close I could see the slight stubble emerging on his chin, giving him a raw look that made my stomach flutter.

"You just need the right partner," he said. "Maybe you and I could have dinner some time and go dancing."

My heart sped up. He seemed nice. He was good-looking. And his eyes were soft and kind, with little creases underneath that made me wonder if he was a reader, like me. Maybe that bouquet did have magic in it. I glanced at the dance floor. No one was looking my way. "I'd like that. I'm Lizzie."

"Hi, Lizzie." He took my hand in his. It was strong and warm. "I'm Warren."

Warren called the next evening. He told me about his day, working another big wedding at the resort. There had been a bit of a scandal when the groom lifted the bride's gown to remove her garter. He was horsing around and pushed the fabric up too much, revealing momentarily that the bride had gone commando. The bride roared with laughter, but her mother nearly fainted.

"Wow," I said. "You don't see something like that every day."

"In my job, oddly, you do. Too bad it was over in a flash. Ba dum dum."

Now I couldn't help laughing. "That's terrible."

Then Warren asked about my dinner availability that week. I had planned to turn him down. I'd come to my senses that morning, realizing he'd never pass muster, so why waste his time? But before I knew it, I found myself saying that Thursday would be great for me and I was looking forward to it. And I was. I pushed thoughts of Katie's disapproval away.

I spent the next few days agonizing over what to wear, how to fix my hair, what color to paint my nails. Like a silly teenager. Thursday couldn't come soon enough. When it finally did, I met Warren at an Italian restaurant down by the water. We got a table on the patio and ordered a bottle of white wine. Soon the combination of the alcohol and the salty breeze flowing off the ocean helped me relax, which was great, because my adrenaline had been on overdrive. I kept reminding myself that it was important to figure out if I liked him, not to simply make him like me, but it was hard not to get super excited with hopes and dreams.

After we ordered, Warren began asking lots of questions. I was flattered that he was so interested in me, but my job (performing pre-employment background checks online) wasn't much to talk about. I didn't have many personal stories to tell him, either. So I kept changing the subject back to him. Turned out Warren was much more than a waiter. He was in graduate school, studying to become a marine biologist. I'd always found science difficult but fascinating. And he was planning a career in it, studying ocean animals and plants to discover new medicines.

"What are you smiling about?" Warren asked, a twinkle in his eyes.

Oops. I was grinning like an idiot and practically dancing in my seat, overjoyed because I'd found this great guy—this guy I liked, this guy who seemed to like me, this guy who definitely would pass Katie's test now that I knew he was preparing for a real career. Not that I could tell him any of that.

"I've always loved the ocean, too," I said instead. "It's one of the reasons I decided to go to school down here, even though my family is all up north. Sometimes I come down to the beach late at night to walk in the moonlight. I love how I can practically taste the salt settling on my bare arms and how it feels when my toes slip into the cool sand."

And I stare at the water, out at the horizon, the distant twinkling stars reminding me of fairy tales, and I dream of a day I won't walk the shore alone. Pathetic but true, I thought. But maybe not for much longer.

"What else do you do for fun?" Warren asked, pulling me out of my head.

"I read. I'm reading a pirate romance now. Actually, I read a lot of them." If Katie were here, she'd talk about something more interesting, like how she went on a biking tour of Italy with her husband. (She'd agreed to that trip in exchange for spending last Christmas in Hawaii.) I struggled for something else to say. "I used to go to the movies and do a lot of window-shopping with my friends, but ..." I sighed inwardly. I shouldn't have brought that up.

"But what?"

"Oh, they're just busy a lot these days." Doing actual shopping and going on couples' date nights.

Warren cocked his head to the side. "Are these the same friends who tried to make you feel bad at the wedding for tasting the cake?"

I shrugged. Warren refilled his wine glass, then topped off mine. "Well, it's not for me to say," he said. "But you seem like too cool a girl to spend your time with people who make you feel bad."

"Oh, no, they're nice girls, really."

"Really? How did you become friends with them in the first place?"

"Katie and I shared a room in our sorority, beginning in sophomore year. I used to help her with her homework."

"Help?"

I paused. "Okay, I did her homework." He raised his eyebrows. "And her friends' homework. *Our* friends' homework. Papers and stuff. I was happy to do it. I'm good at research. And they needed time to work on sorority matters."

"Hmm. I bet they were happy to let you."

I lowered my head, embarrassed.

46

Warren took my hand. It was the second time he'd held it. It felt good. Right.

"Enough about that," he said. "Let's talk about something fun."

"Like what?"

He winked at me. "How about buried treasure?"

Turned out Warren was being facetious. He'd said *buried treasure* to entice me because I was reading that pirate romance. But what he mentioned next was just as intriguing. Salvage work. Miami is near the northern tip of the Florida Keys. Many ships have wrecked on the Keys' shallow coral reefs before sinking to the ocean floor, Warren said. Some of them are still down there, with gold and other enticements, waiting to be found. So it's like buried treasure, minus the pirates.

Warren had never actually done any salvage work, but he'd been reading about the missions since he was a teenager. It was what got him interested in marine biology in the first place.

We finished the wine, Warren paid the bill, and we went walking on the beach. He told me grand stories about lost ships, and I told him what I loved about my pirate romances. I'd never talked about them in detail with anyone before. They were my guilty pleasure. But Warren didn't seem bored at all. He'd read a lot of fantasy as a kid, though now he mostly read non-fiction. But still, he was a reader, like me. My girl friends only skimmed fashion and travel magazines.

As we came around a dune where the beach was deserted but for tiny crabs scuttling across the sand, he grabbed my hand for the third time. I squeezed his hand back, rubbing my thumb across his palm. A breeze came up, rustling my skirt and caressing my legs. Then, under the beautiful full moon, he kissed me. His lips were soft and warm and fervent, and I think, for a few moments, I forgot how to breathe.

Pirates never had it so good.

I must have texted Katie and the other girls fifty times over the next few weeks, bursting to tell them about Warren. We'd gone out several times each week since our first date, and things had progressed, physically and emotionally. We'd even developed a Thursday night ritual: take-out Chinese and a movie at my place. But my friends didn't respond. Or when they did, they were too busy to meet. Or talk. I hadn't told them why I wanted to meet in my texts. I'd wanted to surprise them. But ultimately it seemed I had no choice. So I texted Katie: *I met a guy.* I heard back from her almost immediately: *Lunch at Prime 112. Tomorrow 1 p.m.*

The trendy, see-and-be-seen South Beach steakhouse was way too expensive for me. Thank goodness for credit cards. At least there wouldn't be a wait because it was the off-season. And we had a reservation. I arrived a few minutes early, eager. Too eager. I waited by the bar, taking in the ambiance. Sleek black tables, red chairs, and pale brick columns. I didn't see anyone famous, but their A-list clientele of models, sports stars, and singers probably only came out after dark.

A few minutes after one, Katie and Meghan walked in. Meghan had that radiant newlywed glow, all tanned and relaxed. Katie looked perfectly South Beach, her skirt shorter than decent, her silk, scoop-neck tank revealing much too much, her gold bracelets puddling together at her wrist. The hostess eyed Katie up and down and, approving, seated us right away. Thank goodness, because while Meghan and Katie had the afternoon to kill, I had to go back to work.

They ordered mojitos and salads, and I ordered water and the crab cake appetizer as my meal. Kind of funny that none of us ordered meat, considering the place was known for its steaks. But I didn't have the cash to blow on a steak, and Katie always chose restaurants because of their cachet, not because she actually wanted to eat the food.

Once our orders were placed, Katie asked Meghan all about her honeymoon. Meghan had gone to an island off the Brazilian coast, very exclusive and romantic. She'd been back for more than a month, so Katie must have known all about the trip already. But she apparently wanted to hear the details again. I nearly went mad from not interrupting to share my news, but I reminded myself to practice patience, and to be happy for Meghan. At least I didn't have to try to think of interesting questions to ask. Katie controlled this conversation as she did every other one. I just oohed and aahed when appropriate.

Finally, when we had nearly finished our meals and Katie had coaxed every last tidbit out of Meghan, she turned to me and smiled wide. "So, Lizzie, you met someone? Who? Where? Tell us everything."

And I did, talking way too fast, like a kid visiting Santa at the mall, eager to list every last desire before my time was up. I wanted them to know how wonderful Warren was. How happy I was. How much we had in common. And, most important, I wanted to make it clear that Warren wasn't some no-potential loser. Once he completed his PhD, he'd become a professor at a university. He was someone they could be proud to be seen with. When I finished, I exhaled loudly, and waited expectantly, at long last, for Katie's approval.

She and Meghan locked eyes, then Katie shook her head. "You're dating the *waiter* from Meghan's wedding?"

I blinked repeatedly. That was all she'd heard? "Well, yes, he's a waiter now, earning money while he works his way through school. But he's going to be a professor of marine biology." Of course I'd said that already.

"Like a weather man?" Meghan asked.

"No." God, I'd explained this part, too. "He—"

"Enough, Lizzie," Katie said, interrupting. "He's a waiter *now*. And he has the potential to earn, what, just above minimum wage sometime in the future? This is what has you all excited?" She rolled her eyes and sighed. "After all this time, I shouldn't be surprised. You pick one no-potential loser after another."

"He's not a loser. He's great. He—"

Katie shoved the palm of her hand in front of my face, cutting me off. I ground my teeth as years of little digs and insults emerged from my subconscious. Then, furious, I slapped her hand away. Katie's mouth and eyes hung open. I'd never stood up to her before.

"There's more to Warren than you could possibly imagine, but since you only care about money, I'll mention this. As part of his studies, Warren has come across some very interesting information about buried treasure. He's going to find it. And we'll be richer than you could possibly imagine."

I didn't know where that lie had come from, but it felt good. I was running with it.

49

Katie laughed. "Buried treasure? You must be a bigger fool than I ever thought if you believe a line like that, Lizzie."

I wiped my mouth with my cloth napkin and threw it on the table. "No. I was a fool when I thought you were my friend, instead of realizing you only kept me around to use me and make yourself feel better. I've known Warren for just two months, but he's a better friend to me than you've ever been." I stood up. "I'm so done. Done with all of you." I grabbed my purse, ready to go, but then turned back. "And by the way, in the rest of the country, a size eight isn't considered fat!"

And with that I walked out, leaving Katie with my bill.

My righteous indignation didn't last long. Ten minutes after I returned to my office, I ran to the bathroom and cried in a stall. Over the past few weeks, Warren had helped me see Katie for who she was, but I'd made excuse after excuse for her. I'd considered Katie my first real friend, my best friend. Like a big sister. I didn't want to lose her. I loved Warren—I hadn't told him so, but I did—but I needed friends, too.

"Are you okay?"

I peeked through the gap between the stall wall and the door. It was Dru Ann. She worked in the cubicle next to mine, also doing background checks, though she'd been at it for a lot longer than I had. She was in her late thirties, with short black hair and a figure that hadn't bounced back after she began having children. She came in right at nine every morning, worked like a machine all day, and left at five. I'd never spoken with her much. Not that I'd ever had much to say. Until now.

I rubbed the tears from my cheeks and pushed the door open, trying with all my might to keep it together. That worked for about ten seconds. As soon as I stepped out of the stall, I began blinking as if I'd developed massive tics in both eyes, and burst out crying again.

She pulled me into a hug. "Honey, what happened?"

I breathed deeply, trying to calm down. Dru Ann's cotton top had a floral, comforting scent, reminding me of the fabric softener my grandma washed her sheets in. I used to talk to my grandma whenever I was sad, and it usually made me feel better. So I pulled back from Dru Ann, grabbed toilet paper to dab my eyes and nose, and then I told her everything. Everything. We were in the bathroom quite a while. Good thing neither of us had urgent deadlines.

"Wow, honey," she said when I finished. "You don't talk much, but when you do, you just let it *all* out."

That made me laugh.

"Seems to me, Warren is right," she said. "Why would you want to stay friends with folks who make you feel bad? What you need are new friends. Better friends. Women with the same interests as you. I'm in a book club. You should join us."

"Really?"

"Of course. We don't read too many romances, but I'm sure you'd fit in."

I hugged her. "Thank you."

"Now I have one more suggestion." She scanned the room, as if ensuring no one was listening, even though we'd been the only ones in there the whole time. "Have you ever conducted background checks on those fancy friends of yours?"

"No. Why would I?"

"Oh, you never know what kind of interesting information you'll come across. Not that you should do anything with it, but simply knowing private stuff like that can make you feel better."

"I'd never thought of that."

She nodded. "If I were you, I'd be checking out that Katie girl in a flash. I bet she has some secrets of her own. Everybody does."

Boy, Dru Ann was right. I researched all my friends and learned a number of interesting things. Katie's house was mortgaged to the hilt, three times over. She and her husband were living off credit and prayers. And Meghan had been arrested once for shoplifting! For so long I'd felt inferior to my girl friends. They were hotter than me, and cooler, and ... somehow I'd convinced myself they simply were better. Katie was correct about one thing. I'd been a fool.

But no more. I spent a delicious few minutes that evening thinking about how I could use the juicy information I'd learned to make Katie suffer. Then I realized she was suffering already, being so cold and shallow. It was enough for me. So I put Katie and the rest of my former friends out of my mind as I dressed to go out.

It was the night before Halloween, and Miami always went all-out for this holiday. Warren and I weren't big on the club scene, so we'd decided to go the Monster Splash at the Seaquarium. There'd be carnival rides, marine animals, even a haunted-house-type show called Buried Alive. In honor of our shared appreciation of pirates and salvaging, we decided to dress in pirate garb. I adored how Warren put having fun before worrying about what other people would think.

So with Warren donning a black eye patch, white puffy shirt, and a pirate hat with a skull and crossbones on it, and with me in a red headscarf, black peasant skirt, and an oversized white blouse with a tight black vest over it, we headed out. On the drive over, I told Warren about my blow-up with Katie. He was sorry I'd gone through that but agreed with Dru Ann that I could find better friends.

I watched him as he drove. He drummed his fingers against the steering wheel, singing off tune to "Monster Mash" on the radio, not caring a whit how he sounded. His self-confidence was catching. I could completely be myself with him, rarely at a loss for words, but comfortable with our quiet times, too. I joined in on the song, knowing I'd already found the best friend of my life.

Soon we were wandering around the Seaquarium like a couple of kids, eating candy corn and hot dogs and caramel apples, fitting in just fine. Turned out nearly everyone there had dressed up, including the staff. When we spotted a pirate skeleton carrying a large treasure chest, Warren stopped.

"You know, I have to work another wedding tomorrow night, but how do you feel about a late date afterward?"

"Sure. What did you have in mind?"

"How about we dig for buried treasure?"

And that's how it came to be that at a little before midnight on Halloween night, I was dressed up as a pirate again, but this time in billowy pants, walking hand in hand on the moonlit beach with Warren.

"I'm surprised the wedding ended this early," I said. "I'd figure anyone who'd get married on Halloween would be the type to party late."

"Oh, it's still going on. I got a friend to cover for me during the clean-up phase. I snuck out right after we served the cake."

"Ah, the cake. My favorite part of a wedding."

"And here I thought it was catching the bouquet." He winked at me.

We eventually came to a deserted part of the beach. We walked around a dune covered with salt grass rustling in the breeze, and I recognized the spot. It was where we'd first kissed. Warren pulled me close and kissed me again, long and hard. When we parted, all I could say was, "arrrr."

He laughed. "Wait here. I need to get the shovels. I hid them by those palmetto trees earlier."

"Earlier? You've been a busy boy today, haven't you?"

After he saluted and walked off, I sank down onto the sand and pulled out my phone. This afternoon I'd posted on my Facebook page about my evening plans: "I'm going on a midnight date with Warren. We're digging for buried treasure!" I wanted to see if anyone responded, but the only reply had been from my mom. "Have fun, honey." Boy, did I need more friends.

Warren hustled up with the shovels. "Ready for a little hard labor?"

"You sure know how to show a girl a good time."

He removed a piece of paper from his pocket and unfolded it. It actually looked like a treasure map. He studied it in the light of the full moon.

"Okay," Warren said. "We walk ten paces away from the water line, and X will mark the spot."

I knew Warren couldn't have an actual treasure map. Pirates never really buried treasure. That was a myth. But I also knew he'd gone to some trouble setting this up, so I happily went along with it. We took ten long paces. *Someone* had made a large X in the sand with sticks.

"You're lucky the tide didn't wash this away before we got here," I said.

"Madam, I have no idea what you're talking about, but I do think this is the spot." He smiled. "Besides, the waves rarely come up this high."

He handed me a shovel, and we began digging. Warren started singing the "Dead Man's Chest" song, and I joined in on that, too. We dug and sang and laughed. Warren was a lot stronger than me, so in a few minutes he'd dug a bigger hole than I ever could have made myself. My arms began tiring.

"Are we almost there yet?" I asked, reminding myself of a kid on a long car trip.

"Almost. It wouldn't be as much fun if we didn't have to really dig for it. Just a little bit farther—"

A light suddenly flashed on us from the dune. I stopped digging and looked toward it, squinting, trying to shield my eyes with my hand.

"Oh, please," Katie said, slurring her words. "You could dig to China and never find anything, you dope." She stood there alone, wearing a trashy devil's costume and holding a flashlight. My Halloween nightmare.

"Katie, what are you doing here?" I asked.

She stumbled toward us, a fruity-wine smell preceding her. "I saw your Facebook post, and I had to see this for myself. You actually think you're going to find something." She started laughing, so loudly and meanly that I couldn't believe I'd ever thought she was my friend.

"This is the infamous Katie?" Warren asked.

"Yep." I turned back to her. "How'd you find us?"

"Like you're that hard to follow." She staggered up to me and started poking her finger into my chest. "Anyone who casts that large a shadow in the moonlight shouldn't wonder that people can see her."

Warren stabbed his shovel into the sand, while I began grinding my teeth.

"Don't you dare speak to Lizzie like that," Warren said.

Katie flicked her eyes at him, then rolled them. "So after Jake left me alone tonight for another weeklong *business* trip," she continued, refocusing on me, "I decided to make my own fun, following pathetic Lizzie and her moronic boyfriend. He actually picked you up at your door, as if you were a princess." She

54

laughed, jabbing her finger at my chest again. "But you'll never be anything but a hippo. And he'll never be anything but a no-potential loser."

My fists clenched as heat surged through my body. "He's not a loser. And I'm not fat, you drunk bitch!" And without thinking, I swung my shovel, slamming it into the side of her head. Katie fell to the sand without a sound. Blood began trickling from her ear.

"Oh, my God." I dropped to my knees and put my ear to her lips. "Warren, she's not breathing."

He knelt down and laid two fingers on her neck. "No pulse."

I fell back on my haunches, my breath coming faster and faster. "What are we going to do?"

Warren held his hands wide in a *beats me* gesture.

I couldn't believe this was happening. "We have to call the police."

"No. I won't let you go to prison." Warren's voice was hard, determined. He stood and began turning his head, looking at Katie, then at the hole, then at me. Several times. "What we're going to do," he said when he finally stopped, "is make the best of a bad situation."

Without waiting for me to respond, he grabbed his shovel and began digging hurriedly. Then I heard a *clunk*. He pulled a small treasure chest from the sand. It was the size of a child's toy. "This was for you."

He dropped it beside him and resumed digging. After a couple minutes, when the hole was pretty deep, Warren grabbed Katie by her legs, dragged her to the hole, and rolled her in. "You with me?"

I nodded. My arms shaking, we both began refilling the hole at a breakneck pace, making sure to bury the blood-covered sand along with Katie. When the hole was filled and smoothed out so it appeared like every other part of the beach, Warren grabbed the shovels and rinsed them in the surf. I clutched the baby treasure chest and Katie's flashlight, and we headed back to the car. We kept to the shadowed section of the sand in case we'd cross paths with anyone. We didn't.

55

Katie's shiny red Jaguar was parked at an angle beside Warren's silver Honda, taking up two spots. It had a large dent in the front fender that looked new. She must have hit something while she drunkenly followed us tonight. God, I hoped it was something and not someone.

Warren and I drove from the parking lot at a leisurely pace so not to attract any attention. We passed a number of costumed revelers shouting and stumbling down the streets. For them, this was still a happy holiday. All treats, no tricks. But it would never be that way for me again.

I wiped the flashlight with my shirt, trying to erase the fingerprints, and when we reached an area with no pedestrians, I threw it in the Dumpster behind some business. Finally, we pulled into the small parking lot beside my apartment building. Warren shut off the motor, and I leaned back against the headrest. Neither of us had spoken for several minutes.

He touched my shoulder. "Are you okay?"

Okay? Katie was dead. How could I ever be okay again? I shrugged.

"It wasn't your fault," he said.

"It was my fault. I could have called her names. Told her off. Anything but bash her head in with a shovel."

"You didn't mean to."

"Like that matters." I exhaled loudly, every nerve in my body raw. "And now we've covered it up. Buried her there, like garbage. Even Katie didn't deserve that."

I needed to be alone to process all this. I opened the car door. "I've got to go." I hurried out, not giving him time to respond, and shut the door. Warren stared at me a moment, his eyes sad in the fading yellow dome light. Then he backed out of the spot and drove off.

I kept reading and listening to the news that week, but Katie never was mentioned. Not as a missing person. Not as a found body. Warren and I must have done a good job with that hole.

Days passed, but I didn't hear from him, and I didn't dare call. Not after I'd blamed him for burying Katie, when all he'd been trying to do was help me. I'd messed everything up.

Warren had been right. Katie's death wasn't my fault. Well, not all my fault. Yes, I swung the shovel, but Katie had pushed me to it. Between her continual passive-aggressive digs throughout the six years I'd known her, and her cruelty on Halloween night, Katie had brought her death on herself. I'd never forget what happened, but I decided to try to forgive myself and be happy, even if I'd blown things with Warren.

I was doing just that as I climbed the stairs Thursday night, heading to my apartment. Dru Ann's book club—correction, my new book club—was meeting in two weeks, and I'd just picked up the discussion book from the library, *The Wild Princess* by Mary Hart Perry. It was historical fiction and appeared to be pirate-free. That, I decided, was a good thing.

As I reached the third floor, my mouth suddenly watered from the smell of spicy peanuts. I looked up from the book. "Warren?"

He stood at my door clutching the little treasure chest under his left arm and holding a plastic take-out bag in his right. He gave me a small smile. "Hi, Lizzie."

"What are you doing here?"

"It's Thursday. We always have Chinese on Thursdays. ... That is, if you still want to."

My heart began beating faster. "Of course."

A thousand thoughts swirled through my mind as I unlocked the door, but the most important one was a question. *He wasn't angry with me?* We went inside, I went to my galley kitchen for plates, glasses, and utensils, and Warren set the food on my small dining table. I was tempted to just sit and eat, avoiding the difficult conversation we had to have. But I screwed up my courage as I approached the table. "We should talk, Warren."

He nodded from his seat. I took the chair opposite him.

"I'm sorry," we both said at once.

What?

"What are you sorry for?" I asked.

"Seriously?" His tilted his head. "I put you in a terrible position. I forced you to cover things up, when the cops might have let you off if you'd explained what happened right away."

"You didn't force me to do anything. You helped me. Heck, what are the chances the police would have let me off? It wasn't like I'd been jaywalking." I half-laughed. "I can't believe this. All this time, I thought you were mad at me."

"Mad at you? Why?"

"Hello? Because I killed Katie. How many guys want to date someone who's so ... handy with a shovel?"

Warren laughed, then sobered. "I do. It's horrible what happened. Beyond horrible. But she pushed you to it. And we're in this together." He picked up the mini treasure chest and handed it to me. "This was supposed to be your surprise that night."

I flipped the lid open, finding a photograph of a gold chain necklace with what appeared to be an emerald pendant hanging off the end. I looked up. Warren was holding that very necklace out to me.

"It's my grandmother's. I told her about you. We both want you to have it." He paused. "I come from old money, though my trust fund doesn't kick in until I'm thirty. Grandfather wanted me to earn my way for a while to truly appreciate everything I have. And I do."

"Trust fund? Why didn't you ever tell me?"

"I never tell people at first because I want to make sure they like me for me. But I never had any doubts about you. I'm sorry. I should have told you from the start."

He walked around the table, smoothed my hair aside, and fastened the chain behind my neck. It warmed my skin.

Warren kneeled beside me. "You look beautiful." He cupped my cheek with his hand. "I know we haven't been dating very long, Lizzie, but it feels like this is for keeps. I love you, and I wanted to show you how much."

I stared at him, my eyes watering. "I love you, too."

He kissed me softly, tenderly. I never wanted to be with anyone else.

"You know what's funny?" Warren said as he pulled back. "If Katie had only given me a chance—met me, talked with me, hell, even Googled me—she eventually would have learned that I'd have passed her financial test."

I shook my head. "Nah, Katie wouldn't have figured that out, Warren. She never was good at research."

58

But I was.

Barb Goffman is the author of the recently released short-story collection Don't Get Mad, Get Even *(Wildside Press). Barb's stories often focus on families because the people you know best are the ones you'll most likely want to kill. Or at least that's been her experience.* Don't Get Mad, Get Even *contains fifteen crime stories, ranging from funny to dark, and from amateur sleuth to police procedural. The book has all of Barb's award-nominated stories and five new ones. Barb's short stories have been nominated for the Agatha Award five times, and the Anthony and the Macavity awards twice each. For her day job, Barb runs a crime-fiction editing service.*

In her spare time, Barb serves as a co-editor of the award-winning Chesapeake Crimes *series and as program chair of the Malice Domestic mystery convention. She is secretary of the Mid-Atlantic Chapter of Mystery Writers of America and a past president of the Chesapeake Chapter of Sisters in Crime. You can learn more at www.barbgoffman.com and www.goffmanediting.com .*

The Psychic Temp
By Devon Greene

Sidney Martin visited his psychic every week like clockwork. He continued to see her in spite of all the wrong predictions she made for him. Of all the psychics he had consulted over his lifetime, she was the worst. Her predictions never came true. He was going to give her one last chance today to get it right. If she couldn't get it right on Halloween, when could she?

He pulled up to her house and parked on the curb. Then he grabbed his umbrella from under the passenger side seat. Rain poured down on the streets in torrents. Perfect weather for Halloween night, and the dark clouds suited his foul mood.

For several weeks, Sidney had heard the rumors that he was about to be fired. He'd sensed something bad coming for some time. The company was overstaffed, so he was the most expendable one in the Houston office. He was over fifty and his skills were barely adequate. The younger new hires were faster and more adaptable. Their people skills and language skills were atrocious, but the CEO didn't seem to care if everyone got along or not. He just valued production, and the constant pressure exhausted Sidney. He offered to take early retirement, but his superiors met that suggestion met with cool sneers. The company profited more by firing him and outsourcing his job. No parachute of any kind for him.

His psychic, Gilda, never predicted this turn of events. She predicted rosy days ahead with prosperity and lots of romance. Of course, he didn't believe her anymore. The company moved him into a smaller office, reassigned his secretary to Tom Jesson, a new hire. They discontinued his other perks, too, with no warning or apology. That was the way the world worked these days, and Sidney accepted this system because he had no choice. A bleak future awaited him.

Today, he hoped Gilda would say something positive about his future that might turn out to be true. She never predicted his wife would leave him for a younger man or that his fifteen year old daughter would run away with a Goth idiot, be sent home promptly when she got pregnant, run away again to live with her mother and her mother's new husband who was only a few years older than his daughter. She'd never predicted his stock market losses, his neighbor's dog biting him, his house being burglarized. Nothing! A real cornucopia of disaster, and she never foresaw any of the fun coming. *So*, he asked himself, *does she see what's coming for her today?* Sidney was tired of all the misery dripping on him like a deadly resin. Time to spread it around a little.

When he flung open the door and walked in without even wiping his muddy feet on the doormat, his eyes shot fire at Gilda. Sidney assumed this reading would be as inaccurate as usual. She'd told him before that his anger only attracted negative energy to him. He'd have to lighten up if he wanted the universe to respond to his prayers for something good to come into his life. Sidney always laughed at the New Age babble with a sneer and usually walked out in a huff when she said these foolish things. But her inane predictions gave him some hope for getting through one more week. That's why he kept coming back. Plus, she was prettier than the other psychics he'd known.

"Hello, Sidney," Gilda sighed. "How is it going for you this week?" He knew she dreaded his answer.

Sidney scowled and shook the water off his umbrella onto her nice fake Persian carpet. He caught her stealing glances at his muddy footprints, and he could almost see her blood pressure rising at the thought that she'd have to spend thirty minutes cleaning the rug after he left. Then he saw her smile to herself, and he figured he'd pay for his rudeness somewhere down the line.

"Please sit down, Sidney. Some hot tea? Good day for it with all the spirits around tonight."

"No thanks, Gilda. Let's just get on with it." He put down

62

his umbrella, took off his raincoat and tossed it onto the sofa. Then he sat down across from her at the card table covered with a red velvet cloth that hung to the floor.

"Palm or Tarot today?"

"Tarot."

"All right."

Gilda took a deep breath and straightened imaginary creases in the cloth on the table before handing the cards to Sidney to cut. Then she grasped Sidney's palm in her hand while she closed her eyes for a minute, continuing to take deep breaths and exhale.

"Your hands are warm and moist today, Sidney. They're usually cold and dry."

He caught her opening one eye to peek at his face. He looked down at his hand, pretending he didn't see her. Then she closed her eye again and started chanting in a slow, calm rhythm. When she finished her chant she spread the cards across the table.

"Oh, spirits, guide me today in reading this man's life and help me give him wisdom to live a life of love and spirit." She hummed the same old chant in her low voice, supposedly waiting for the spirits to inspire her and reveal Sidney's future.

He assumed she'd give him one of her good readings today to cheer him up. He probably looked like he needed it. Even a slug needed a break now and then.

"I see a silver lining appearing for you, Sidney. At long last." She smiled at him.

He scowled back, certain that she could recognize the anger and desolation in his bloodshot eyes.

"Really? How big a lining and when?"

"Soon. Soon. Your money problems will ease. A new, beautiful woman enters your life very soon." She pointed at the Queen of Hearts. "She will change your life completely. You will never be the same again." She paused as if watching Sidney's reaction to the good news.

He stared at her without blinking, which seemed to make her nervous. His mouth tightened and his cheeks flushed. He breathed faster, but his eyes never left hers.

"Sidney, are you all right? You want some water?"

"No. Keep going. Tell me 'bout the woman. When do I

meet her? What does she look like?"

"Ah, okay." She glanced down at the cards again. "You will meet her very soon. I see a fair-haired girlish woman. Young. Tall. A person of strong emotion… like you, Sidney." She looked up and smiled at him again, but her smile froze.

With his hand, Sidney pointed a .22 automatic straight at her heart. There was a cold smile on his lips. His eyes were dilated and staring at her as if he could no longer see Gilda, the person, but simply an annoyance that must be dealt with. Despite his lack of stature, he gripped her hand with the strength of a pit bull.

"Too bad you never gave me a single prediction that came true, Gilda. Now it's too late to matter. I just feel like killing someone today. I'm getting shit on everywhere I go so now it's payback time, and you are the easiest one to hit. No one will connect me with you so I'll get away with it, too. Even better."

Gilda tried to pull her hand free, but he wouldn't let go. He squeezed it hard, twisting her wrist. She winced and cried, "Sidney, I only see possibilities. You make choices that change the outcome of things. I can't predict those choices. Let my hand go. I can't help you anymore."

Sidney squeezed her hand tighter, pulling her forward over the table toward him. He laughed at her now.

"Help me? Where'd you ever get the idea you helped me? You never got anything right. Some psychic you are. Well, did you foretell this today? Huh? Did you see me coming in with this gun? To kill your ass? What does it say in *your* hand?" He twisted her hand around to expose the palm. "Read it, Gilda. What does your palm say about your death?"

"Nothing, Sidney, nothing." She lost her balance and fell across the table. Sidney wrenched her arm behind her back. "Sidney, let me go. You can fix everything. I saw big money coming to you… like the lottery or something. It will all be better for you. You'll love this girl. I promise you."

Sidney lost all control now. He pulled her off the table and dragged her by her arm behind the velvet curtain hanging in the doorway to her living quarters.

"I've had enough, Gilda. You've made a fool of me for too long. All of you so-called psychic leeches have used and manipulated me. Now it's my turn." He pushed her down on her bed. As Gilda tried to wiggle away from him, he grabbed her foot and pulled her back.

"Say goodbye, Gilda, to whoever it is you pretend to talk to when you're fleecing people. Say goodbye, now."

"No, no, Sidney! Don't be crazy. You have everything to live for now. Don't be foolish now of all times. Please, Sidney. Let me go."

"Shut up and say goodbye. It's over for you, babe!" He pointed the gun at her head while holding her down. She started to cry. Sidney fired the gun point blank at the center of her forehead and wondered if Gilda, the psychic, ever saw it coming.

Sidney tossed the bedspread over her body, but blood seeped through the thin fabric and dripped down to the floor, forming a puddle that fit well with the Persian design. He took a deep breath and put the gun in his waistband. He couldn't quite describe the odd sensation he felt, but he didn't want to leave the apartment yet. Sidney's breathing was too fast, and he felt clammy. Wouldn't do to pass out on the pavement in front of Gilda's place. Sidney didn't want to attract any attention to himself, so he decided to wait until he calmed down before he left. He went to the bathroom and tried to wash off the blood splattered all over his clothes. He removed his clothes and rinsed them in the sink.

Sidney glanced into Gilda's closet and saw the gauzy dresses, gypsy blouses, and skirts she wore as her "professional" clothes. He went into the closet and stroked the filmy dresses and smelled them. They carried Gilda's strong perfume, which he liked. She was a large woman and Sidney was an average size man, so he pulled a dress out of the closet and crossed to the mirror. He held the dress up in front of him to see how it looked on him. He liked what he saw.

I could wear this to a Halloween party tonight. Just walk down the streets in Montrose until I find a good one and go in. No one ever asks for ID anyway.

He'd always wondered what it felt like to wear a dress so he decided to find out for himself. He slipped into the dress. Then he opened a drawer, pulled out one of her scarves, wrapped it around his head the way Gilda did. Added some lipstick and jewelry. He was amazed at the transformation! He laughed at his reflection.

Sidney's life had taken a strange turn in just a few moments. When he opened another drawer, his jaw dropped. Piles of money. Wrapped, neat stacks of hundred dollar bills!

"What the hell?" *Where would Gilda get this kind of dough? The psychic scam must be better than I thought.* He counted one pile of hundred dollar bills. There were ten rows three piles thick of hundreds all neatly arranged.

"Good God! We're talking big money here, Gilda. Maybe I should have married you instead of killing you. Too late now." He chuckled and pulled off the headscarf.

Sidney found a large bag in the closet and stuffed money into it.

"It must be a million or so," he said while licking his lips. Then he opened another drawer--same thing. More money! Sidney had never been so happy as he continued transferring money into a second bag.

As he laughed and made plans for a new future, he heard the front door open when the bell on it tinkled. *A customer! Uh oh!*

A young female voice called out for Gilda. He had to do something fast to keep her out of this room. So he did the only thing he could think of. He pushed the bags of money under the bed, wrapped the scarf around his head again, and sauntered into the front where he saw a beautiful young blond girl standing in the middle of the room.

Her huge hazel eyes stared at him with an intensity that made his knees quiver. Their outrageous beauty struck him speechless. His thoughts fired randomly, and one of them yelled at him, *"This is the girl, you idiot! The one Gilda promised!"*

For the first time, Gilda had said something that came true. Lots of money and a beautiful new woman to spend it on. The girl wore blue jeans and a tight blue tee shirt showing off her ample curves. She smiled at Sidney and appreciated the effect she had on him.

"Hi. Where's Gilda today?"

His speech slowly returned, "Uh . . . well . . . she took off today. Family crisis or something. I'm…" And then he stopped. He suddenly remembered he was dressed as a woman. What should he do? He couldn't lose this girl. Not now. He desired her more than he'd ever wanted anyone. He had to think of a name… fast.

"I'm Jimmie."

"Jimmie?" She looked skeptical, eyeing him closely from head to toe.

"Jimmie Sue. I'm a friend of Gilda's. Told her I'd sit in for her today while she was out. You know-- just helping out a friend." He knew the story was ridiculous and she'd never accept the lie, but he hoped she'd find it funny. Women loved men who made them laugh.

"Like a temp?" She laughed at the idea.

Sidney smiled, too, glad she had bought the story. "Yeah, like a temp. A psychic temp. Funny, huh?"

"Yeah. Funny." She moved toward the table like a panther circling its prey.

"Well, can you read my cards?"

"Cards?"

"Tarot cards."

"Oh, of course. Sure, I can. Let me clean these up from the last suck… uh, customer."

He picked up the cards and shuffled them. He didn't have the slightest idea how to read them. So he'd make it up. He was sure Gilda and all the others who'd read his had made up most of their nonsense babble. Maybe the girl wouldn't know the difference. He hoped not. He had to keep her--forever.

He took the cards and spread them all over the table haphazardly. The girl was already sitting down with both hands in her lap, and she watched him closely as he laid the cards out. He knew there was supposed to be some pattern for the cards but, right now, his brain was too frazzled for him to remember.

Then the girl started laughing. A cold, hard laugh out of those soft beautiful lips. Sidney didn't care. He just wanted to kiss them and soon. Then he glanced at her eyes. Cold and hard, too. Angry. Narrowed like a cat's before it struck. They looked green now.

She slowly lifted one hand above the table, and it was holding a gun. A large one that made his small one look pretty puny. Sidney couldn't take his eyes off the gun now.

"Ok, Bubba, where is it? What did you do to Gilda?"

"Huh, where's what?"

"The money, dope! The money! Where is it?"

"What are you talking about?"

"You only have a few seconds left to live. Gilda's not gone. She's dead, isn't she? How did you know about the money? She wouldn't have told anyone about it."

"I, uh, don't know what you're talking about."

"Okay, stupid. Last chance." She stood up and yelled, "Mother! Mother! Where are you? Are you all right?" A loud silence reverberated through the house now. Sidney slumped in his pretty dress.

It's not fair, he thought to himself.

The blonde went to the front door, locked it and picked up a throw pillow to muffle the sound of the shot. Sidney could not move. He'd left his own gun in the other room beside his own clothes.

"What have you done with her?" She held the gun about twelve inches from his brain, which was suddenly flooded with bad memories of his entire life. As he started to stand up, she hit him with the barrel of the gun, knocking him off-balance. He fell back into the chair.

"You're a dead man if you hurt my mother."

He was a dead man.

She moved to the side and glanced into the back room searching for her mother. Then she said in a low blood-curdling voice, "Get up, you son of a bitch. Get up."

He placed his hands on the table and pushed himself up for the last time. Sidney mused how such a small gesture became so important when he faced a deadly gun. The blonde motioned for him to turn and go into the back room. Sidney put his hands up and walked ahead of her. He figured he had about ten more steps left in his life.

She spotted the blood on the carpet beside the bed and then saw Gilda's feet jutting out from under the bedspread. She gaped at the body's shape under the covers for a minute, and then sobbed.

Sidney turned to grab the gun while she was distracted, but she was too fast for him. She backed up and aimed the gun at him. He stopped.

"What did you do with the money? It's ours. We did the work. It's ours."

"Work?" He was curious. Psychic work paid that well? That was hard to believe.

"You must've read a helluva lot of Tarot cards for that amount of money, kiddo. And, frankly, she wasn't that good."

"You bastard. It's not from palm reading or Tarot. That was just a front for suckers like you. We launder money for drug dealers. "

Sidney now felt foolish for thinking palm reading was the source of the money.

"Oh. I get it. Did she hold it for you? Something like that?"

"Something."

"I won't tell anyone. Just let me go."

"You're right about that. You won't tell anyone--ever!"

She raised the gun and Sidney crossed his arms in front of his head. The blast was loud in spite of the pillow, and it was the last sound he heard. His blood ruined the real Persian rug in the room. As he died, he realized, ironically, that all the positive predictions Gilda promised him had finally come true. He came into a lot of money, met a beautiful new woman, and she changed his life.

Devon Greene writes and sweats in Fort Worth, Texas. As far as she knows, none of her writing has appeared on restroom walls but if she runs across any submission guidelines for a particular wall, anything is possible. Several stories have appeared on mystery ezines in the past and one humorous piece won first prize at a writer's conference held at Weatherford College in 2012. She also writes plays which have been produced both in Houston and Los Angeles including one full length play accepted and produced in the Edward Albee workshops in Houston. She is currently working on three novels, which she hopes to finish this year if the cats will stop distracting her.

The Creepiest House on Witch Hazel Nook
By Marianne Halbert

Corwin Hill pedaled his heart out up the ramp. It wasn't a ramp anyone had built. Other than God, if you believed in that sort of thing. Or developers if you didn't. Just a steep dirt rise at the highest elevation in the subdivision. For that two-point-six seconds (he'd timed it) he could see all seventy-four homes in the neighborhood. While the sun peeked over the horizon, a speck of yellow bobbed at the neighborhood's entrance. For a moment, the canvas sack carrying his newspapers flew skyward, the straps digging under his armpits and yanking across the tops of his shoulders. Then the entire load slammed onto his fourteen-year-old back as the tires of his hybrid bike bit into the dirt on the downhill side.

He veered left, avoiding the elm tree, then swung back to the right. Dried leaves, crimson, bronze, golden, crackled satisfyingly under his wheels. Suddenly, the crackling stopped as Corwin approached the creek. The sound became sodden, soggy. He had to pump double-time, plowing through the mud. Dammit. *The rain. Last night's thunderstorm.* He hoped it wouldn't rain tonight for Halloween. Globs of cold mud spattered on the lower part of his jeans, chilling his shins. His tires rumbled over the wooden planks of an arching bridge across the creek. Corwin sped down Mr. Bixler's back yard, and passed him on the driveway as the man wheeled a boxy trash can to the curb. Mr. B. waved. Corwin took his right hand off the handle, reached over his shoulder to snag a paper, and flung it toward Mr. Bixler, who caught it and smiled.

Corwin squeezed his right hand to brake at Mrs. Dair's mailbox next door. She preferred hers in the newspaper box. He smiled and shook his head when he saw her concrete lawn goose with black pointy ears. *A bat, or a cat?* She'd apparently decided on rust colored mums this year. *Too bad about the dead grass in the front corner of her yard.* Over the summer, during the neighborhood covenants dispute, someone had written GET OUT with Round-Up on the lawn. The GET was in Mrs. Dair's yard, the OUT in the Hodges'. As he'd done his summer paper route, he'd watched that grass wilt and wither to a dry dead yellow.

Now he passed the Hodges' place since they were on vacation. He'd be back to feed and walk their Yorkie later. He skipped the next two houses (one because it had been repo'd, the other because they didn't subscribe to the paper). He flung three in a row onto driveways…*whop whop whop.* Placed another in the paper box. He continued down Witch Hazel Nook toward the entrance of the neighborhood. He saw Becca Baines in a bright yellow rain slicker. She had set up a stand on the sidewalk near the end of her driveway. Selling bushels of apples from her uncle's orchard. Cider. And at sixteen years old, she made the sweetest apple pie Corwin had ever tasted. He tossed a paper in her direction, careful not to hit her or her products.

"Apple pie today?" he heard her yell as he sped away. On the school bus or in the hallway, she usually ignored him. He figured most sophomores ignored the freshmen. But when she was selling, there was a tone in Becca Baines' voice that was almost as sweet as her pies.

"Maybe later," Corwin shouted over his shoulder. He turned left onto Chokeberry Mews, and by the time he'd gotten to the end of that cul-de-sac and back to Witch Hazel, his load was a lot lighter. He crossed over onto his own street, Burning Bush View. He emptied his sack except for one paper, then headed back to Witch Hazel. He glanced toward his left, and saw Becca and her pies. He turned right toward the dead end where Mr. Bixler's house sat. To the right of Mr. Bixler's house was Mrs. Dair's, and to the right of her place, he saw Maxi, the Hodges' Yorkie, sitting in the window. But he was going to the house on the left of Mr. B.'s. He sped up the U-shaped driveway. Mr. Warlon liked his paper left on the porch. He was old, and his hip might give out walking to the end of the driveway. Or so he'd told Corwin probably a dozen times. Corwin tossed the paper onto the porch, glimpsed the strobing light of the television through the front window, and cruised back down to the street.

Mr. B. had set the ramp up for him in his driveway. Corwin pumped his legs, and headed straight for it. His aim for the ramp had been perfect, and he soared over the woodpile feeling the wind in his hair. The soar lasted point six seconds. (He'd timed it). And that was all it took to see Mr. B. laying prone behind the woodpile. With his eyes frozen skyward, his neck twisted grotesquely backward, his hand still clutching the newspaper, and a wood splitter embedded in his spine.

Corwin Hill pedaled home as fast as he could. His property backed up to Mr. Bixler's back yard. He raced over the bridge and through the woods they shared. A breeze sent dry leaves fluttering down around him. He dropped his bike on the driveway, and ran inside through the garage. His mom was in the kitchen, piping orange icing onto cut-out pumpkin-shaped cookies. The familiar smell of fresh baked cookies enveloped him.

"Hey sweetheart. Can you take the trash down to the curb for me?" she asked. But when he plopped down on the kitchen floor, hugging his knees to his chest, she paused, and said his name. When he began crying, she dropped the icing bag into the bowl, and the next thing he knew, her arms were around him. Five minutes later, he heard the sirens approaching.

The police questioned him for about fifteen minutes. They wanted to know what time Corwin began his paper route that morning.

A few minutes past eight, I guess.

And Mr. Bixler had been alive at that time?

Yes, he caught the paper I threw him. He set up the ramp for me.

You didn't actually see him set up the ramp?

No, it was just our routine. Biking was his passion. For a guy in his mid-thirties, he was still really good. He even did the Hilly Hundred a few years ago. Taught me how to fix a broken chain. Gave me an old spare pump. We built the ramp together last spring out of extra plywood he had left over from a room addition.

And you said your bike route takes no more than about ten minutes, twelve at the most?

Right.

Did you see anyone else nearby?

Corwin thought of Mrs. Dair's concrete goose, and Maxi staring out the Hodges' window. Mr. Warlon's television flickering through the window. Of Becca Baines and her apple pies.

No.

The cops left shortly after that.

Corwin had been sitting on the sofa. He looked down and realized he'd been sitting on the sofa – in his mud-spattered jeans. Corwin's mom had added a little water to the icing. It had begun to stiffen. She was stirring, and looking at the bowl when he spoke.

"Mom, I'm sorry, I got some mud on the couch." His tone had been deadpan with the officer, but now it was quivering. He was thankful his dark hair was long enough to partly shield his eyes.

"Want a cookie?" she asked as she began decorating them again. Her tone was normal enough, but his mom never let him have a cookie before lunch. And she'd normally freak over anything staining the furniture.

"I'm not hungry." Corwin's mom gave him a look that said, *you're never not hungry*. All was not right in the Hill household.

"I'm going out for a ride," he said, snatching his jacket from the back of a kitchen chair, and a key on a gray shoestring from above the fridge. Suddenly his mom wasn't so nonchalant. She stepped between him and the door, planting her feet. She had a dab of orange icing drying above her left eyebrow.

"Corwin, that's not," and she turned her head, as though looking for something over her shoulder. "That's not a good idea. It might not be safe out there. You can help me carve the pumpkins, and change out the floodlight to the orange one. I need you here, buddy."

74

"Just for a while. I need to feed and walk Maxi. And I need to ride." He could tell by the crease in her brow, the way the dried icing cracked above her eyebrow, that she didn't like it, but she stepped aside. She suddenly reached for his face as he passed by her, and he paused long enough to let her plant a soft kiss on his forehead. They were about the same height now, and before too long he knew she'd have to lean up to kiss him. Corwin was pretty sure she was about to cry. He kissed her back, on the cheek. Something he hadn't done in a long time. Not because he didn't love her, it was just that kissing your mom usually seemed so juvenile. Today it seemed grown-up. It seemed right. He walked out, and closed the door behind him.

Instead of taking the back way, he went down Burning Bush View, then turned right onto Witch Hazel Nook. He pulled his bike into the driveway. Maxi was sitting quietly in the window as usual. He let himself in the front door, and opened a can of mushy, smelly dog food. Maxi kept her eyes on him until he stepped away. Then, very daintily, she ate her breakfast. While she was eating, he pulled open a drawer near the fridge, and grabbed a plastic blue baggy. He stuffed it in his pocket. When Maxi was finished eating, Corwin washed out the bowl and set it to dry. He grabbed the smallest leash in the world from a basket near the door.

"So, lady, you ready for a walk?"

They walked along the sidewalk, heading straight down the street toward the neighborhood entrance. He approached Becca, who got out of her chair and started fawning all over Maxi.

"She's adorable, I didn't know you had a dog."

"I don't," Corwin said. "Petsitting for the Hodges while they're out of town."

"You want some pie?" she asked, turning her hazel eyes up to look at him. Her sandy blonde hair fell in loose waves over her shoulders.

Corwin sat down on the grass. He plucked a piece of it, and started slowly breaking it to pieces. "Mr. Bixler was murdered this morning. I found the body."

"What? How?" Becca asked.

Corwin explained about his bike route, and about seeing the body behind the woodpile.

"He had an axe in his back. And his head didn't look right. I think maybe his neck was broken, the way his face was twisted back. And his hair looked, darker than it should. Wet."

"Oh, Corwin," Becca breathed. "I'm really sorry. I saw the cop cars pull in earlier, but I had no idea." Becca stood up and prepared a piece of pie for him. She handed him the plate.

"I just can't figure who'd want him dead. Everybody liked Mr. B." He took a few bites of the pie. "I'm going to ask some of his neighbors if they saw anything."

Becca shook her head. "Don't you think you should leave that to the police?"

"They don't know anything. Just took the report, took his body and left. He deserves to have whoever did this caught. I've got to do something."

"Wait here," Becca said. She took her cash box and walked up the driveway and disappeared into her house. A few minutes later she came back out. She was wearing UGGs, jeans, a pea coat, and a beret the color of cinnamon sugar. "So where do we start?" she asked.

Corwin said he wanted to talk to Mr. Warlon and Mrs. Dair, the neighbors on either side of Mr. Bixler's place.

"Perfect. Mrs. Dair called me little while ago and asked me to drop a bushel of apples by her house." She started to reach under the card table for the apples, but Corwin offered to carry them. Becca carried Maxi, and they began walking toward the dead end of Witch Hazel Nook. If Life is fair, Corwin thought, one of my friends will look out the window and see this.

"Corwin," Becca said. "Not everyone was crazy about Mr. Bixler. It was his room addition last spring that kicked off the flurry of meetings about making the neighborhood covenants more restrictive. You know, the dead grass on Mrs. Dair's lawn, and the Hodges'—"

"He wouldn't have done that."

"Maybe not. But if someone thought he had, that might be all it took."

"Three months later? That's a long time to wait for revenge. Besides, the Hodges aren't even in town." They'd made

76

it about halfway down the street. An *I just got an idea look* dawned on Becca's face. She stopped walking and faced Corwin.

"What if they aren't out of town?"

"Of course they're out of town. I'm petsitting their dog. Bringing in their mail."

"What if that's what they want you to think, because they need an alibi? What if they're still in the house, hiding upstairs? Have you checked their garage to see if their cars are gone?"

A chill shimmied across the back of Corwin's neck. "No, that's crazy," he said. But his voice didn't sound too confident. A car slowed down alongside them. Mrs. Dair rolled down her window.

"Hey kids. Becca, you can just leave those on the porch. I've got to run an errand, be back in a jiffy."

They walked on down the street, and Corwin set the bushel on the porch. Then they crossed the street and rang Mr. Warlon's doorbell. Maxi had practically fallen asleep in Becca's arms. The door swung open. Mr. Warlon looked Corwin up and down, then slammed the door. Becca rang the doorbell again, and they switched places. This time when the door opened, it didn't close.

"What do you want?"

"Sir," Becca asked carefully. "We were just wondering if you'd seen anything unusual this morning."

Mr. Warlon paused, narrowing his eyes. "You mean other than the coroner taking my neighbor away in a body bag?" He tilted his head slightly.

Corwin stepped forward, "Mr. Warlon, we're just trying to—", but the door slammed in his face. Corwin rang the bell again, and was surprised when the door opened again. "Trick or treat," Corwin said.

"Trick or treat hours don't start until six p.m. tonight. Besides, you're too old for that kind of thing, and you don't have a costume. No costume, no candy."

Corwin looked at Becca. He was desperate. He slipped his shoes and socks off, and wadded the socks up, shoving them under the shoulders of his sleeves. He bent over and grabbed a wad of dirt, swiping some under each eye. Mr. Warlon looked disgusted.

77

"A football player? A scrawny kid like you? Let me give you some advice kid, you can't pull off that look. But I'll give you an A for effort. Hang on." He walked away, leaving the door ajar just a crack. A minute later he came back and held out a bowl. It contained an individually wrapped package of Fig Newtons, and a sample size tube. Corwin picked up the tube.

"Denture adhesive?" Corwin said.

"Put that back boy, ladies first."

"But she doesn't even have a costume," Corwin protested.

"No costume, no candy."

"Sure she does," Mr. Warlon said, smiling a little for the first time that morning. "She's playing the part of the pretty girl next door. And doing a mighty fine job."

Corwin turned to Becca. "You're older. You'll need dentures sooner."

She smirked. "I floss," she said. She took the Fig Newtons.

Mr. Warlon reached out to pet Maxi on the head.

"Hey there, little feller."

"Actually," Becca said, "it's a she."

Mr. Warlon shrugged his shoulders. "Uh well, nobody's perfect."

Corwin wanted to get back to the investigation now that Mr. Warlon had begun to warm up a little. "Sir, did you see anyone at all this morning before the cops showed up?"

Mr. Warlon was stroking the back of Maxi's neck. The dog's eyes were closed. "No. Like I told those cops who came by, sirens woke me up."

"Well, we appreciate your time."

Mr. Warlon nodded and closed the door softly behind him. Corwin whispered to Becca.

"His television was on before I found the body. He's lying."

"Just because the light is on, doesn't mean anyone is home. He's more ancient than the Sphinx. Old people fall asleep with the TV on all the time. The TV being on isn't proof he was awake." She flipped a wave of her hair over her shoulder. He hadn't eaten anything except that slice of pie this morning, and her beret was still making him think of his mom's cinnamon toast.

"You're just trying to defend him because he liked your costume and offered you first dibs. He probably doesn't even have a bum hip. No one's ever even seen him leave his house."

Becca brushed him off, and wanted to check out the Hodges' garage. They walked back across the street. Corwin glanced to his left, to the house at the end of the cul-de-sac. Yellow crime-scene tape surrounded the wood-pile at the top of the driveway. By the time they got to the Hodges' door, Corwin's stomach was in knots. He didn't want to be anybody's alibi. And in his mind he was now convinced they were hiding upstairs. A bouquet of Indian corn hung from the door. *Would killers actually be the kind of people to take the time to hang Indian corn?* They walked in the house and Becca set Maxi down on the floor. The Yorkie shook her fur out, and hopped up onto her perch at the windowsill. Becca urged Corwin toward the garage.

Corwin reached out his hand, and touched the cool doorknob. He sucked in a breath, and swung the door open. Both cars. Both cars sat in the garage. Corwin's eyes were fixated on them.

"Maybe they took a cab to the airport," he said.

"Or a rental car, or had a friend give them a ride," Becca added.

They backed away from the garage, and Corwin closed the door.

"Let's not freak out here," Becca said. "This is still our same neighborhood, still our same neighbors. We shouldn't jump to conclusions." She went into the kitchen and ran some warm water. She tore a paper towel off a roll hanging from the underside of a kitchen cabinet.

"Come over here," she said. Corwin obeyed, and she began cleaning the dirt from under his eyes. She stood back and looked his face over. "Better," she declared.

"Funny, I would've thought you'd prefer the football player look."

She laughed as she tossed the paper towel in the trash. She was careful then when she spoke. "Not on you." She plopped down on the couch, and rested her UGG covered feet on an ottoman. "So if we assumed for a minute it's not the Hodges," she said, and Corwin agreed it was way too creepy to keep thinking it might be them, "then who? And why today? Why Halloween?"

Corwin had a thought. "Did you have any customers this morning? Or see anyone coming and going in the neighborhood?"

"I'd been out there maybe twenty minutes before you rode by on your bike. And no, until the cops drove in, I hadn't seen anyone else. Other than the Earles setting their pumpkins out, and Mrs. Curdy tying a cornstalk to her mailbox post. But no one wandering the neighborhood. No one suspicious."

Corwin felt wistful, remembering how cool Mr. B's house always was at Halloween. "None of the other families around here came close to Mr. Bixler's stuff. The tombstones in the lawn, the witch on a zip line over his walkway."

"Mrs. Dair comes pretty close. She usually makes the effort at least."

"Yeah, she's got Auntie Goose dressed as a black cat this year."

"Auntie Goose?" Becca asked. She sat up straighter, taking her feet off the ottoman.

"You know, that lawn decoration of hers. She calls it 'Auntie Goose'. Puts a bonnet on it in the spring, bathing suit in summer, raincoat during a storm. I saw it this morning. Black pointy ears."

"No," Becca said, shaking her head. "I saw that thing when we dropped the apples off. It's a ghost."

"Black pointy ears means cat."

"White sheet equals ghost." She said the words slowly, like she was talking to a five-year-old. "It's my keen sense of observation that will help you crack the murder case. Auntie Goose is dressed as a ghost."

"Wanna bet?" Corwin asked.

She held out her hand to shake.

"Stakes?" he said.

"The loot from Mr. Warlon. Winner takes all. The fig newtons *and* the denture cream."

Corwin knew she didn't want either, but he had to admire her competitive spirit. "You're on." They shook on it.

They left Maxi on the windowsill, and Corwin locked the front door behind them. As soon as he turned he could see Auntie Goose in the yard next door. Covered by a white sheet.

"That's weird," he said. "This morning it had black ears. Maybe she's saving the big reveal for trick-or-treat hours. That ghost costume isn't even a costume. No eyes, no hem. Sloppy, sloppy, Mrs. D." They walked up to it. Corwin grabbed a stick, hunched over a little, and lifted the edge of the sheet up. Becca leaned down with him.

"Is that-?" she asked.

"Hair?" he answered. They inched a little closer. Corwin squinted his eyes, trying to get his mind to wrap itself around what he was seeing. Becca's voice sounded nauseous when she spoke again.

"And is that-?"

Brain matter? Corwin heard the car pulling up to the curb behind them. He dropped the stick onto the grass, and the sheet dropped back down. A car door slammed and Mrs. Dair waved a meaty arm at them.

"Hey kids."

"Mrs. Dair," Becca said. "We brought the apples you wanted."

"Great," she said, a large grin plastered across her face. "I need some help here."

Corwin and Becca walked down toward the car. Mrs. Dair handed them each a bag of groceries out of her trunk. Her red shock of hair glimmered in the morning light. But it didn't move at all. *She must go through a can of hairspray a week.* They followed her up the driveway. She was wider across than the two of them combined. She yanked open the garage door and hefted it up. Then she went around to the porch and came back holding the bushel of apples.

"Well, come on in. See what I've got in store for tonight."

Corwin's brain kept telling him to run. *We'll just put these groceries down, say polite goodbyes, and get the heck out of here.* As they put the groceries down on a table near the back of the garage, Becca was signaling him with her eyes. He looked

81

behind him and saw a container of Round-up, with a hose and nozzle attached, sitting on the shelf. He heard the garage door slam shut behind him. Then the lights went out.

The regular lights that is. A moment later blacklight shone down from the ceiling. Becca's teeth glowed, and looked so perfect and white, Corwin was sure she was right. She'd never need dentures. Spiraling orange plastic streamers hung from the rafters.

Corwin felt a hand clamp around his wrist, forcing his palm into something slimy in a bowl.

"Eyeballs!" Mrs. Dair declared. "Really just peeled grapes, but pretty good, right?"

"Oh yeah," Corwin sputtered. "Pretty good."

"Try this one," she said, moving his hand to another bowl. "Cat intestines. Or cooked cold spaghetti noodles. Now all I need is a severed head for that table over there. Any volunteers?" She laughed that full throated waddling laugh of hers again. Then the laugh subsided, and she sighed. "You know, there's a lot of pressure on me to put on a good show for the trick-or-treaters tonight. With Scott not being able to participate."

Corwin looked at Becca, whose eyes were wide under the blacklight. *Scott Bixler*.

"We used to have so much fun, he and I. And he was such a thoughtful man. He felt so bad when someone vandalized my yard over the summer. But at least that put an end to that crazy talk about stricter covenants and an aesthetics committee. I don't need anyone to tell me how tall my shrubs can grow, and Scott loved his home improvements. I couldn't let them interfere with that. What's a little dead grass compared to his happiness? But Halloween. That was *our* holiday. Trying to out-do each other every year. It was like a dance. Did you know he was going to have a fog machine this year? Can you imagine that?" She sounded genuinely impressed. "A fog machine. Anyway, we used to compete to see who had the creepiest house."

"Uh, I don't think you have anything to worry about there, Mrs. Dair," Corwin said. "I'd say hands down, you've got the creepiest house on Witch Hazel Nook."

Becca nodded in vigorous agreement.

82

"Oh, you kids are so sweet," Mrs. Dair said, getting choked up. "You don't know how much that means to me. You know, I heard him taking his trash to the curb this morning. I walked over to show him Auntie Goose's costume. He was in such a good mood, but then he said he's started seeing someone. She was going to come over tonight to help him pass out candy. Well, I can tell you, Auntie Goose didn't like that kind of talk one bit. No siree. After the conversation she had with Mr. Bixler, there was no more talk about new girlfriends."

No, Corwin thought. After the conversation Auntie Goose had with him, that was pretty much the end of all things Bixler. So he was hit in the head with a concrete goose. That would certainly explain the way his neck was twisted, and why his hair was dark and bloody, if his skull was crushed in. So why had she planted the axe in his back? One last moment of rage, and it was a weapon of opportunity laying by the woodpile? How many weapons were within reach here in her garage? *We have to get out of here.*

Mrs. Dair picked up the bushel of apples, and dumped them into a barrel. Corwin could hear the slopping and splashing sound they made as they plopped into the water. He lunged forward, and grabbed her around the waist.

"Becca, run!"

Becca let out a blood-curdling scream as she ran for the garage door. The neighbor on one side was out of town, the neighbor on the other side out for good, the one across the street was more ancient than the Sphinx, yet still Corwin prayed someone would hear the cry for help. But Mrs. Dair was fast for a meaty woman. She grabbed an apple and flung it at the back of Becca's head. Corwin heard the thud, and saw Becca drop to the floor mid-run. In the silence that followed, Mrs. Dair spun in his grasp, and put a hand around the back of his neck.

"Too bad about your bike accident. I hear you drowned in the creek."

She slammed his head forward, into the cold water in the barrel. Apples nudged against his head as he struggled for breath. His hands gripped the side of the barrel and he tried to push himself away. His lungs were burning. He sucked in a quick breath, but all he got was water in his lungs. He hands flailed and gripped something. One of the bowls. He tried to hit Mrs. Dair over the head with it. He could sense the cold slimy feel of cat intestines on his hands. Frantic, he kicked at the barrel, and managed to get his head above water. He heard Becca's voice.

"Let him go, or I'll blind you." She practically growled it. The fierceness in her voice scared Corwin. *Thank God she's on my side.* He turned his head enough to see Becca glowing in the dark, the bottle of Round-up in her left hand. The nozzle in her right, pointed straight at Mrs. Dair's face.

There was a large booming sound and the garage door flew open. Three policemen stood on the driveway, their guns drawn. Corwin could see Mr. Warlon across the street, headed down his driveway toward them.

Becca put down the weed killer. Corwin explained what happened, and considering how soaked he was, the cops didn't doubt that Mrs. Dair had tried to drown him. Corwin saw Becca's beret laying on the garage floor. It must've fallen off when she'd been pelted by the apple. He bent over to grab it, then held it out as he turned to her.

"You OK?"

She took his hand and moved it toward the back of her head. He could feel a small raised bump where the apple had connected with her skull. "I think I'll live." She took her beret and put it gently back on her head.

The police called their parents. Becca's dad pulled up in his pickup truck. She started walking toward the truck, then turned back.

"Corwin, maybe on Monday, you could stop by my lunch table. You know, just to say hi."

"Sure," he said, water dripping from his shaggy hair down his neck. "Maybe." He smiled, and he was sure she knew he'd stopped by. After all, she was Becca Baines.

He watched her run toward her dad, and saw them embrace. Then he turned and walked up to Mr. Warlon, who had made it about halfway across the street. Maybe his hip really was going to give out. Corwin's mom drove up just then, and she leapt from the car, not even bothering to turn the engine off or close the door.

After she'd hugged him half a dozen times, she turned to Mr. Warlon.

"The police say you're the one who made the 9-1-1 call. How did you know?"

"Well, these kids put the idea in my head to be on the lookout for anything suspicious. That little pooch has been sitting quietly in the window across the street for nearly ten years now. But, a few minutes after the boy looked up the goose's skirt and that garage door slammed shut, the poor pup was going nuts. Scratching at the window, yipping like crazy. Couldn't hear her but I could see her plain enough. After the way Bixler took out of here this morning, I didn't figure to take a chance. If I was wrong, senile old man made a mistake. Besides, no love lost between Mrs. Dair and me. Not ever since I made fun of that goose of hers a few years back."

Auntie Goose. The unwitting accomplice to murder. Corwin looked up toward the yard where she hid under a scrap of a white sheet. The more he thought about it, the more he realized the axe hadn't been in anger. It was a decoy, so the cops wouldn't look for the real murder weapon. At least until Mrs. Dair and Auntie Goose had had this one last Halloween together. The police were putting up a small line of yellow crime scene tape around the goose. They lowered Mrs. Dair, handcuffed, limp spaghetti noodles clinging to her hair, into the back of the cruiser.

"I don't know how we'll ever thank you," Mrs. Hill said.

"Well, I've got an idea about that," said Mr. Warlon. He pulled out his wallet and peeled off several bills. "Way I figure, the responsibility for putting on Halloween in the Nook has fallen on me. Most kids in the neighborhood probably going to be too scared to even venture down this way tonight. Those brave enough to risk it, deserve some candy. Maybe even a little denture cream." He winked at Corwin. "So let the boy pick out some candy, and a couple simple decorations. Friendly ones. Smiling ghost or pumpkin. And of course I'll need to borrow the boy at six o'clock. If I try to get up out of my chair every five minutes for three hours to answer the doorbell, my hip's likely to go out." Corwin was smiling, and he could tell by the look on his mom's face, she'd agree to Mr. Warlon's request. "Oh, and boy, bring that little feller over with you if you want. He can sit on the recliner with me while you take care of the trick-or-treaters."

Corwin didn't bother to correct him again about Maxi not being a feller. He retrieved his bike from the Hodges' driveway, and promised his mom he'd come straight home, for a hot shower and dry clothes. Even though he knew he'd be back on this street tonight, he was relieved to have escaped from the creepiest house on Witch Hazel Nook.

Marianne Halbert is from Central Indiana. She loves all things weird and dark, and has had dozens of short stories published in magazines and anthologies. You can now find those stories in her "Wake Up and Smell the Creepy" series. She was also a panelist at AnthoCon 2011 and 2012, and is currently working on her first novel, "The Lady's Pocket". Follow her at https://www.amazon.com/author/marianne.halbert and http://halbertfiction.webs.com and Halbert Fiction on Facebook.

Pact of the Lantern
By Daniel Hale

There is a place where the monsters live. A low, cold, dark place, closer than the shadows that trails behind you at dusk, and further than the wind that scatters golden leaves into the night. It is a hollow place, without a soul, where every moaning ghost, every shuffling ghoul, and every shrieking, toothy, long-legged beast scraps and scrabbles and bickers, fighting for space around tiny, glimmering pockets of light; minute windows, peepholes into the higher realm. They huddle round them, peering into the daylight world.

And they wait, without patience, for the day when the windows begin to widen into doors, large enough to pass through. They watch with eager, greedy eyes until they can squeeze through the holes and into our world, while the ether of the Hallowed Realm trails along behind them.

Halloween is when the walls begin to wear thin and the cold can seep into the walls, and the monsters can come to play.

The first trick or treaters left their homes and dashed excitedly into the streets. Costumes of all kinds were in sight: gleeful witches and cherubic devils, miniaturized movie stars, hobos and hippies, clowns and super heroes, ninjas and fairy princesses and angels. They ran and skipped happily in the streets, their parents trailing along and watching anxiously for cars.

The neighborhood was completely transformed; front yards were lined with ominous signs and fake tombstones. Hedges and bushes were coated in cotton cobwebs. Papier-mâché ghosts and bats hung from skeletal trees. Pumpkins sat on every stoop, carved with hollow grins and cartoonish faces, lit from within by flickering flame. As the first families set out, porch lights began to turn on; a friendly beacon of invitation, a longstanding etiquette.

Not everyone joined in the celebrations. One particularly surly old soul had gone to the lengths of painting NO CANDY in large black letters on a plywood board across his door.

Every year the traditions die a little more, as parents spread scary stories of children made ill by poisoned candy, or worse. They talk about masked kidnappers and keep their children in on Halloween night. They do away with monstrous masks and fake blood and orange lights and plastic skulls and Jack o' Lanterns.

In seeking protection for the sake of their children, they destroy it.

This is the face of Halloween: a sideways grin with wide eyes and a single tooth, hinting slyly at secrets discovered and fears reborn anew. It is a grin that can charm the most stoic of souls into acts of mischief and malice, and can stare into the face of the Devil itself without ever once wavering. It is the grin of someone who knows where all of the bodies are buried, and does not promise to keep them a secret. It makes no promises you can trust it to keep. It is a grin that implies everything, and reveals nothing.

As the night began to wear down, the children were guided home, dragging sacks of candy. Already many of them had sampled their treasures, and were walking with a post-sugar high exhaustion. Still they tumbled on, fighting to keep their eyes open, eagerly anticipating the moment they could dump their takings before friends and siblings and count every delicious piece.

A little girl dressed as a princess screamed and cried as her father carried her home. "Something took my bag!" she bawled. Her father, too tired to care, marched on.

The bushes along the sidewalk rustled strangely. From the way the leaves were shaking, it looked as though something— perhaps several somethings—were hiding, trying their best to go unheard.

"You didn't, you *didn't*," croaked one rather raspy voice. It was harsh and bestial, and it spoke in a tone of fearful disbelief.

"Oh shut yer snout, you fuckin' crybaby," was the snarled response. "Or I'll give ye somethin' to bitch about."

"Well you've only gone and broke it now," stated a third voice. "That was a bloody pact violation, you stupid shit."

"And just 'ow do ye figure that, eh Scabus?"

"Because," continued the one called Scabus. "You stole the lass's bleeding sack! You only darted out there when she dropped it and bleeding well snatched it! And that's not allowed, isn't it, Founger? Ye ain't allowed stealing from the marked."

"Yeah," grunted the raspy voice. "No stealin' from the marked."

"Well she wasn't fecking marked, was she?" complained the thief. "Not a mark on her. And what about the sack? You two see any lanterns on here? No? Right. It's just that sparkly pixie wench all over it. And she didn't see me anyway, so it's no harm."

"It damn nearly was," retorted Scabus. "That was too close by half, Pintley. You needn't have chanced it so."

"Didn't see you coming up with anything otherwise, Scabus." Pintley leered and a glint of something like teeth could be seen in the darkness. "We've been out here for hours with no luck. Might as well have something to show for it. Now you two shut up or you won't be getting nothing from my lovely sack."

"Any tootsies? You knows how I likes those," Founger asked. The bushes shook and shuddered once more, and the voices did not speak again.

It was late. A tiny bonfire spat and cackled beneath the wooden bridge of the local park, surrounded by three figures. Though it was difficult to make out many details in the dark, the flickering light revealed flashes of scaled hides, pointed ears, and pales eyes. One figure was crouching inside a large sack, muttering and sifting through the contents, while another held something on its lap that seemed to be twitching.

"Ooh, lots o' lovelies in 'ere," the voice of the figure in the sack was slightly muffled. "There's always something worth nicking at that Lucile wench's apartment." The sack sifter, whose name was Pintely, pulled a long slender bottle out of the sack. "Oo wants some champers?" he said in a high-pitched voice. His friends guffawed sickeningly.

"I still can't believe nobody saw us, in that crowd," snickered Scabus, the breeze blowing through his long, mossy hair.

"I reckon that one bugger did," mused Pintely, needle-grin glinting in the light. "That pale chappy with the greasy dreadlocks. Though I don't think he was in a position to do much, with the whiff I was getting of him…"

"'e smelled like a skunky, 'e did," croaked Founger, his blunted snout sniffing at the twitching thing in his lap.

"'Ere, Founger. Why don't you just go and kill the little blighter already, eh? Put it out of our misery."

"I likes to sees it twitch, Scaby." Founger dragged his tongue across the poodle's fur, once artfully curled and now crusted with blood and dirt "Makes it more fun."

"Little shit deserved it anyway, the way it was yapping at us." Pintley glared at the small dog. "Besides, look at it. It's like a fecking rat, it's so small and mangy. Why'd these humans have to go and make their dogs look like rats, eh? That's real class, that is." He turned back to the sack and resumed digging.

"Aye, and you'd know all about class, Pintley," responded Scabus. "I saw what you did in their milk."

"Just topping it off with some lovely brandy!" Pintley's and Scabus' shrieks of laughter disturbed the night, sending owls and foxes fleeing.

Founger looked up, concern scrunching his reptilian features. "We won't get into trouble for that, will we? Cause…they's had a pumpkin…"

"Nah, Founger, I told ya," Pintley explained. "It wasn't carved or nothing. No grin. No lantern. Means no protection, which means they's free for us! So no trouble, see?"

Founger looked doubtful, but nodded. He started up at the sky. "We's should be getting off. The windows'll be shrinking soon."

"Yeah, all right," Pintely said and straightened up, the sack over his shoulder. "Till next year, lads."

The fire went out and the three were gone. In the darkness under the bridge another light briefly flickered and faded. The afterimage suggested the shape of a grin.

Another year passed, with little to mention. There were the days that passed as any other, and the days where our world pulled a little closer to the Hidden Corners. The sleigh tracks and hoofmarks on the roofs quickly faded beneath falling snow. Gifts of chocolate and painted eggs appeared in the bushes with a twitch of leaves and the distant scent of fresh tilled earth. The impossible folk of the Hidden edged between realms, not yet prepared to fade away, leaving their mark once again to let us know how much goes on and how little we will ever see.

And when the leaves started to change color and fall into thick blankets on the lawns, and when mischievous winds curled through the streets, the people of the Hallowed Realm began to stir again. Some woke early, to scout ahead and see what fun could be had this year.

"What do you reckon, Pintley?"

The three goblins peered from a sewer grate at the old house across the street. It was old-looking, compared to the other houses in the neighborhood, and distinctly Gothic. Its gray roof jutted alarmingly in the air, and the largely black exterior made it look extremely somber. There was even a black Bentley, somewhat like a hearse, parked in the driveway.

"Well the way I sees it is, 'e's got to be a posh bugger, what with buying a house like that." Pintely grinned eagerly. "Should be plenty to loot come Hallows' time."

"Dun't look too posh to me," rumbled Founger. "Looks like a bleedin' wreck. Haunted, I shouldn't wonder."

"Nah, I asked Robby, up in the Llewellyns' attic," replied Scabus. "No ghosts in there, he said. It's just a bloody old house. Nobody in there since the 20's, he said, and they didn't stick around long."

"All the better for us then, innit? There'll be a right lot of lovelies in there, ripe for the picking."

"You sure about that, Pintley?" Founger scratched his head, bursting several boils. "Dun't recall a moving van or anything."

91

"Course I'm sure," Pintley replied haughtily. "'s a big house, innit? Bound to be food an' silver an' all sorts in there to steal or wreck. Bound to be."

Scabus looked back to the house. "'es coming back!" The other two leaned forward eagerly through the grate as the front door opened.

He was a tall, burly figure. He had a big bushy beard of a sickly orange, and long stringy hair of the same. His broad form was covered by a big brown trench coat and he wore big black boots. In his arms he carried an orange pumpkin with two triangular eyes and a crooked, single-toothed grin.

"'es a big one," Scabus whispered as the man walked forward.

"Oh no," Pintley moaned as he placed the Jack o' Lantern on the edge of the porch. He struck a match, lifted the stem and lit the candle within. Then he walked down to the Bentley and drove off.

"A Jack o' Lantern," whispered Scabus, astonished. "An honest to goodness, Jack o' Lantern. Proper one, too, with ol' Jack's grin an' all. First I've seen in these parts in ten years."

"We's won't be getting in there, then," Founger muttered. "Tha's the pact, true enough."

Pintley snarled at the house. "That fucking pact. What's the bloody point? The one bloody time of the year we's get to 'ave a bit o' fun, and we have to leave some bastard alone jus' cause 'e lit a fucking pumpkin on fire."

Scabus looked sideways at Pintley, surprised at this outburst. He patted him on his spindly shoulder. "That's the way of it, mate. Nothing we can do. Best to just leave it as is."

Pintley calmed slightly, but continued to glare at the house. "Yeah…s'pose you're right."

Founger sniffed the air. "Never mind. I think I smells some rats. Let's 'ave a nibbles, eh?" He shuffled down the tunnel on his knuckles. "Come on, Pintley," Scabus called as he followed.

Pintley glanced back at the house, and the hateful Jack o' Lantern, before running after his friends.

Halloween was two days away. The goblins spent their time stalking the streets. Though they could physically exist in places where humans couldn't see them, out in the open they reverted they became unreal and ghostly, streams of wind that eased through the open and slid into bushes or sewer grates, places where they couldn't be seen.

As they came to rest in a shrubbery, Pintley peered through the leaves. "'ere, you two. Look." He pointed to the sidewalk, where a piece of paper lay crumpled. A picture of a Jack o' Lantern was just discernible. "Wonder what that is."

"Looks like a piece o' paper," Founger said, and whined as Pintley smacked the back of his head.

"I can *sees* that, you stupid lump. But what *is* it?" He glared at it. "I want a closer look. Go and get it."

Founger rubbed his head and sniffled as he crawled out of the shrub. He vanished into the wind, and a gust blew the paper up and above. Scabus snatched it from the air and read it while Pintley read over his shoulder. Founger rematerialized beside them.

It appeared to be some kind of flyer: white with yellow letters, with a large grinning Jack o' Lantern in the background. The words COMMUNITY HALLOWEEN PARTY sat at the top, followed by a list:

- COSTUME CONTEST!
- BOBBING FOR APPLES!
- JACK O' LANTERN WORKSHOP!
- GHOST STORIES!
- ALL ON HALLOWEEN NIGHT!

And an address: the house of the first man to light a Jack o' Lantern in the neighborhood in years.

Pintley, Scabus and Founger were quiet for several minutes as they each finished reading (Founger taking slightly longer than the other two).

"Wha's that mean?" Founger asked. "Wha's a Jackie lantern workshop?"

"It means," Scabus said at length. "That he's gonna teach em 'ow to make em."

Founger blinked once, looked down at the ground, and then up at the leaves of the bush shading them from sight. He blinked again, slowly. "Oh," he said. Another moment passed, and this statement was followed by another. "Fuck."

"'e can't do that!" Pintley teared the flyer out of Scabus' grasp and crumpled it in his fist. "Fifteen bloody years in this bloody little town where the bloody people are too bloody *stupid* to keep up the bloody traditions. *Fifteen bloody years we've 'ad it good. And now....*" He stopped, his reptilian features furrowing into angry determination. He leapt from the bushes. The furious gusts of his non-physical form breezed away.

"Pintley!" shouted Scabus. "Oh, bloody hell. Come on."

Pintley streamed through the streets as an ethereal wind, followed by Scabus and Founger. From their own perspective the ether of reality was blurring around them as they moved through visible space invisibly. From the perspective of the people in the streets, a blast of wind tousled their hair and blew off their hats.

At last, the house was in plain sight. The wind seemed about to blast against the door before diverting to the storm drain across the street. The winds of Scabus and Founger darted in soon after.

"Oo the flyin' fuck do ye think ye are?!" shouted Pintley from the drain.

"Shut it, ye stupid-" Scabus tried to say.

"You shut yours and all, Scabus Scumsticker." Pintley flared his pinhole nostrils. "This bastard is going to take everything we've had. This is our place! 'e's got no bloody right..."

"Someone's coming!" Founger hissed.

There was indeed a man walking towards the house. He was portly, in a sports jacket and tie, with glasses and a shiny, bare scalp ringed with short, stringy hair.

"Bugger me," whispered Scabus. "That's that Anderson chap, innit? That ponce bugger what does the neighborhood association thingie."

"What's he want?"

Mr. Anderson proceeded to walk up the steps and onto the porch, and rapped sharply on the door. He pulled a folded piece of paper from the inside pocket of his jacket. The goblins saw a flash of orange.

"'e's there about the party!" Pintley chortleed with glee. "Hehe, I think our mister Jack o' is in fer it now!"

The door opened, and the man with the orange beard greeted Mr. Anderson with a warm smile.

"Never did like Anderson," mused Founger as Anderson spoke primly to the bearded man. "'e's a picky bastard. Remember when 'e went off at the school fer puttin' together that haunted house? Damn near went postal."

"All the better for us, then, innit?" Pintley rubbed his talons together in anticipation. "No way he'll be puttin' up with this bugger's 'alloween party!"

The bearded man still smiled as Anderson talked at length. He still smiled as he invited Mr. Anderson into his house. Anderson appeared to hesitate, and began to say something else. The bearded man laughed and drew Anderson in with an arm round his shoulder.

"What the bleedin' heck is going on now? Why's 'e going inside? I dun't like the look o' this, Pintley…"

"Shut it, Scabus! It dun't make no different." Pintley continued to peer out of the drain. "Whatever 'e may do, 'e ain't gonna hold no 'alloween party round 'ere. Ol' Andy ain't gonna stand for it.

Pintley ceased talking, and continued to watch. Scabus looked at Pintley, sighed with resignation, and sat down against the wall of the tunnel.

The goblins waited. Scabus continued to sit, and muttered under his breath. Founger found a centipede, which kept him amused as he pulled off each of its legs one at a time. Pintley kept to staring at the house. And then—

"It's opening!"

Scabus and Founger looked to the house. Mr. Anderson was indeed walking out the door. In his hand he had a big, sticky caramel apple on a stick, and was laughing joyfully as the bearded man showed him out. He shook his hand, continuing to speak with a sincere smile and a gleeful energy that, the goblins realized with growing disquiet, was *joy*.

As Mr. Anderson walked off, still munching his apple happily, Scabus glanced sideways at Pintley and said "Looks like it went well."

"'e's lettin' 'im do it." Pintley's voice was an astonished whisper. "He's only going and letting 'im do it…"

"Looked damn cheerful about it, too," commented Scabus. "Not like the bugger at all."

There was silence, save for Pintley's shocked mutterings and the *crunch* of Founger eating his centipede.

Scabus looked to Pintley, thinking of what to say. "Well," he started. "And so what? 's just a bloody party anyway. So he teaches a few brats 'ow to make Jack o' Lanterns. So we lose a few houses. So what?"

Pintley lashed out. Scabus shrieked in pain as wicked talons nails scraped his face. He clutched his cheek, hissing and snarling. "What the fuck, you bastard?!" he screamed.

"It may start," Pintley whispered, low and menacing. "With just a few Jack o' Lanterns. A few more people remembering the old ways. Remembering the pact. But then there'll be more, and more, and *more….*" He barred his teeth at Scabus and Founger, both visibly trembling in fear.

"And then it's all of them. All of them remembering, *and we get left in the cold.*" Pintley shook his head slowly, before casting his eyes back to the house. "We ain't gonna have that. Get ready, lads. Tonight, we's *sorting this out…*"

"I don't like this."

"You shut your maw, Founger."

There was silence in the neighborhood, on the night before Halloween. In other places, the people of the Hallowed Realm were creeping out from the shadows, grinning and eager, ready to pillage and defile the homes of humans, to steal and trash and wreck and laugh in those places untouched by the omniscient grin of their despotic king, the lone guardsman at the edge of the shadows.

Normally, this would have been the way of things here. But Pintley, Founger and Scabus, the goblins who had long since claimed this town for themselves, who had been a tiny yet persistent wave of dread there for fifteen years, had more important things on their minds.

"Come on, Pintley, it's well after midnight! We's could be out there right now! We's could be 'avin' an evenin' o' it."

96

Scabus protested. "Instead, we's lurking in these bushes like a load a bloody badgers!"

"I don't care! We're not letting this bastard take the town away from us." Pintley stared up at the house, and the shimmering light of the Jack O' Lantern.

"But it's *marked*," Founger moaned. "No stealin' from the marked, no messin' with the marked, no *nothin'* with the marked. Them's the *rules*..."

"I told you to shut it, you great pustule!" Pintley hissed before scurrying through the bushes and across the road. Scabus and Founger hurried after him.

Pintley stopped short of the porch and stared at the pumpkin. His body froze almost of its own volition. He had planned to walk right up and smash the stupid thing, destroy it in front of the others to show them how stupid and cowardly they were. He had intended to caper and dance on the squashed remains and throw seeds at Founger and Scabus in mockery.

"Pintley?" whispered Scabus behind him.

He stared into the fire at the heart of the pumpkin, his body rigid with a terror that his mind screamed to rebel against. But sense flees in the face of fear, and the habits of centuries, avoidance, and reverence for the grin had Pintley in its grip, and he could feel himself backing down as the words reverberated in his head. *No nothin' on the marked....*

He stared into the flame. He began to shake. His teeth clenched together. Far away he heard Scabus. "There'll be other houses. Other towns."

He almost gave in. He almost turned away.

At once, the hate and fear and frustration rose inside of Pintley and he leaped at the lantern. Snarling and spitting he tore it apart, orange rind and seeds flying through the air. He crushed and gouged at it until the flame was gone and the pumpkin was nothing but a juicy orange pulp.

Scabus and Founger watched in silence, unable to process this unthinkable blasphemy.

At last, Pintley stood, breathing deeply and glaring at the greasy remains of the lantern in triumph.

Founger's jaw worked silently, his black eyes wide. "*You didn't...*" he moaned.

Scabus whispered. "*Pintley...*"

Pintley hesitated, momentarily at a loss, before he forced a confident grin. "Whatcha say, lads? No lantern here! Let's have a browse!" His affected excitement and enthusiasm, hiding the sheer horror and shock he felt at what he had done, fooled nobody.

Founger sat on the ground, holding his head in his hands, rocking back and forth. Scabus shouted a nonsensical litany, "Youstupidshitlookwhatyoudidfeckfeckitalllookatititsovernowwe 'redead—"

"It's nothin'! Pintley's cheer turned into a strained shriek. "No silly lanterns 'ere!"

Scabus paced back and forth, his face scrunched in frustration. He squatted by the sobbing Founger, trying to reassure him. "Founger, hold it mate! It's, c'mon, it's not that bad! We, um, we'll run off! Right now! Just keep runnin', keep movin'. They won't find us!"

"They will!" Founger cried, tears and yellow snot streaming down his face. "'e's fucked us, we're dead we're *dead...*"

"No! We, ok, maybe, um, oh! We'll get another pumpkin! *Yes that's it!* And we'll carve another lantern, nobody will know!"

"*Dead dead dead, we's dead n' dead, we's gonna get skinned and carved and burned—*"

"WE'S GOING IN THE BLOODY HOUSE!" Pintley screamed.

Scabus lunged at Pintley and gripped him by the throat. "*You shut up, just shut the feck up you stupid toad shit nothin'*," he hissed in anger. "*You's can go in that bloody house and face the bleedin' Hollowing alone, but me an' Founger is getting out of here now, we're not gonna be burned cause you were too stupid and greedy to listen to us.*"

"*Ssscabusss,*" stammered Pintley as Scabus throttled him. He pointed a quivering talon over his shoulder and stared wide eyed at something. Scabus turned sharply around

"My oh my," whispered the orange bearded man in a breathy voice. He dropped Founger's prone body to the ground. "What is this? A couple of mischief makers, come to egg and teepee the place and spoil everyone's Halloween?" He grinned at the two remaining goblins.

The twisted body of Founger stared sightlessly at Scabus and Pintley. Scabus reached for his friend's face and cried. "Founger, oh fucking fuck no, Founger why—"

"The fuck are you?" Pintley growled defiantly. "Why're you here? What you playing at with these pumpkins?" His angry bravado masked his fear. He barred his fangs. "This is our place!"

"Not so, Pintley Gormellow." The man continued to grin, arms folded behind his back. "This was never your place, though you've certainly made your mark here." He sneered at the supplicating Scabus and stepped forward. Pintley backed away.

"It's been quite a flush decade and a half for you three," he mused. "You've done quite a bit to make Halloween a hated and feared custom here. People forget the old ways so easily, don't they? The parents think they know what's best for their kids, and then needlessly destroy the things that keep them safe. I blame the Internet myself." He shook his head and sighed.

"How do you know my name?" Pintley whispered. Scabus stared wide-eyed as the man advanced and stammered desperately. *"Please, oh lord, please have mercy."*

"Why, don't you recognize me, Pintley? Mister Scumsticker here certainly does." In a swift movement he grabbed Scabus by his mossy hair and held him up. Scabus struggled and cried in pain. *"No oh no please please don't please..."*

Krrrk.

The man dropped Scabus, his head now twisted completely around on his crooked head. Pintley stared at the corpse that had once been his friend. He wanted to flee, but his body was locked in terror. A tiny animal whine escaped his lips.

"I'm the Hollowed King, and the Hallowed Beast," the man intoned. "I am the Overseer of the Under Realms, and the Autumn Kingdom. I am the flutter of leaves on October breezes, and the cackling of witches under the full moon. I'm Stingy Jack, the Drunken Smith, and the Lantern Lighter. I'm the sneak-thief that tricked the Devil himself, who escaped from Hell and was denied Heaven. I'm the wandering soul, and the grinning fire that

99

keeps you and yours at bay." He stood close enough that Pintley could see his teeth; yellow and black, with a single tooth missing from his jaw.

The man reached down and lifted him up, gently, by the neck. Pintley struggled, scratching and trying to bite, but the man took no notice.

"And now I've come to remind one and all of the pact. You lot have had your fun, but you've gone too far. You've grown greedy and reckless. Now it's time to put a bit of humility back into you."

"*You tricked me, you bastard!*" Pintley spat and shrieked, kicking and scratching at this creature, this being who had kept him and his people in the darkest lands for millennia.

"Tricked you?" The Hallowed King seemed angered by this accusation. "*Tricked you?*" He squeezed, slowly crushing Pintley's windpipe. He began to choke.

"You destroyed that lantern, Gormellow. You would violate the pact. This world isn't your playground, your treasure trove to rape and plunder." He hissed at Pintley's quivering face. "It is not beholden to you, or to any of the Hollow Children. Your kind may choose to spend the fleeting moments of glorious physicality you have on this plane by despoiling everything you can get your slimy little hands on. But without the pact—without a *balance*—all of you would be *exterminated*. You understand?" He shouted in rage. "*Stamped out like the blind, greedy, opportunistic vermin you are!*"

Pintley's vision darkened, his head throbbing as he gasped desperately for air.

"You and your friends are going to be an example, Gormellow," the King's voice was getting fainter by the second. Just before blacking out Pintley heard, "The pact will be honored."

Most of the neighborhood had turned up for the Halloween party. Though the members of the neighborhood association had been somewhat nonplussed at Mr. Anderson's enthusiasm, they dutifully spread word. Community fellowship overcame prejudiced suspicion: wary parents and excited children donned their costumes and headed to the party.

The orange bearded man—he called himself Jack—welcomed each guest heartily and showed them inside. Tables were draped with orange and black cloths and laden with mugs of fresh apple cider, homemade pumpkin pies, caramel apples, popcorn balls and bowlfuls of candy. The decorations had all been handmade; a threaded spider web with a grinning stuffed spider hung on one wall, while paper bats and ghosts bobbed from the ceiling. Cutout figures of monsters and grinning pumpkins plastered the walls.

Jack got on well with the children, performing magic tricks and telling scary stories. Their kids' laughter did much to warm the parents to this strange man. They listened to Jack's ghost stories and laughed at his jokes. They bobbed for apples and chanted along in the Snap Dragon game, plucking burning raisins from the brandy fire.

Jack told them about Samhain, the Irish festival of the dead, when food was left out for vengeful spirits, to keep them from harming houses and crops. He told them how Jack o' Lanterns were once carved from turnips, and lit to keep evil spirits at bay. He told them the story of Jack of the Lantern, who had conned the Devil and escaped a fate of eternal damnation, but was denied access to Heaven in the process.

As the party drew to a close, Jack announced the winners of the costume contest: a teenage girl in a black witch's dress with a bristly broom, an armored space warrior, and a boy in bluish gray zombie makeup. He presented them with their pick of the prizes: one of three green goblin masks.

"They're practically antique," Jack explained as the zombie marveled at his mask's smooth, scaly feel. "Made from genuine goblin skin!" His guests laughed, and he grinned.

Daniel Hale is an amateur storyteller living in Massillon, Ohio with a penchant for tales of the bizarre and disquieting. He's also a dedicated bibliophile and Anglophile, always seeking to expand his book collection and perfect his English accent. Other stories he's published can be found on Beorh Quarterly *and* Revolt Daily.

The Murderer At The Cabin
By Robert Holt

Lexington moved through the overgrowth with a steady and precise step. He held the hatchet firmly in his hand. It was Halloween; time to start a new hunt. His last one had just come to an unfortunate end with a car crash. He had stalked Lisa Barnes for four years, systematically killing everyone that she cared about, stalking her but never killing her. Killing Lisa wasn't the objective. Killing was never the objective, just a tool to the means of developing a lively competitor from the least likely of people. That was what Lexington did--he killed to help one unfortunate soul learn to live. Lexington smiled to himself; he liked how that sounded.

He could recall seeing Lisa on that first day at the camp grounds. She was a poor, confused young lady. After years of killing her friends and family, Lexington had turned her into a ruthless, take-no-prisoners, bitch with a chip on her shoulder. When she died, she was driving a stolen police car and firing a shotgun one-handed out the window at him. She never saw the turn in the road. Lexington had pulled over and wept in the woods over her death for three days.

Three days of eating nothing but the bugs that were trying to eat him and drinking nothing but rain water, and then he heard it. Music, the eerie sort of music that always accompanies the depraved holiday. He grabbed his hatchet and rose to his feet. Time for a new mission. Time for a new subject to train into a competitor.

LaRose stood up, and the music died away. "Ladies and gentlemen," his voice was an eerie combination of Rod Serling and Vincent Price. "I am afraid that there has been a murrrderrrr." The group around the table began to clap in anticipation. The price tag for an active role in one of LaRose's events often peaked in the tens of thousands, and the patrons gathered around the table had likely been telling their friends and colleagues about this for weeks. The hidden camera recordings of reactions alone would later sell for twenty dollars a pop.

LaRose slammed his hand down on the table, and everybody began sitting more upright while they listened. "One of you is the murderer." The group began to squirm in their chairs in discomfort. The discomfort was due to a minor electrical current being delivered to the backs of their legs through a bolt in the chairs. It was perfect for setting the mood and getting the hairs to stand up. "Ten suspects," LaRose continued, "ten possible murderers. Maybe you were all in it together. Maybe it was the act of a pair of lovers. Or maybe it was the act of a single depraved person." As he talked, LaRose was scanning the faces, selecting his murderer. At the exact moment he said "person" he was standing behind a fidgety young lady named Marissa Bloch, and this was the cue for the prop planner, director, and two FX boys to start planning to make Marissa the murderer. LaRose had a sixth sense for being able to spot the person in the group that would always be the best murderer. It was crucial to choose somebody that could be the most innocent and the most spastic. They would let her scare the others into a frenzy before telling her that she was in fact the murderer: typical horror movie bait and hook.

Lexington came out of the woods. He faced a large log cabin with a wide window. Through the window he saw, at a quick count, ten seated people and one man walking around the room talking. Lexington's eyes scanned the faces. There was one, a perfect one: a young lady, plump but not fat, with a nervous tension about her. Her hands even seemed to tremble as she sipped from a flute glass of white wine, Riesling, Lexington guessed. She would be the perfect one.

Lexington watched as a man amongst those sitting got up and excused himself. The standing man gave a wicked grin and pointed towards a door that would lead the man within arm's length of Lexington. Lexington started to move back towards the woods before he realized where the man was going. He was heading towards the outhouse. Lexington snorted. This collection of obviously wealthy people were going to be using outdoor shitters. This was just…grand.

Lexington moved swiftly towards the outhouse, which was completely stereotypical with a crescent moon carved into the door. He stood stock-still on the side and waited for the heavy man to enter. It was Lexington's intention to wait until the door reopened before attacking, but when he heard the roaring flatulent explosion, everything changed. Lexington went to the door. It wasn't locked. He flung it open. The fat man was sitting with his pants around his ankles and a smile upon his face.

"Hot damn, am I going to be the first down?"

Lexington did not hear this statement. He was too preoccupied with holding his nose with one hand and swinging the hatchet with the other. The hit was perfect. It caught the big man at the back of the neck, severing the spinal column. Couldn't ask for a better kill shot. Lexington quickly finished cutting the head off and stuffing the rest of the body down the toilet. The hips needed a few hacks, but soon the outhouse shithole had about two hundred and seventy-five more pounds of waste down in it. Lexington then placed the head on the toilet seat, careful not to allow it to fall in. The scene was a bloody, gory mess, and that was just how he wanted to leave it. He wanted his presence known. He wanted the horror to begin.

Lexington turned around to see two young men staring at him. They didn't look scared or horrified. They looked impressed. Lexington twirled the hatchet in his hand. He didn't want to kill these two yet, he wanted them to run in terror to the others. He wanted them to be cowering in the corners. Instead one of them held out his hand. Lexington hesitated, and then shook it.

"The name's Burt. This is Eddie, but people call him Ernie. We weren't expecting help on this one."

Lexington did not respond. His eyes just took in the two men, one after the other. They looked like nerds, but nerds would generally piss themselves in this type situation.

Ernie moved to Lexington's side and looked past him into the gory outhouse. "Nicely done. That is a sweet blood pattern on the walls."

Lexington squirmed a little. "Do you think so?"

Burt placed a hand on his shoulder. "We are professionals, and we know a good murder scene when we see one."

Lexington tilted his head at him, like an interested dog. He always wondered what it would be like to be a professional and kill exclusively for money. The idea left a dirty feel in his mind, but Lexington had little doubts now about the lethality of this pair. He would need to bide his time.

"You hungry?" Ernie asked.

Lexington did not answer, but he fixed Ernie with an intrigued stare.

"We called in a pizza. It got here about an hour ago, and we don't have a microwave, but if you want some…"

"I do," Lexington said.

"Cool, lets head back to the van before they start looking for Mister Shithead," Burt said, indicating the outhouse and its occupant. "What was your name again?"

"Lexington," said Lexington.

"Is that your first or last name?" asked Ernie.

"Last."

"So what's your first name?"

Lexington clammed up for a moment. He didn't want to say it. He never wanted to hear it again. But then again, these were professionals. They would understand. He stopped walking so that the seriousness of his confession could be appreciated. The other two took a step and then turned back towards him to see why he had stopped. He met each man's eyes. "My name is Elmo Lexington."

The two men smiled broadly. For a moment, Lexington feared that they would laugh at him, as everybody does when they hear his name. He gripped his hatchet tightly, waiting for it. But they didn't laugh. Burt stepped towards him and placed a

106

hand on his shoulder. "Lexington, I think you are going to fit right in with us." The three continued towards the pizza.

LaRose had them separated into three groups. "We must solve this mystery! But first, it seems Mister Heldridge has disappeared. We must find him, wherever he is." The three groups of three were all smiling, all except Marissa Bloch. "You will search the cabin," LaRose said as he pointed to a group of three young professionals. "You will search the yard," indicating the older group that had arrived with the late Mister Heldridge, a better shock if they found the murder scene. "And you three need to explore the fruit cellar." He pointed to Marissa's group. The plan was to separate her from her boyfriend, and to leave a few remains of him to find. She would surely crack. It would be after this that they would reveal to her that she was the murderer. LaRose entertainined himself with the plans. "Happy hunting, kiddos."

Lexington was finishing his third piece of cold pizza and practically drinking the garlic butter sauce when a voice came over a push-to-talk phone. "The girl is in the fruit cellar with two others. Isolate her."

Burt pushed the button. "On it, chief."

Ernie started to get up, but Lexington held up his hand. "I will take care of this."

"Sure you don't want any help?"

Lexington shook his head. "I have handled such things many, many times." He took his hatchet and climbed from the van. He instantly saw a group of three older people going towards the outhouse. Spurred by urgency to get out of sight, Lexington hustled across the driveway and down the open exterior cellar door. He paused to close it behind him.

The darkness below the cabin was absolute. He felt his way with outstretched hands, turning corners, and finding that he was in a maze of plywood walls. He continued moving until he heard whispered voices. Then he saw a soft glow and the walls became a kaleidoscope of dancing and jumping shadows. He hunkered down and watched as Marissa, his target, his competitor, came into sight. She was carrying a candle. Close behind her was another woman, younger and stronger, and behind her was a man, the man Marissa had been sitting with back at the dinner table.

Lexington knew his mission would need to be performed swiftly. He hid until the three were within slashing distance. Then he simply leaned around the corner. All three saw him then, and they saw him blow out the candle. There were screams, lots of screams. Lexington, acting on his memory of his surroundings, grabbed Marissa by the back of the neck and threw her forward. The other woman tried to follow her, holding onto the back of Marissa's shirt, but she ran into Lexington instead. He gripped her by the throat and lifted her from her feet with the single arm. The man, her man, was swinging wildly and repeatedly hitting the woman that Lexington held with haymakers. Lexington waited for a count of ten, then he felt the snap and the woman's body went limp. He tossed her to the side and held the hatchet out. The timing could not have been better. He felt a swinging arm collide with the hatchet. Blood gushed into Lexington's face.

The screams continued. Lexington grabbed the man by the hair and yanked his head back. A swift slash and the screaming stopped from him, but Marissa, blinded by the darkness, continued to scream from the sounds that she heard. Lexington then kicked at one of the walls and felt the board come loose. He pried it free and felt inside. It was perfect. He tossed the dead man into the crawl space. He then grabbed the dead girl and dropped her on top of him.

He heard a clicking sound. He froze and listened. It was a lighter. Marissa had a lighter. Lexington replaced the board, grabbed his hatchet and vanished around the corner as he heard another click and saw a soft light follow him. He stopped and peeked around the corner. Marissa was on the edge of hysterics as she saw the severed hand on the floor. Lexington followed her eyes. They were locked on the wedding ring on the finger. He smiled. His training of her begins now, he thought. Happy hunting.

When Marissa came falling into the cabin, she was screaming and frantic, with blood smearing her skirt. Her hair had fallen in front of her face, where it stuck to the tears on her cheeks. LaRose broke off of a monologue about the murder and decapitation of Heldridge and ran to the girl. She was nearing a state of shock. To think, LaRose used to work with actors. Who needed actors when you could simulate true terror like this? "Are you all right, my dear?" He was beginning to switch entirely to his Vincent Price voice now.

"There is someone in the cellar. Someone killed Donna and Bill. Oh Jesus," she cried.

"There, there," he said as he pulled the girl into a comforting squeeze. "Tell us all what has happened."

The girl couldn't, though. Sobs and cries wrecked her story, which was all the better for both the DVD audience and the other dinner guests. A few words squeezed their way through, and Marissa would get caught on these words and repeat them like a mantra. Among these words were hand, wedding ring, and candle. Other than those, she spoke only incoherent sobs.

LaRose sat the girl down on a loveseat where she continued to cry and whimper. "It seems, from this girl's testimony, that the murderer may not be of our little party, but an outsider. We need to split up the remaining six of you and find the bastard that has cut down three of us. I will stay with Marissa. She shouldn't be alone."

Lexington got back to the van to find a short, stern-faced man looking at him over the rim of a martini glass filled with seltzer water. Ernie and Burt were sitting off to the side with an attractive props coordinator. The man cleared his voice with a sound that resembled a 1963 Ford Fairlane trying to start with the choke pushed all the way in. He then took another dainty sip from his martini glass. "I don't know who you are, or who hired you, or even who paid for the high dollar props you have been using, and to be honest, I don't give an upside-down possum fuck. This is my production! This isn't LaRose's! Whatever salary you negotiated with him will be coming out of his salary!" The director had been slowly inching towards Lexington with fists clenched. He got so close that Lexington could feel the shorter man's breath on his nipples. "Do I make myself clear, Elmo?"

The name was spoken with such mocking, with such spite. Lexington instantly heard the years of the high-pitched voice being used to taunt him, felt the dead gold fish being flung at him behind, saw the crayon drawings passed to him, and smelled the red hair and industrial strength rubber glue that was smeared over his body every year as a spring break joke. He was unaware of anything. He just saw red, Elmo red. The hatchet fell and fell and fell. When he stopped, he was winded and tired and standing in a van filled with dismembered limbs and brutalized carcasses.

Lexington dropped the hatchet and fell to his knees; the fall was cushioned by one of Ernie's ears. Lexington stayed there and cried. He did not look up until the push-to-talk phone spoke up.

LaRose held Marissa's hand in his own. "I know you are scared," he said, "and I am sorry, but it is part of the show."

Marissa's sob caught in her throat. "What?"

"That's right," he patted her hand. "This has all been part of the show. Have you never seen one of my DVDs?"

Marissa shook her head.

"Well, you see Marissa, we have chosen you to be our star." He brushed the hair out of her face and tucked it behind her ear. "*You* are the murderer at the cabin."

Marissa shook her head and opened her mouth to speak, but LaRose hushed her into silence. "I know you are confused. We planned that. You see, by making you scared and pathetic you become the least likely suspect. *That* is when we let you in on our surprise."

"I don't understand what you are saying." She broke into a new fit of tears.

LaRose cleared his voice, and tried again. He was aiming for a soft yet stern voice, not unlike John Wayne, but in his frustration and excitement his effeminate lisp crept into the voice. It didn't exactly reveal him as a flamer, but changed the stern courageous sound into a weird perversion of the spoken language, and he ended up sounding like Peter Lorre in his later works. "What I am trying to tell you is that your husband and friend are being safely held at the post mystery party hall a

110

quarter mile down the road. This is a play, and you are in the lead role. And I need you to play along. Do you understand?"

Marissa nodded, but her face showed that she did not understand.

"You need to stay as you have been, frightened and shocked. But when the last man confronts you…" LaRose set a pistol on her lap. "Put a bullet in his guts."

Marissa picked the gun up and put it between the couch cushions.

LaRose took this to be a good sign, but he pressed on. "Think of what you would say if you were a killer. The clearer your dialogue, the better. Think it through. Give us a real hoot. Show us how good of an actor you can be." LaRose told her a brief back story of her motives, and a list of clues that the other patrons could have noticed. When he was certain that she was ready, he went over to his hidden phone and pressed the push-to-talk button. "The spider has caught the flies, the lion is in the den, and the virgin has her panties around her ankles. Next move is on you."

LaRose's words over the device was the encouragement Lexington had needed to pull himself from the blood-and-sinew littered van and continue with his mission. He stumbled out of the rear door of the van, hatchet still in his hand, blood dripping from everything. He was face to face with three of the dinner guests. They eyed him suspiciously.

"No way this is the murderer," one of them said. "It is way too obvious, and besides, this would hardly be a mystery if the murderer was somebody we never saw before."

"Maybe that is the logic LaRose is counting on us having," another countered.

The third in the party opened her mouth to counter this argument, but Lexington had grown tired of the conversation. He played a quick, live action version of Whack-a-Mole, and moved towards the cabin to have his first face to face confrontation with his target.

He stopped just shy of the door as he saw three other dinner guests going back into the cabin. It was time to bring the terror with full gusto.

LaRose was at the door to welcome the other three guests back inside. "Did you have any luck finding the murderer?"

The man of the group spoke up. He had been drinking heavily of the wine and his voice slurred as he spoke with a posh, blue-blooded, East Coast accent. "We found nothing, not a damn thing. We didn't even find…" His witticism was abandoned as glass shattered in the main dining hall of the cabin. A ball flew through the window, bounced on the table, and landed on the cushion of one of the high-backed chairs. Only when it came to rest did the four dinner guests see that it was the head of one of the other attendees.

"What the hell is this?" LaRose shook his head. This was not a part of his script; this was most certainly not in his script. "That fucker will be directing tampon commercials in Japan when this is over." The break of character went unnoticed by the other guests, who seemed to be thrilled by the startle and the gore.

Another window on the side of the house shattered as another head of another dinner guest came hurtling into the house. This one landed at LaRose's feet. He was astonished by the complexity of detail and texture. This was effects far beyond his budget. His first thought was that he was being pranked, but when the director's head came through yet another window, he finally realized the severity of the situation.

He darted to the fireplace and grabbed the poker. He whirled around to face the door. One of the girls had backed into the door, hoping to avoid the rain of glass shards that littered the cabin. When the hatchet burst through the door, it sunk itself into the middle of her spine. She fell to the floor twitching and moaning.

The door was then bashed entirely open, and the blood-stained Lexington stepped confidently into the cabin. LaRose dashed forward with the fire poker held like a fencing sword. Lexington glanced at him, and then swung the hatchet at the remaining male dinner guest. It caught him at the hairline and took off the scalp like an Indian brave. The allusion was not lost on Lexington, who turned back towards LaRose, raised his hand, and patted his mouth while he let out a high pitched sound.

112

LaRose looked quickly over his shoulder at Marissa. Unbelievably, she was smiling. LaRose then looked at the other guest, and she was sobbing and crying as she hid behind a chair. He was closer to the murderer than either woman, and that was how he wanted it. It was time to be the hero, rather than the twisted villain. He darted towards Lexington and swung the poker with menace. Lexington blocked the blow with his forearm. He grunted at the pain. LaRose seized the momentary shock of pain to attack again. His aim was to break the murderer's kneecap, but Lexington turned his leg away from the blow, catching it in the back of the knee. He stumbled a few steps to the side and half-heartedly swung the hatchet. LaRose ducked under the high swing and lunged in with a stab. It caught Lexington in the midsection and penetrated to an inch below the skin.

Lexington howled in pain and knocked the poker to the ground. LaRose twisted and kicked with a side kick directly into the wounded stomach. Lexington doubled over, and as he did, the hatchet in his hand collided with LaRose's thigh. LaRose screamed and tried to step back, but his leg gave out under him, and he fell backwards against the chair that sheltered the girl.

She screamed and ran for the door. Lexington held the hatchet out and the girl ran into it, catching herself in a wrestling style clothesline with deadly effect. Lexington took a troubled step towards LaRose and raised the hatchet over his head.

Marissa began to laugh louder. Lexington paused and looked at her. He had never seen one of his subjects laugh. This girl was special. He knew that now. He was in…in love.

Marissa slowly got to her feet once she realized that the attention was on her. Both LaRose and Lexington were looking at her with deep consideration.

"That's right," she said. "It was little ol' me all along. I murdered the others. I hacked them down one by one as they discovered my secret, and the secret of this cabin." She stepped forward, and Lexington retreated a step. "You see, this cabin sits on nearly a billion dollars of oil. You would have known that had you bothered to look down the outhouse shit hole."

Lexington turned towards the window that offered the view of the outhouse and wondered what he had missed in there.

"Or had you checked behind the plywood walls in the basement," she went on. "Or if you had even bothered to look at any of the books on the mantle."

Lexington's eyes darted to the bookshelf. They were all books about oil wells.

LaRose had sat up and was in the process of standing. "Marissa," he said, "run. This is real. This isn't a game."

"Damn right it's not," she said as she raised the pistol that LaRose had given her. She leveled the gun at Lexington. "Any last words?"

Lexington smiled. "I love you."

She pulled the trigger, and the ball of red paint fired out towards Lexington's face. It struck him on the bridge of his nose, shattering the fragile cartilage and sending paint over his wide open eyes. He screamed wildly and began swinging the hatchet recklessly around the cabin. Marissa side stepped his clumsy and blind charge. His momentum carried him to one of the shattered windows. He fell onto the broken shards with all of his weight. They pierced through his stomach and protruded through the back of his shirt. They broke from the frame and his limp body fell forward, out the window, and onto the dirt below.

LaRose limped over to Marissa and hugged her. "It's over," he said. "It's over."

Marissa smiled. "How did I do?"

Robert Holt is a St. Louis native where he lives a stone-throw from the muddy banks of the great Mississippi with his wife and daughter. His writings of horror and speculative fiction have been flooding the markets lately, appearing in seven anthologies this year. Follow him at www.facebook.com/holthorror .

A Eye For A Eye
By Wenda Morrone

A uniform in Little J.'s subway car had commenced to hover, which meant one of two things. One, the cop had an idea Little J. was on a job, or two, Little J. was headed for a neighborhood where a black kid stood out just by being black. When the subway screeched into the Fourteenth Street Station, he hit the doors.

By the time he zigzagged half a dozen blocks to shake the cop, he had figured out it wasn't number two. Amongst the other people heading toward the Greenwich Village Halloween Parade, Little J. was invisible. Who would look at a ten-year-old kid in jeans and a jacket and a t-shirt--even one with a Stegosaurus on the front--when they could stare at a breast four feet tall? He saw a boob per block, minimum, and the four-footer was the smallest. He considered asking one of them for directions to Sixth Avenue--where the parade paraded--or Spring Street, where it started. But asking might get him remembered. Besides, why would you ask a boob anything?

Plus, Greenwich Village was south. Manhattan was a reasonable place; south just meant following street numbers down. One block after another full of paraders with wallets just waiting for his fingers: he had to keep reminding himself he was on a job. That wasn't the worst, though. Greenwich Village didn't get the memo on using numbers. A dozen blocks, and the streets commenced having names. He could read numbers okay, but letters didn't line up for him.

They never stopped him, though. If Greenwich Village was south, Sixth Avenue had to be west. Sure enough, a couple blocks over, and there he was.

Once he hit the official parade, it turned out everything he'd seen before was just the prelim. Along came a bat ten feet tall with outriders holding up the wings, followed by a skeleton at least a story high and as wide as a building. A dragon half as long as a city block. Some kind of giant hawk lit up from inside like he was made of fire. Before and after and around the big puppets walked people who were mostly naked, but painted like tigers or zebras or just purple with strategically placed blue polka dots. They looked nearly as invisible as Little J. needed to be.

Finally he spotted what he'd been sent to find: a giant eyeball. Blue. It rode atop a black robe about ten feet tall, which seemed about average by this time. The eye blinked. It was bloodshot. It had eyelashes a foot long. Most important, someplace underneath the robe was a person with a package not much smaller than the one inside Little J.'s jacket, except the eye's package was full of money.

Little J. sidled into the street and over to the eye. Quick once-around stare. He was still invisible. He ducked under the robe and whispered, "A eye for a eye."

The man underneath, both hands on a bamboo pole, kicked out at him. "Get away from me, you stupid little git!"

Little J. dodged as the pole--which had to mean the eye up above it, too--swooped dangerously. "Watch youself, fool. You going to drop you eye."

"Whose fault is that?"

Little J. grabbed the pole, too. The man didn't kick him this time. When the two of them had it upright again, Little J. said, "Honest mistake, mister. I looking for a brown eye." He bobbed back out onto the street again, nearly tripping over the big flat foot of a clown. Talk about boring: he wasn't ten feet tall *or* naked.

Once he was out of the parade line, Little J. surveyed up and down the avenue. Sure enough, there were almost as many eyes as boobs. How many would he have to whisper to before he hit the right one? He began listing: in easy sight were three brown, five--no, six--more blue, only two green, one bruised and black with a ginormous glittering Band-Aid across one corner. This delivery could take a while.

116

Worse: On the far side of a line of roller-skating skeletons, he spotted a cop who actually knew him and what he did for a living. Theo Taylor. Shit. He was already on his way to Little J., shouldering skeletons aside.

Little J. took off, weaving through zombies and spiders and a few women baring real boobs. Well, tasseled. Still.

He warded off yet another nearly naked purple-painted gent, said "Sorry," and ran on--guarding his now-purple hand-- and came face to face with another giant puppet, a dinosaur that straddled most of a block.

He took a personal interest in this one. He tagged along museum tours so often, he could give one himself better than most. The puppet's big head weaving from one side of the street to the other on a long snaky neck had the gaping jaws and saw-teeth of a T. rex, only it had a row of plates poking up all the way down its back like the Stegosaurus on Little J.'s t-shirt. No little T-rex front claws, either: it was built like an Apatosaurus, ginormous body, four big splayfeet, dragging a tail as long as its neck. Little J. went with Apatosaurus.

It must take at least two dozen men to keep it in the air. They were herky-jerky, but in a funny way that helped it move the way you expected a city-block-sized dinosaur to move, ponderous and unstable at the same time.

Plus perfect for what Little J. needed.

Halfway along Apatosaurus' underbelly, Little J. paused beside a man wearing cargo pants and jacket, tucked his package in the man's back pants pocket, and patted the jacket sleeve with his purple hand. "Good job."

"Thanks," said the man, blotting his sweaty forehead with the sleeve. So now he had two purple smears. Twice as easy to find again.

Little J. moved past Apatosaurus quickly so Taylor wouldn't find him there and went back to his job: locating the right eye. Though he didn't want Taylor spotting him doing that, either. This was getting complicated. He almost welcomed Theo Taylor's big hand coming down on his shoulder.

"Aren't you out of your territory, Little J.?"

"Who you calling little? I a three hundred fifty pound white guy. This a costume."

117

Taylor held in a smile, Little J. could see it took work, but he kept his hand on Little J.'s shoulder. "That's no answer."

"A man can take a night off. Tell me this, Sergeant. Halloween always this crazy down here? They so many fake boobs, the real ones ain't seem worth looking at."

"There's a twelve-foot spider climbing a clock tower a few blocks farther along. Only you won't get to see it unless you tell me why you're here."

"This harassment, clear and simple. I call my lawyer. All us white guys has one."

"Let me rephrase. I know why you're here. Tell me who you're carrying for, maybe I can help you."

Little J. looked past Taylor's big black-clad shoulder at Apatosaurus, a good block away now and wobbling farther out of reach by the second. The whole damn night was getting out of reach.

Apatosaurus dipped to its right, only instead of righting itself, it dipped farther. Still farther.

Little J. said, "Ain't you got better things to do? Like keeping a eye on Apatosaurus up there? He look like he about to roll over."

The left front foot went up in the air. Its handlers must have let go. Apatosaurus threw up its head as if panicking, and then in slow motion settled down to the street, head coming to rest last of all, like any dying creature. Of course, no scream. Even if there had been one it would have gone unheard. Everybody was screaming.

Then and there Taylor showed how he once got the big bucks running for the Giants. He went through the crowd like a hot knife through butter. Little J. kept in his wake. Past the tail, the hind legs. Taylor stopped abruptly mid-belly.

When things went wrong, they just kept going. Little J. almost wasn't surprised when Taylor squatted beside a man in cargo pants sprawled on his belly. No jacket, so maybe not the same guy. A man could hope. He wouldn't know for sure until Taylor turned him over, looking for clues to how he died. No blood. Maybe just a heart attack.

Taylor had a big hand on the man's throat, just under his chin. He shifted his hand a little, then back where he started, then put a phone to his ear.

Before he said a damn word, a voice like a buzzsaw, the female kind, yelled at him loud enough for the dead man to hear. "Sergeant, WTF? We've stopped moving. The parade director's having a shit fit."

"Where are you?"

"Sheridan Square."

Taylor looked up and down Sixth Avenue. "Tell her to re-route west to Seventh Avenue, then back over here on Christopher Street."

Little J. was impressed. He intended to know Manhattan from one end to the other and side to side before he was through. Taylor appeared to be way ahead of him.

"Will do, Sergeant," said the buzzsaw.

"Hang on, Detective. I called you, remember? We need a murder team, murder kit, forensics."

"Who? How?"

"Let's start with where, shall we, Roxanne? I'm at Sixth Avenue and West Fourth."

"Sixth Avenue. You don't mean the vic was actually in the parade."

No crowd noise now, everybody close was eavesdropping along with Little J. It hadn't occurred to him that if he wanted to learn Manhattan, he had to learn its voices, too. Taylor's partner had a voice a trucker could use.

"Afraid so."

"Sergeant, there are fifty thousand just in the parade. They're estimating two million watching. We can't shut down--"

"No, we can't. Have the team confine the cordon to this block only." Taylor gave Little J. a sideways glance. "Bring a drug-sniffing dog, too. Tell the teams where to find you, Roxanne, then guide them in to me."

"Getting through this crowd will take a while, Sergeant."

"Yes. Warn forensics I'll be starting without them. Any security footage in the area?"

"I'll check."

"Call Shelby Only. He's the whiz kid in the puzzle palace at One Police Plaza. He'll find whatever there is faster than anybody else."

"Will do."

"And keep me updated."

"Likewise."

It was spooky listening to Taylor--safe in one way, threatening in another. Little J. had been standing with Taylor when Apatosaurus went down; he couldn't have killed the man. On the other hand, any minute now Taylor would go over the body and find Little J.'s package. If it was the same man.

"Why you thinking murder, Sergeant? I ain't see blood."

The crowd murmured as if he spoke for them, too.

Taylor ignored him, but he cradled the man's head, tilting it just enough that Little J. could see blood trickling out of his ear, down the lobe, down the side of his neck.

Not enough for Little J. to see a purple smear on his forehead. If there was one.

"That ain't happen on account of his heart give out?"

"Not in this case," Taylor said curtly. He stood and got loud. "Everyone in the immediate area, your pictures may be helpful. We'll need to collect your cell phones. Anybody have a shopping bag? Maybe trick-or-treat?"

Little J. said, "You joking? In this crowd? What fool comes here with kids?"

One, at least--a kid dressed as Superman--and one was all Taylor needed. Superman howled when his mom (Wonder Woman) dumped his candy in the trash and handed Sergeant Taylor the bag. She managed to make it very personal. Little J. couldn't see that Taylor took notice.

If ever there was a chance to disappear. A sensible man would. Where would he be if Mr. Sullivan heard he helped a cop, particularly Theo Taylor? But how could he fade without Mr. Sullivan's money? He'd have to stick, get his package back somehow, then deliver it somehow and get paid. Somehow.

Somehow figured too damn much into whatever came next. He studied his hands, flexing his fingers, hoping they felt clever.

Taylor handed the bag to him. "Collect the phones, Little J. I want you where I can see you." He raised his voice. "This boy will be coming around for your phones."

Little J. commenced circling the crowd for trick or treat. Most of the watchers weren't in costume. Who would have thought he'd be relieved not to get stared in the eye by four-foot boobs?

He didn't know whether he wanted or dreaded to see Taylor find his package. Both. He snuck glances as he worked his way around, watching Taylor use his cell-camera to record the dead man top to toe and up and down his arms. Then--finally--he turned the man right side up.

Purple smear on his forehead.

But even now Taylor didn't search him. He had to record the dead man's front side. Then he had to scrape a bit of the purple smear and put it in a little plastic envelope and label it. Little J. tried and failed to imagine going everywhere equipped for unexpected murder.

Halfway around the crowd, a man said, "Shouldn't you be taking our names?"

Like Little J. would let them watch him try to write names down and discover he couldn't.

"They get it from you phone." It might even be true.

Little J. couldn't bear to watch Taylor and couldn't look away for long, like touching a sore tooth with your tongue, knowing you were making yourself hurt but you couldn't stop.

Finally Taylor commenced going through the dead man's clothes. Shirt pocket: nothing. Front pants left side: nothing. Right side: wallet. From where Little J. watched, it looked neither fat nor empty. Average.

Pause while Taylor went through it. Of course: ID, credit cards, how much money or had his killer stripped the cash? Doubtful. Little J. wouldn't even trust himself to be that good that fast.

Collecting the phones would have been slow even if Little J. hadn't been looking over his shoulder, on account of most of the crowd wanted to keep taking pictures of Taylor. He didn't blame them, but that didn't mean he had to take any shit.

121

One brass-voiced woman said, "I don't want to give it to you."

"Ain't giving it to me. It for the black dude over there. Trust me, you ain't want to mess with him."

"What if I keep it?"

Little J. nipped it out of her hands. "You got a sister named Roxanne? Take it up with her."

Taylor was on his phone again, talking, not listening, so he must have found ID and was giving it to his trucker partner. Start checking for friends and enemies.

Taylor eased the dead man on to his front again to get at his back pockets. They looked bone-flat. Little J. hadn't had the right angle to see that before. The right pocket should have been sagging with the weight of Mr. Sullivan's package. It was as limp as the other. Taylor slipped his big hand in each pocket in turn and waggled his fingers: nothing.

Nothing.

Little J. had to keep going. Blood hammered in his ears. Looked at one way, now he had neither Mr. Sullivan's package nor his money. Without one, he couldn't get the other. Without the money, he was a walking dead man.

Looked at another way, he now knew two things Sergeant Taylor did not: one, the dead man had been wearing a jacket, which Little J. could describe in detail, down to the purple body paint he had smeared on one sleeve. Two, the dead man had been holding Mr. Sullivan's package, though he never knew it. Just the same, it might be why he was killed. Somebody could have seen Little J. pass off the package and guessed it was worth taking.

It happened fast, though. More likely somebody *knew* Little J.'s package was worth taking. Which would mean the somebody was likely Mr. Sullivan's buyer.

How could Sergeant Taylor do his job if he didn't know what Little J. knew?

How could Little J. tell him?

All that was left was for some helpful Lookie Loo to remember seeing Little J. with the dead man before he was dead and sing out what he'd seen.

Sure enough: somebody on the far side of the street said, "I saw your kid there talking to one of the dinosaur-men."

Taylor gave Little J. the evil eye. "Is that a fact? Would you please step forward, sir, and tell me what you saw?"

Easy enough to read what Taylor thought the guy saw: Little J. making a delivery and getting paid. Which was half-true, in an ass-backwards way.

Shit. He hadn't been thinking straight. His buyer hadn't just happened to bring his gun to the parade, he had come equipped--like Taylor--for death. Only dishing it out, not working to solve it.

What if the fucker never had any money? Had planned all along to take delivery from Little J. with a gun, maybe to kill him? He'd been told what Little J. looked like, just as Little J. knew what his buyer looked like. Well, his eye-costume. That should be Little J. lying there with a bloody ear.

What took him so long to see it?

Because up in Mr. Sullivan's territory, everybody knew his deliverymen were under his protection. Greenwich Village must not have that memo. Little J. wasn't the only walking dead man here.

He must have been thinking at the speed of light, because Taylor was still waiting for his volunteer. Or maybe he'd been standing there a while and the volunteer had faded.

Taylor raised his voice to a bellow. "I want all workers who supported the dinosaur to come to me. Now. Your names are on record; not showing up will get my attention."

How did he get the names so fast? A cop had an unfair advantage.

Taylor dropped his voice and told his partner to move to Plan B, he needed her assistance forthwith.

Little J.'s mind was splitting in two, one half following Taylor, the other half trying to work out what he needed to do himself. He watched men in drab pants and shirts gather around Taylor. If somebody dressed as a ten-foot eye had leaned down and shot a man in front of or beside them, they'd notice. They'd already have said something.

Somewhere nearby was an abandoned eye costume. If he could find it and show it to Taylor, Taylor could work it out his own self. Little J. wouldn't have to explain anything.

Taylor's hand closed on his shoulder again. "Not so fast, Little J. Let's see if anyone can identify you."

Okay, here's hoping he really had been invisible.

Apparently he had. One of the men said, "I'd have remembered the t-shirt. I mean, a dinosaur."

There was a hum of agreement. Whew. Temporary, though. Somebody could have seen something and kept it to himself in case he could use it.

Little J. said, "Satisfied, Sergeant? On account of, I has to take a leak."

Taylor said, "Pick someplace close. On second thought, never mind. The dog will find you."

In his dreams. Mr. Sullivan packaged better than that. Well, he'd better.

Little J. couldn't fade into the crowd right away--get past the first row, and he was too short to see over anybody. He needed to check off whatever eyes he could so he'd have some idea what he was looking for. He should be able to go with his previous count--the murder had frozen this particular part of the parade in place. Three browns. Check. Both greens. Check. The black-and-blue eye. Check.

So now he knew: he was looking for a heap of cloth, probably black, topped by a blue eyeball.

Good thing Taylor's voice carried. As Little J. disappeared into the crowd, he heard Taylor asking the dinosaur men if they planned to celebrate together after the parade was over. They might not know how to translate that, but Little J. did. Party meant drugs. Taylor figured the dead man for Little J.'s client.

Eye-puppet man could have fled to the side of the street opposite the dead man, but he'd probably left his costume on this side--spend the least possible time as his recognizable self. He wouldn't drop it at the parade, where too many people would notice, or amongst the spectators, same reason. Little J. figured he was looking for a doorway, better still an unlocked door. Probably a block away his odds were better.

The crowd was only about four deep--anybody else was too far away to see anything, they'd have moved on to the parade's detour-route.

124

Easiest would have been just dumping the costume in a doorway, but Little J. didn't expect easy. Instead he checked for doorways deep enough to pull off a costume without being seen, then doors. On the first block, all locked. Pushing buttons till somebody buzzed you in probably wasn't something a murderer would care for. The second block halfway down, a door shifted, not quite locked. Little J. pushed, and it gave, but nothing dumped inside. Down to the end of that block, and he was into the new parade route crowd--he could see a freaking caterpillar's head bobbing up above their heads. He crossed and headed back. No luck. Worked his way one block down and started in again. Almost at the corner of that block, another door gave to his touch. Inside, under and behind the radiator, was a black heap. Over to the side closer to the mailboxes, a huge bloodshot eyeball. Blue.

Little J. snuck out as quietly as he had snuck in and pulled the door until he heard the lock snick. Looked up and memorized the apartment house number to tell Sergeant Taylor later. If he still needed to.

When Little J. wanted to hide something--his savings, for example--he wedged it in the upper branches of a tree, an evergreen for choice. When he wanted to get rid of something-- say a gun--he ran for blocks at random, then picked the first dumpster. But he didn't see a dumpster, and the available trees were bare. Unusable. The next logical choice was storm drains. Though he probably shouldn't expect logic. Amateurs got their ideas from crime teevee shows. Druggies could do anything, and probably would.

Cops would have teams and search the whole neighborhood at once. Cops meant telling Taylor.

He worked his way back to the parade crowd and found nothing in the drains but matted leaves. Commenced the up one side and down the other routine, feeling like a fool, but at the far corner of the second block, in the storm drain, past the grid but snagged on something was--not the gun. Not the package of drugs. The jacket.

If he hadn't seen it close-up, would he have recognized it? It looked more like an animal torn limb from limb. That told him something else Sergeant Taylor needed to know.

The thing about storm drains, the corner ones were nearly always under a light pole. When you stuck something down, if the light was still working you could check to be sure it had actually gone down. This fool hadn't taken the time to check. Or maybe he hadn't had anything to give the jacket a poke. Amateur.

The jacket still looked get-at-able, but it wouldn't be easy. He tried stretching flat on his belly and reaching down the length of his arm. Not quite. And the grid openings were too narrow to get more than his arm in. He needed a stick with a claw on the end. Good luck. Belt? He didn't wear one.

At the curb end, there was a cutaway, probably so leaves and small branches could wash down. He could squeeze his whole self through that, but what if he ended up down the drain with the jacket?

The other thing handy about the light pole was it gave him something to hook his legs around.

He lowered himself by careful inches, so far bent over he couldn't actually see the jacket. One hand on the grid just in case, the other arm flailing until he hit cloth and could grab hold. Getting back up was trickier. He squirmed sideways as much as he dared and worked his free hand until he had it curled his fingers over the metal frame edge, gripping with all his might.

Which was handy, because at that exact moment, somebody commenced kicking at his feet to knock them loose.

Nothing like a scare to make a man move fast. Little J. doubled in the middle like a fish and heaved himself upward. Head and one shoulder now out, but one foot already pushed down the drain. He couldn't even spare a look to see who he was fighting for his other foot. Another heave, and he had enough weight out on the street to roll over, sobbing for breath, and face the man trying to hurt him. Kill him.

The man had that bug-eyed look a jock got when he was playing out of his mind. That plus his thin-lipped grin made it easier to look at his clothes than his face. No jacket of his own. A cutoff sweatshirt and baggy jeans. A bulge in the front that could be the gun or the drugs--maybe even Mr. Sullivan's money. Or maybe the idea of a second killing gave him a hard-on. His expression fit any of those things.

126

He looked down at Little J. "Where's my coke, little man?"

"Like you ain't already have it," Little J. said to keep the talk going. His mind was turning over a mile a minute.

"Who did you give it to?" said pop-eyed eye-man.

It was tough to talk while Little J. was flat on his back and he suspected the fool looming over him had a gun. He had to pretend it was easy. "You come ready to pay?"

The guy's laugh was off. "Or what? I kick you back down the storm drain?"

"Depends if you has a death wish. You diss me, you dissing Mr. Sullivan. He a businessman. That bad for business."

"Ooh. I'm scared." He prodded Little J. with his foot. "The blow? Before I lose my patience?"

Little J. thought he had all he was going to get. He worked up a sneer. "Going to use your popgun again? Only work if you stick it in my ear, fool."

The man lost his smile and his pop-eyes. He reached down, hands like claws. Little J. rolled and tried to jump to his feet. Not fast enough. The guy grabbed him by his jacket. Little J. managed to shuck it and still keep hold of the rags of the other jacket, the dead man's. He feinted left and took off right.

Little J. had been chased down and beaten by pros. This guy might be an amateur, but his damn legs were still longer. He caught up and grabbed Little J.'s shoulder--one-handed. The other one now held a gun, so Little J. had guessed right. And he was ready. The jacket-piece with the zipper was now wrapped tight around his fist, teeth facing out. He turned in his attacker's hold and raked the zipper teeth across his eyes.

Fool dropped his grip on Little J. and commenced screeching and wailing. Hands to his eyes, too, which meant he had the gun head-high for all to see. Amateurs never knew to keep fighting no matter what.

One more street crossing and Little J. would be . . . back to Sergeant Taylor.

To tell him what, exactly? He had half a block to figure it out.

Plenty of time. Time, too, to stuff the gunman's cash bundle down the back of his pants. Fool shouldn't have carried it down his front. Plus he shouldn't have put both hands to his head.

The crowd seemed smaller. Little J. pushed through and caromed into Taylor, just to be sure he had his attention. He bounced off. Man was built like a brick shithouse, it practically hurt.

"Little J., what's the matter?"

Little J. would have protested, but he didn't have the breath for it. "You saying you has a whiz kid with the cell phones?"

"He's not having much luck, I'm afraid. Nobody seemed to have caught the exact moment our man went down."

"I thinking something different. The shooter have to be in the front row, right? Or somebody remember him shoving."

"Makes sense."

"So he have some of the best pictures. Except he ain't be taking them while he doing the shooting."

"Damn." Taylor poked his cell and clapped it to his ear. "Shelby, try looking at it this way."

Little J. tugged at his coat. "Course they a guy waving a gun down that street yonder. Might be quicker."

Taylor's look couldn't be described as trusting. "Tell me."

"While he getting away?"

Taylor gripped Little J.'s shoulder harder than the gunman had. He looked around and waved at somebody. It must be his partner, because she looked like she sounded. Trucker to the bone.

Taylor said, "Roxanne, I have a report of a guy with a gun over on West Fourth. Check it out."

Little J. said helpfully, "His face be bloody. Just in case he already throw the gun."

She had her own gun out. "On my way."

"Now, Little J."

Little J. said, "Tells you I taking a leak, right? Storm drain usually work best. Only when I looks down, what do I see but--" He unwound the ripped up jacket. "I sees a purple smear, like the dead guy's forehead. So what if I pissing on a clue? I goes after it, and a guy go after me."

128

Taylor spread the jacket pieces out with care. "You ripped it up between you?"

Little J. shook his head. "Like that when I find it. They may be blood on the zipper. On account of I has to go at his face a little."

Taylor gave him a sideways glance. "Maybe the shooter thought he'd find drugs in it somewhere."

Little J. embiggened his eyes. "That a fact?"

"But we didn't find money. He used his gun to get them for free. He thought."

Little J. kept his mouth shut. Somebody besides the shooter must have found the drugs, and Taylor still had that guy to look for. Little J. couldn't point that out, Taylor was already looking for an excuse to pounce.

But as Little J. had learned the hard way, Taylor was no slouch. He called his whiz kid again. This time he told Shelby to check if one of the people helping the murdered guy might actually have been patting him down and taken something. All those Smart Phones? Somebody must have caught it, maybe a few. Had the thief had a chance to get away? The cops would have pictures to circulate. They'd ID him. He'd be found.

So the cops would have the killer and the drugs and a drug receiver. Not the kind of delivery Mr. Sullivan had assigned him, but Little J. would be bringing the money back. He hadn't had a chance to check it, but it felt about thick enough.

Little J. raised his voice. "I see you has you hands full, Sergeant. I be on my way."

"Hold it." Sergeant Taylor squatted down so he actually had to look up a little to meet Little J.'s eyes. Nice change.

He said, "Looks like you'll get away clean this time, Little J. You're lucky."

"Think I ain't know that? That fool came here tonight ready to kill somebody. What if it be me?" There, he'd said too much. Taylor always seemed to get him.

He didn't pounce, though. Instead, he said, "But he did kill somebody," and swiveled on his heels to watch two men loading a black body bag into a black Maria. Little J. couldn't keep from staring, too, until the doors closed and it moved slowly through the crowd.

Taylor said, "You know why the victim worked on the dinosaur puppet, Little J.?"

Little J. had a feel for where this was going. His stomach already didn't like it. "Had a thing for parades?"

"His friends say he had a thing for dinosaurs. Specifically, he had two kids--boys--who liked them. Four and seven. He took them to the Museum of Natural History nearly every week. That's your home spot, isn't it?"

Little J. wanted to say, "Best bathroom in the city." He knew he couldn't get the words out. He kept his eyes wide so Taylor couldn't tell he couldn't see a damn thing. He cleared his throat. "He so expert, why ain't he tell them not to put Stegosaurus plates on a Apatosaurus? And I ain't even mention the T. rex head."

You'd think Taylor was deaf. He said, "He didn't plan to risk anything. He didn't plan to be part of your business. You didn't give him a choice."

Trust Taylor to see what he wasn't meant to. He whipped out a big white handkerchief and held it out. Little J. mopped himself up as best he could and handed it back.

"Keep it, Little J."

"Right. I wash it in my washing machine back in my apartment. Oh, I forget. I ain't have a washing machine. Or a apartment."

Taylor took the handkerchief back and stuffed it in a pocket, his mouth twisting. "If you decide to make some changes, Little J., you know where to find me."

Little J. fired up at that. "You the one who need to know where to find *me*, Sergeant Taylor. How else you going to get help the next time you in over you head?"

He took off before Taylor could catch sight of the money bulging in the back of his jeans. If he made good time, he might even make his delivery and get back down to Greenwich Village before the parade was over. All those wallets.

Wenda first met Little J. while she was working a thriller with a protagonist whose history resembled her own--New York fashion magazine career side-railed by cancer--only in the heroine's case, someone was meddling with her chemo. She had

130

a few ideas how it might go. None of them included a homeless, streetwise ten-year-old, but Little J. popped up on her computer screen--complete with leather jacket, Rolex watch, dinosaur t-shirt, and passion for BMWs--and took over. Wenda had to know what his life was like and how he came to be who he is. Three or four times a year he'll let her sneak a look.

When the call went out for All Hallows' Evil, *she immediately thought of Greenwich Village's Halloween Parade. During the years Wenda worked for a cooking school in the Village, she never missed one. Little J. plus the kind of over-the-top spectacle only Greenwich Village could come up with: what could go wrong? Well...*

Making Contact
By Marilyn Pierce Patterson

After getting Stuart's distressed phone call around sunset, I rushed out of my house just as I was, in a tee shirt and yoga pants, and sprinted to Meredith Bell's house next door. I knocked on her front door. When she didn't respond, I turned the knob. The door was unlocked, and I walked into her living room. I found Meredith sitting cross-legged on the hardwood floor beside a low, square table draped with an orange cloth. She cradled a framed photograph in her hands and didn't look up when I entered the room.

"Meredith, didn't you hear me knock? What's going on?"

"My mother—she's trying to make contact, Georgia." She stroked her finger over the photograph.

Stuart's phone call had prepared me for Meredith's claims about her mother. I looked down at the photograph and saw Meredith and her mother, Karen, captured in smiles. Karen had died two months ago at forty-two, a few years younger than I am, after a long fight with multiple sclerosis.

My immediate concern was not Karen's visitation from beyond, or lack thereof, but the very real lack of warmth in Meredith's house. I walked over to the thermostat on the living room wall, rubbing my bare arms. Our October weather had been relatively mild for Central Minnesota, but some nights the temperatures were dipping close to or just below freezing. Meredith and I both lived in drafty old houses. My furnace had been on for a while to take the nip out of the air. Meredith's thermostat was set to heat. The furnace should be running, but the temperature display registered 48 degrees.

"When was the last time the furnace kicked on?"

"What? Oh, I don't know. It's not a big deal." Meredith placed the photograph on the table. A silver bud vase on the table held a small bunch of pale blue asters. A lit pillar candle sat next to the vase. Meredith's long, black, wavy hair flowed down her back and over a red patterned silk shawl wrapped around her shoulders.

"Meredith, it is a big deal. It's freezing in here."

Meredith waved away my concern, her shawl flapping with her arm. I gasped, fearing an edge of it might end up in the candle flame. Meredith turned from her altar and looked at me as if just realizing I was in the room.

"Why are you here?"

I stood silent for a moment, startled by her blunt question and the frank look on her face. Since her mother's death, Meredith had welcomed and even sought out my support. I had spent more time with her in the past few months than with my daughter, Fiona, and more time than Meredith and Fiona, friends through high school, had spent together. Fiona had started her first year of college in September at a nearby university and was living in a house off campus with several roommates.

"Stuart called me and said when he talked to you on the phone today, you said something about your mother visiting you and then hung up on him." Stuart Opatz, who considered himself another of Meredith's guardians since her mother's death, owned the Flashback Cafe a few blocks away in downtown Granite Bluff. Meredith had been waiting tables at the Flashback since turning sixteen three years ago. According to Stuart, Meredith had called in sick the last two days. He called her today to see how she was doing, and her comment about her mother had him quivering with alarm. Only my agreement to check on her immediately had kept him from rushing over.

"Like I just told you, my mother is trying to reach me. She would choose Samhain to return to me, when the veil between our worlds is lifted. She knows what that would mean to me." With her mother's blessing, Meredith had started studying and practicing paganism as a young teen.

I, on the other hand, was a skeptic and suspected grief at the root of her current claim. As a widow, I knew firsthand the peculiar byways grief could lead us down, and the peculiar people we could become as we traveled them. I settled into a burgundy antique armchair, then pulled a gray afghan off its back and wrapped it around my shoulders. Somehow, I needed to make sense of her ramblings and guide her back to the real world so we could deal with her malfunctioning furnace.

"What exactly has she been doing?" I asked.

Meredith took a deep breath and let it out with a noisy sigh. "The details don't matter. What matters is the ritual I need to do on Samhain as the veil lifts."

"So, tell me the details, and I'll help with this ritual."

A look of joy spread across Meredith's face. I had no idea what I was getting into with my less than sincere offer, but at least I seemed to be reaching her.

"Okay." Meredith scooted around on the floor to face me. As she did, her shawl fell open, revealing the blue jeans and thin, pink camisole she wore underneath it. She was barefoot. Before she went on, she sniffled, and I noticed how wan she looked.

"First, she started moving things, photos, my shoes by the back door, dishes on the counter, things like that."

"How long ago did this start happening?"

"I don't know for sure—I didn't catch on right away. But I finally did about a week ago. Then the gifts started."

"What gifts?"

She lifted a smooth, black river rock from her lap, which I hadn't noticed before. "First, this rock. I found it on the mantel by our favorite photo." She set the rock on her altar by the photograph she had been holding earlier.

She continued. "Next, I found two apples on the kitchen counter. And three days ago, when I came home from work, I found a bunch of wildflowers on my bed—these." She pointed to the vase of asters on the altar. I realized with a start they looked a lot like the asters still in flower amid the decaying summer blooms at the side of my house.

"Anything since the flowers?"

The smile that had swelled on Meredith's face as she recited her finds receded a bit. "No, but that's not unusual. That's why I haven't left the house since the flowers and have been trying to contact her. She needs to know I'm okay with her being here, that she isn't scaring me. That's why I need to do the ritual."

A creeping dread began to work its way into my brain and warn me this was more than confused illusions triggered by grief. "Did the gifts appear while you were out of the house?"

Meredith scrunched up her eyebrows. "Yes, of course. She left them while I was gone so she wouldn't scare me."

I suddenly wanted us both out of her house as quickly as possible so I could process what she'd told me. What Meredith fancied as harmless gifts from her mother, I was starting to fear were signs of a much more sinister invasion of this world. Visions of a shadowy intruder placing flowers on her bed hammered through my mind. "I think you should come and stay with me. Until we get this sorted out."

Meredith's smile disappeared completely. She narrowed her eyes. "What do you mean? Get what sorted out? I told you what's going on, and you said you'd help me. I'm not going anywhere." She tried to maintain her scowl, but a sniffle interfered. She wiped her nose on the back of her palm.

I tried a softer tactic. "Meredith, for practical reasons more than anything, you need to come home with me. The furnace isn't working, and we probably won't get anyone out here to fix it until tomorrow. You can't stay here another night without heat. You're already catching a cold. And you need to eat."

"Who says I haven't eaten." She resumed her scowl.

"The fact that you haven't been at work for two days. Will I find any food in your fridge or cabinets if I go look?" I already knew the answer to that question. Stuart made sure she ate at least one good meal at his cafe when she worked. If she hadn't been at work or outside her house, she likely hadn't been eating much or at all.

She shrugged, then turned back to her altar, shutting me out.

"Just for tonight then. Until the furnace is back on. Have a good meal at my house, get a good night's rest, and we'll come back tomorrow night on Halloween—Samhain—and do the ritual. You can keep me company." That last bit popped out before I could stifle it. I hadn't said out loud to anyone how much

I was dreading this Halloween, which marked the first anniversary of my husband, Wade's, death. Meredith's altar and her talk of contact with the dearly departed were getting to me.

I finally persuaded Meredith to come home with me, and we walked the short distance from her front door to mine. While I made a salad for our supper, she sat on a barstool in my kitchen and played catch with my Dobies, Shadow and Stella. We ate at my dining room table and later snacked on a bowl of organic black grapes as we watched a sitcom in the living room. While I was in the kitchen doing the dishes, Meredith fell asleep on my leather couch. I pulled a blanket off the bed in Fiona's room and draped it over her, leaving her to sleep where she was. Then I called Stuart to tell him Meredith was safe with me.

The next morning dawned with a touch of fog, putting dew on the carved pumpkins on my front porch. After scheduling someone to repair Meredith's furnace that afternoon, I left my house and walked downtown. My first stop was city hall to sign some documents in my official capacity as mayor of Granite Bluff. Less than a week after Wade's death, I won the mayoral election, which made my life even more surreal. Now ten months into my four-year term, I was finally getting used to being called Mayor Farraday.

After discharging my official duties, I walked a few more blocks to the old, red brick building that housed our local library to see Ruth Glenn, the head librarian. Meredith had volunteered at the library while in junior high and developed a special bond with Ruth. I knew she'd be concerned.

"What can you tell me about Samhain?" I asked her after relating the details of last night's visit with Meredith.

Ruth swiped her short, white hair behind her ears, and then started tapping on the computer keyboard in front of her. I leaned against the wooden front desk and watched her work. She studied the search results on the computer screen through her purple, rhinestone-studded eyeglasses.

"According to this website, Samhain signals the end of summer and is a time when the mundane rules of time and space are suspended. It's a time to honor the ancestors who came before us and contact loved ones who have crossed over, while the veil between worlds is thinnest. That sounds like what Meredith told you."

"Which doesn't mean her mother is actually behind what's going on at her house," I said.

"Stranger things have happened."

"The skeptic in me just can't go there."

"It is quite a remarkable possibility," she said.

An older man walking with a cane approached the desk, two hardcover books stuck under his arm, and I backed away. A bit of mild flirting passed between the two of them as Ruth checked out his books.

After the man left and we were alone at the desk again, Ruth continued. "Okay, so if we discount the paranormal for the moment, what's your theory?"

"I have a few theories now that I've had time to think about it, but no proof. After Meredith fell asleep last night, I went back over to her house and looked around. No sign of any break-in, no damage to any doors or windows, all windows locked, nothing suspicious."

"I'd say, then, you have yourself a mystery. Whatever's going on, tonight will get you closer to the truth. Help Meredith with the ritual, and if nothing paranormal happens, you're left with the alternative."

I frowned. "Which to me means either Meredith is planting these things herself in a grief-stricken fantasy or she has a stalker."

"Do you think she could be doing it herself?"

I shook my head. "The rock and the apples, maybe, but the flowers on her bed—those set off alarm bells in my head."

"So, a stalker then. Any ideas who?"

"No one I can name. I'm still puzzling over how a stalker might be getting in."

Ruth arched an eyebrow. "An old boyfriend with a grudge and a key?"

"I thought of that, but I talked to Fiona, and she said there haven't been any long-term boyfriends in Meredith's past that she knows of, and no boyfriend who she thinks Meredith would have given a key. That doesn't mean one didn't take a key somewhere along the way."

"Have you talked to Matt yet?"

Talking to Matt Turner, Wade's brother and Granite Bluff's police chief, had briefly crossed my mind the evening before, and I had quickly pushed it aside. "And tell him what? Meredith is getting strange gifts at her house, things are being moved around, there's no sign of a break-in, and she thinks it's her dead mother communicating with her? I suspect he would think Meredith and I have both finally flipped. I'm going to do my own surveillance for the time being until I have something more concrete to share with him."

A woman and her two children approached us, and I stepped aside again so Ruth could check out the items they piled on her desk. The little girl was dressed in a pink fairy costume and the little boy in a pirate's outfit.

"Great costumes," Ruth said. After checking out their items, she picked up the pumpkin-shaped bucket of candy sitting beside her on the desk, looked at their mother for approval, and then offered each child a piece. "Off to trick or treat tonight?"

The children nodded and giggled as they burrowed through the bucket. After a few minutes, and with some harried prompting from their mother, they made their selections and left.

"Count me in," Ruth said when we were alone at the desk again.

"For what?"

"The ritual, the surveillance. I can offset your skepticism at the ritual, be another set of eyes and ears to witness what does—or doesn't—happen. And any black belt superhero needs a sidekick for surveillance." She winked.

"Probably a good idea on both counts." Ruth was a star pupil at the weekly women's self-defense class I taught at our community center. She would have a level head if our surveillance landed us in trouble.

Noises coming from the children's room drew Ruth's attention. "Sounds like trouble brewing," she said. I told her I'd call her later and left.

I ran a few more errands before returning home. When I arrived, I found Meredith asleep on the couch again. A technician showed up soon after to fix her furnace. I made supper a little before sunset. Following our meal, Meredith insisted on going back to her house alone to prepare for the ritual. Even though I wasn't happy about it, I decided arguing with her was useless. Her sniffles had increased, and I consoled myself by convincing her to take a megadose of Vitamin C before she left.

I spent the next few hours handing out bite-sized dark chocolate bars and organic lollipops to the costumed children who rang my doorbell, feeding Shadow and Stella peanut butter doggy treats to appease them, and looking out my kitchen window at Meredith's house for any signs of trouble.

Gradually, the stream of children gave way to teens in more elaborate and scarier costumes. Then the span between doorbell rings grew longer until I declared my Halloween treating over. I turned off my outside light, stored the candy so Shadow and Stella had no chance of getting into it, and headed over to Meredith's.

I had asked Meredith if Ruth could join us, and she'd agreed. Ruth drove up in her red Smart Car and parked it in front of my house as I walked out my front door. After getting out of her car, she swirled a gold, lacy shawl around the shoulders of her maroon tracksuit. I was much less flamboyant in my black yoga pants, black hoodie, and black canvas shoes.

Meredith greeted us at her front door and ushered us into a dramatically warmer living room lit by the flickering glow of white pillar candles placed throughout the room. The scent of nutmeg and candle wax hung in the air. She again wore the red patterned silk shawl, this time over a long, flowing, black skirt.

She had instructed me to pick up something with apples in it for the meal we would have as part of the ritual. I carried into the kitchen one of Stuart's homemade deep-dish apple pies that I had picked up while downtown. I had given Ruth the same instructions when I phoned her. She had brought apple cider, which she poured into a pan and set on the stove to warm.

When it was time to start the ritual, Meredith directed us to sit on the living room floor around her altar. An expression of expectation filled her face as if she was waiting for the doorbell to ring announcing a tardy but honored guest. She lit the white pillar candle on her altar, and then recited a bittersweet, lyrical poem she had written for her mother. After the poem, we joined hands, and she recited a Samhain prayer to her ancestors.

Next, she led us into the dining room. Four places were set, two on each side of her oak table, with white dessert plates and white mugs.

"This one is for my mother," Meredith said, pointing to one of the settings, which had a gold fabric square beneath the plate.

Ruth and I brought in the pie and cider and then sat at the two place settings on the opposite side of the table. Meredith cut the pie and slipped the first piece from the metal pie tin onto her mother's plate. She dished out pieces for the rest of us and poured the cider. We ate our pie and drank our cider in silence.

As I ate, I kept sneaking a glimpse at the piece of pie on Karen's plate. I wasn't sure what we were waiting for, but so far nothing unusual had happened during the ritual. The expectant look Meredith had worn at the beginning of the evening was slowly turning to sorrow as she picked her piece of pie apart and spread it over her plate.

"I really thought this would work, that she'd let us know she's here," she said. Tears began rolling down her cheeks. Ruth went over to Meredith and hugged her as her tears flowed.

After crying herself out, Meredith went willingly back to my house. Ruth and I helped her to bed in Fiona's room. Her cold was getting worse. Ruth said she would stay with Meredith for a while, so I went to let Shadow and Stella out into the backyard. I turned the lights off in the kitchen and living room and left the outside light off. I grabbed Wade's old hooded sweatshirt off one of the hooks by the French patio doors and joined my dogs outside.

A crisp chill hung in the night air. I was warm enough wrapped in Wade's big sweatshirt. I sat down on a black metal chair belonging to the bistro set on my patio. Drawing my arms to my nose, I sniffed the sweatshirt fabric, catching Wade's musky scent. Real or imagined, I didn't care. I felt tears pressing at my eyes. It was official. My husband had been dead and gone one year.

The memories of the night Wade died had been growing more vivid the closer the end of October loomed. On that fateful night, long after all the trick or treating was over, I went to bed, deluded that my little world was safe from goblins and ghouls.

Wade said he would join me soon—the last words he ever said to me. A little after midnight, I woke up in our bed, Wade not by my side. I found him on our living room couch where he had suffered a massive stroke and died alone.

For one fleeting moment during tonight's ritual, while Meredith read her poem, I had wanted to join in her boundless belief and defy the skeptic in my head. One wild, improbable hint of contact from Karen, and my grieving heart would have been ready to kindle a glimmer of hope that Wade could reach me from beyond this world.

Exhausted by the paranormal and whatever else might be lurking around us, I put my head down on my arms on the bistro tabletop. I closed my eyes and, Wade's sweatshirt soft on my cheek, gave into my sorrow.

I dozed off, and some time later jerked awake when someone touched me. Ruth stooped at my side, her hand on my shoulder.

"I heard something," she whispered close to my ear. "Noises over by Meredith's house. Maybe footsteps."

Shadow and Stella were quaking at my feet and on alert. I didn't move and tuned my ears to the night sounds: a few cars humming along a downtown street, a dog barking in the distance—nothing out of the ordinary. The high privacy fence walling in my backyard prevented a view of the surrounding area.

"I'm going to check it out," I said.

"I'm coming with you," Ruth said.

I put Shadow and Stella back into the house. If there was someone prowling in the darkness, keeping Ruth and me safe and accounted for was enough to worry about. I grabbed a flashlight from a kitchen drawer and Meredith's house keys from a hook on the side of my kitchen cabinet. I rejoined Ruth in the backyard. We headed toward the gate at the back of my fence.

Outside the gate, I turned on the flashlight and aimed it toward the ground just ahead of our path. The streetlight at the end of the block gave off an eerie glow. We approached Meredith's house from the back. Three ancient bur oak trees with corky, gnarled, leafless limbs dominated her backyard. A crumbling sidewalk led from the back door to the single car garage along the alley.

We stopped at the perimeter of Meredith's yard. A breeze shivered through the trees. The house was dark just as it had been when we left it earlier. I looked toward the garage.

A moment later, Ruth seized my arm. "I saw a light, Georgia, in the window. Just a flare and then it went out. It could have been a reflection. I'm not sure."

I turned my gaze back to the house. "Which window?"

"Up there." Ruth pointed to one of the windows in Meredith's bedroom on the second floor.

My heart raced. I strode toward the back door. Ruth followed along. Before inserting the key, I tried the doorknob. It turned freely. We had exited through the front door earlier, and I couldn't be certain now that the back door had been locked.

I pushed the door open and crept inside, Ruth on my heels. We were in Meredith's kitchen. I clicked off the flashlight. The streetlight threw hazy beams through the window at our backs. I looked around the room.

After our meal, while Meredith cried in Ruth's arms, I had cleared the dining room table and washed the dishes. I hadn't been able to bring myself to throw away the uneaten pie on Karen's plate, and after covering it with plastic wrap, I had set it aside on the kitchen counter. The plate was where I had left it, but it was now empty, the plastic wrap pulled off and discarded beside it. I pointed to the plate. Ruth nodded, her eyes wide.

I didn't have my cell phone and considered going back home to call the police. Footsteps shuffling across the floor above and then starting down the stairs stopped me. We were directly in the path between the intruder and the door he or she had used to enter the house. I scanned around us for a safe place to avoid an encounter, then grabbed Ruth by the arm and dragged her over to the small bathroom off the kitchen. The door was open, and we popped inside. We crouched down and peered out the doorway. Ruth clutched my arm. Adrenaline flooded my body.

Footsteps landed heavily on each riser down to the bottom of the stairs, then creaked along on the hardwood floor of the living room. Then the footsteps stopped.

The next thing I heard was a lock sliding open at the front of the house. A light came on in the living room. "Ruth, Georgia?"

I sprang up and bounded into the living room. Meredith stood in the doorway staring at her couch. A man stood before it extending an arm in her direction. I sprinted toward him and pushed his arm away, then kicked behind his knee. He yelled and started to collapse. I grabbed his wrist nearest to me and rolled my other hand over his shoulder, bringing him to the floor. He landed facedown. I put my knee on his neck applying just enough pressure to hold him in place. Meredith was screaming. Ruth ran to comfort her.

"Ow. Let me go," the man said in a muffled tone around my leg. I still had hold of his wrist. He wore a shabby tan coat with a ragged hem at the sleeve. The back of his blond hair was matted.

"Shut up and hold still, or it will get worse. Ruth, call the police."

The next morning, Meredith and I met with Matt in his office at the police station. We sat in front of his desk in stiff-backed chairs. Matt's dark hair looked as though it hadn't been combed yet this morning, and his eyes were bloodshot. Lack of sleep didn't sit well on him. I hadn't slept much myself and doubted I looked any better.

He got right to business after asking Meredith how she was doing. "His name is Jeremy Long, and he's from Colorado. He's twenty-three and has a history of mental illness, although he claims he's taking his medication. He came here hoping to find a place to stay." Matt paused for a moment before going on. "Your place, specifically, Meredith."

Meredith gasped and huddled deeper into her chair, pulling the down jacket she wore around her like a cocoon. She had cried most of the night. Her intruder had left another bunch of asters and a childish love poem scribbled on a scrap of paper on her bed, confirming beyond a doubt that the strange happenings in her house had not come from her mother.

"What do you mean?" I asked.

"Jeremy's grandparents lived in your house, Meredith, before your mother bought it. It was over a decade ago, but I vaguely remember the Longs, nice couple, had a few kids as I recall. Jeremy said he used to visit them at the house in the summer.

"His grandfather died a few years back, and then his grandmother last year. They had moved to Colorado, but they still had keys to the house here with the address labeled on the keychain. Jeremy found them while helping his mother clean out their house, and he took them. He says he left home about a month ago after a fight with his parents and has been on the road ever since. He decided to come here and see if the house was still standing and if anyone lived in it. When he found it, he tried the keys to see if they would work."

"And Karen didn't change the locks," I said, stating the obvious. I shuddered thinking of my own house and the locks Wade and I hadn't even considered changing after inheriting it from Wade's great aunt.

Matt ran his hand through his hair, making it more unruly. "Apparently not."

Meredith finally roused. "But why was he leaving me things, moving things around? Was he trying to scare me out of my house? Was he planning to hurt me?"

I put my hand on her shoulder. She was trembling.

Matt leaned forward and rested his elbows on his desk. His face grew stern. "He can't hurt you now, Meredith. You are not in danger anymore. We've called his parents and they are coming to get him. We have the keys so he can't get back in. But for all we know there could be copies. You need to change the locks. Right away." He directed that last bit to me. I nodded.

We got up to leave. Meredith headed out the door, and I followed. Matt came up behind me and took hold of my arm to keep me back.

"Meredith, go talk to Amanda out front about getting those locks changed. She can give you the names of locksmiths in town. I need to talk to Georgia about city stuff for a minute."

Matt led me back into his office and closed the door. He stepped behind his desk but stayed standing. I stayed standing, too.

"What city stuff?"

He ignored my question. "This Jeremy guy built a huge fantasy in his head about Meredith. At first, he was just going in the house because he could. Then he saw Meredith and everything changed. He thought the two of them were kindred spirits on the same path, lonely and searching for each other. He had quite elaborate plans for how they were going to live happily ever after. As far as I can tell, he wasn't going to hurt her, but, of course, if she had resisted, who knows what he might have done…" He crossed his arms over his chest. "You should have told me what was going on."

I shook my head. "It was complicated. I hardly knew myself what was going on until it was too late to call for help. Anyway, I handled it."

A smile flitted across his face. "Yes, Jeremy told us, repeatedly, about the crazy woman who came out of nowhere."

Then his expression sobered. He scrutinized me with eyes that were almost identical to Wade's and had unnerved me a time or two since his death. "How are you?"

It took me a moment to shift gears and understand what he meant. I realized at the same time that some of his weariness might be due to his own grief and the anniversary we had just passed.

I felt tears welling and pushed them away. "I'm not sure yet," I said, the tremor in my voice giving me away anyway. "How are you?"

Matt shrugged and turned to gaze out his office window. I fought an urge to go around his desk and give him a hug. After a silent pause, he shook himself back to the present.

"There's something I think you should see. Jeremy said Meredith wrote him a note. He found it when he brought her the apples." He opened his top desk drawer and pulled out a slip of pink paper. He handed it to me. I opened it and read Meredith's words.

I knew someday we'd be together again. Please don't leave me alone.
M.

I folded the pink paper note in half and then in half again and set it on Matt's desk. It was suddenly clearer why a lonely, unstable young man might think he had found his soul mate. I

146

understood, too, the desperation fueling Meredith's plea. Over and over in the last year, in the terrifying silence of my home, I had cursed Wade for leaving me and begged him, against all logic, for one more day together. I had whispered. I had screamed. But never raised the slightest response—or believed it was possible.

I looked out the window and saw Meredith standing in the parking lot, tilting her face up to the sky. And I hoped, beyond reason, that one day, somehow, she would make contact.

Marilyn Pierce Patterson lives in Minnesota with her husband, two inquisitive dogs, and a cat with all the answers. This is her first published short story. She is a member of Sisters in Crime and is working on a novel.

Bill's Chair

By Jason Purdy

Work had never been an easy thing for John, at least not until he found his calling. He'd ran away from home at sixteen, because he'd grown up working his fingers to the bone on his father's farm during every waking moment that he wasn't at school or asleep. John wasn't afraid of hard graft, but he was afraid of spending the rest of his life being paid in *gratitude*. Gratitude didn't pay the bills. Gratitude didn't put gas in your tank, or whores in your bed.

Money did that. Money makes the world go round after all. John would know that from a song, if he had ever bothered to fix the radio in his car. He was one of those people. On the road in his old Impala, he didn't need the noise of some schlocky *sumbitch* (as his dad would have put it) yelling in his ear and shoving rock and roll down his throat. All he needed was the roar of the engine and the silence of the open road. So he left home at sixteen, and for a long time, he floundered, struggling to find a job that would engage his brain, his hands, and his *heart.* Of course, this was a common desire of the high school dropout. The quest for that job that didn't exist. The people who got paid well to do little work were born into that sort of thing. From cradle to grave with a silver spoon in their mouth and a wooden stick shoved up their ass.

Not John. John had a redneck name, one that was worse than "John". John wasn't his name, it was just a word. Nobody ever remembered a John. The name was unremarkable as unremarkable comes. His birth name screamed redneck, more so than his sunburnt neck and slightly off teeth did. He didn't smile much. If he kept his champers hidden, he was a handsome guy. Not excessively so. Just handsome enough for a young lady to

149

give him an appreciative glance, and then forget him entirely. In appearance, he was the one item on your shopping list that you really needed but always forgot. That was the essence of John.

He was a ghost, until that bar fight. After that, you'd probably describe him as a ghoul. The bar was your usual road side piss hole. Somewhere bordering a highway not remarkable enough to name, between two small towns in the middle of America, in the heart of the Bible Belt. The signs would ask you to drive carefully, just in case you happen to run over one of the less than five hundred inhabitants, and the bar would go deathly silent when you walked in. Like you were sweet creeping Jesus raised from the dead again, back to see how the church goers fared on a Saturday night with a few beers under their belts and the nightmare of Sunday service a blessed few hours away still.

John walked in, walked to the bar, and ordered a beer. He wasn't looking for a lot of drink, just one or two so he could sleep in the back seat of the car without the noise of squealing rubber and revving engines along the highway keeping him up. He'd just been paid for a bit of moving work. Helping shift some furniture into a house, and then shifting it out when they realized it was the wrong house, and then shifting it back somewhere else. He didn't get paid any extra for those wasted hours, and at that moment, when he realized the mistake his moving buddy had made, he had one of those flashes of white hot rage. The kind that back on the farm would have made him punch the side of the old barn until his fists bled, or would make him grab one of the old turkeys and push his fingers into its throat until blood spilled over his grimy, chewed fingernails.

He bit his tongue and held it back. He knew that if he lost it, it'd all be for nothing, and he'd never see the money that he busted his hump for. So here he was, looking for a beer, sitting in a free stool close to the bar between two big guys in overalls. They smelled like beer, sweat, and shit. The typical aromas you'd find on any farm. Part of John felt at home, the little kid inside of him. The rest of him was on edge, tense, rage flashing like a car alarm, sending pulses into his head and down his spine and bringing on a real hurricane of a migraine. He asks for a Miller's. Thank God they have it, because that would have pushed him over the brink.

He knows, sitting here in this bar with the imaginative name of "Joe's", that he'll have to let it out eventually, this sort of rage could eat you alive. He's about five miles as the crow flies from the moving job. He'd bet that if he went back in the morning, he'd see his good old buddy sitting there, looking for more work. A badly rolled cigarette hanging from the side of his mouth, his hand rubbing his rough stubble, making a hiss of sandpaper. That stupid grin plastered on his face, as if to say *sorry buddy, it's an easy mistake to make! I mean, who'd have thought to double check the address eh? Nobody's perfect, and I ain't no saint, that's for sure! Did I ever tell you about the time I-*

Even though they'd worked together for one day, he'd know the time that dim witted bastard meant. He told the same stories over and over again, to the point where you thought this guy was a robot, just planted on earth by some alien race. He tries to fit in, see? So he comes up with this one story, a real dinner party anecdote, and he spews it out over and over again, grinning and nudging you on the shoulder. Eh? Ain't that a real hoot, ain't that a real pisser?

The bar man sets the Miller's in front of him and the sound near makes him leap out of his skin. Everything in the bar is too close and too loud, like the walls are closing in and the burly meat bags on either side of him are leaning closer and closer, pushing their words into his head like they're hammering a nail into a piece of wood. He pays for the beer and sinks half of it, straight up. There's a tap on his shoulder, and he turns, his face curious, slightly surprised. He doesn't notice the silence in the bar; he's more worried about the fist coming towards his face. It makes contact, the sound of meat on meat, and John hits the floor, slipping off the stool and taking his Miller with him.

He peers through a haze of pain and indignant anger at the man standing above him. The two guys in the stools look down at him, as if this is the sort of thing that happens every night. It's no big deal.

"You're sitting in my seat." The one staring down at him says. The one who is currently frantically shaking his right hand, as if that punch hurt him more than it hurt John.

"I *was*." John says, spitting out blood, and waving his arm at the empty seat. The bar is so silent you could hear a mouse fart. No one dares to laugh, John feels outnumbered. Someone even turned off the jukebox. Real life isn't meant to work like that. This sort of thing is an urban myth.

"Check out the mouth on this one." The big guy has a Yankee accent to match his look. John wishes that just for once, he'd see the tourist's version of Middle America instead of this happy horse-shit.

"Didn't mean nothing by it." John says, slipping back into his father's drawl instead of using that New York accent he'd been working on. He had plans to head there when he'd gathered enough money. Seemed more his scene. Throw on a suit and get paid a big wad to look the part. He could do that. John was all about looking the part.

"Sorry stranger." The big guy says, offering a hand to John, who takes it. He gets pulled halfway to his feet, and then right into another fist. John goes down harder, his head hitting the tiled floor and his teeth clacking together like a bag of marbles.

"That's enough." The bar man says, pulling a rifle down from the top of the bar and pointing it at John, as if he's the problem here. "Take this outside."

"With pleasure." The big one says, grinning. He's missing a few teeth. He'll be missing more than that by the time they're through.

2.

John finds himself standing in the empty parking lot, his hands covered in blood, and the big guy lying on the asphalt in front of him. The big dope's trucker hat lies a few feet away, covered in blood. Teeth litter the ground around his head like pocket change, and there's a glass bottle wedged through the guy's throat, coated with sticky blood and phlegm. The bar is closed; the car park is empty except for John's Impala, and the big guy's big rig parked right beside it. *What are the odds?* He bends over; hands on his knees like a jogger getting his wind back. He vomits blood and, well, *vomit*, onto the tarmac in front of him.

He'd expect the big guy to laugh at him, but the big guy is quite dead. John runs his hands through his sweaty, dirty mop of blonde hair, and he sniffs up a wad of blood and snot from his nose and hawks it out onto the big guys face. Later in his career, he'd be more concerned about DNA. Right now he just finds himself concerned that he doesn't seem to give a flying Frisbee - another one of his dad's, Frisbee instead of *fuck,* what a kidder - about the dead man before him. He drags the body to the truck, fishing into the dead man's pocket for his keys. There's a whole bunch of them held together with a faded little trinket telling him that Jesus Loves You. John snorts. The lucky sumbitch has his pick from several nice rides, and still takes a shit heap of a truck out to drink. Probably doesn't want the boys to know he's a made man. Well, they'll never find out now.

John gets the right key and tosses the body onto the front seat. He takes the man's wallet, his license, his Johnny Cash cassettes, and raids the glove compartment, nabbing a packet of Juicy Fruit, a small pistol, and a few cans of beer. He takes everything else that might identify the guy, and then climbs out of the truck. He takes the plates from the front and back and tosses them into his own boot. He does this with a grin on his face, whistling while he works. Headlights appear in the distance and he ducks behind the truck as a cop car passes, sirens flashing, not sparing a glance for the empty car park and the stranger behind the truck. This would unnerve most folks. John just resumes his whistling, a reedy and tuneless sound.

He tosses the rest of the stuff into his passenger seat, grinning at the beers and the tapes. Maybe he'll get drunk tonight after all. He climbs back into the old truck, which is starting to stink to high heaven already. Ducking under the dashboard, he rips down the cover and looks at the tangle of wires. His dad taught him how on the farm with their old tractor. You couldn't start it with a key, but if you knew the right wires, then you were sorted. If you knew the wrong ones, his pa reckoned you were likely to start an engine fire. A real dirty one, the kind that would eat up the car and spit out nothing but tangled metal and melted seat covers. John grabs the wrong wires and he does it the wrong way. The fire starts.

"Fuck you, pa." He mutters, as the whole thing starts to burn merrily. He sits back, cracking a beer, watching the flames rise. He sticks Johnny Cash blares from his own cassette player, which

153

he's never used, but still works, despite the radio. He knows this one.

He reckons he knows what he's going to do with his life now, too. Once he's sure the car is going to burn without supervision, he jumps into the Impala, turns Johnny up a little bit louder, and he vanishes into the night, putting a good hundred miles between himself and the charred remains of the big guy before the sun comes up. For a few months, he lays low, taking odd jobs here and there, some heavy lifting, some security work, nothing during the day, and nothing that exposes him much. He rents a small one bedroom one room deal, with a cot, a sink, and just about a pot to piss in. He expects a knock on the door any day, and two officers standing there, in the typical cream to gray uniform you see in this neck of the woods. Hell, they'll probably be holding the cuffs out ready for him, all he needs to do is hold out his scrawny little wrists and let them snap them on.

They don't show up. He passes back through, past Joe's bar, to see a small shrine erected in the spot where the big guy burned. He heads to the library on a whim, checking through old newspapers, back to the date that's become etched in his mind, even more so than his birthday. Which might be sometime in January, he's not sure. They've got a well-kept edition of the local news rag from that date, telling him all he needed to know. Front page news, a big headline.

BIG BILL DEAD IN TRAGIC ACCIDENT

He skims the article, his chest seeming to inflate like a bullfrog's throat. Police not treating it as suspicious, Bill was a heavy drinker, verdict: misadventure. John thought that was the best way to describe it. He asked to see a few other random papers from several years before, telling the librarian he was writing a paper for his college. When she asked what on, he told he was interested in the history of the town fair, which happened to be the same day the news broke. He noticed little things like that now. She helped him find more information, and he dutifully pretended to read every paper she gave him. She was beautiful, in a plain sort of way, and she seemed to like him too, even though she couldn't quite remember the details on his face every time he

154

turned away. He considered asking her for a drink, but he was pretty sure the only bar around was Joe's, and he was already risking enough hanging around here.

He left it, handing the papers back to her at closing time. She asks what college he went to.

"The worst one," he says.

"Really?" She says, with a laugh. "Me too. Cafeteria food was good though."

"Must have gone downhill since your time. It's like dog food now."

"Really?"

"Really." He says, grinning. Part of him wonders if he can make her say *really* a third time, but he resists the urge. He knows how to play the game.

"Aren't you a little old for college?" she says, giving him a smile he can't figure out.

"You're never too old to learn something new." He says, winking and turning to leave. She expects him to be back the next day, doing more research. She spends a bit more time getting ready that morning, figuring she'll ask him out for supper if he doesn't bite the bullet first. She never sees him again, and by the following day she's pretty much forgotten what he looked like at all.

3.

John went to New York and he became a cleaner. He figured there were two ways to go about this, and his decision boiled down to jail time. Accomplice to a murder was less serious than *actually* committing the act. Maybe God would disagree on that one, but to John, God was a man who sent his son to earth to die, so the son in question, Jesus, of course, could hang on John's kitchen wall back home and watch with a demure smile as his dad beat him around the room because he hadn't done his homework again. John always had the comeback on the tip of his tongue; that it was hard to get your homework done when you were worked like an old horse until your body ached with agony and you were numb from exhaustion, but Jesus seemed to tell him to bite his tongue on that front, too.

155

John wasn't a cleaner in the traditional sense. He didn't battle dust bunnies or take out the trash, he got rid of evidence, of sorts. He disposed of bodies. The fiasco with Big Bill had shown him that he had something of a talent for it, or at least a streak of black luck. It was something he'd always been good at. Not murder of course, but not getting caught. The few times he got beat over the homework were rare times. He always had dodges, he blamed the dead turkeys on foxes, and he blamed his teachers for the work, and blamed his father for his tiredness. It rarely fell on him, and now he could make a career out of it. He found his contacts easily. When you're poor and you live out of your car, falling in with the wrong crowd is as easy as getting laid on prom night. You just need to know where to slip your hands.

For five years, he got rid of bodies and got paid well for the privilege. He didn't change his car, but instead kept it in tip top shape, replacing the ragged old seats with nice leather, putting a false bottom in the boot to hide his tools, and even adding a CD player well ahead of the curve. He only listened to Cash now, but it seemed that Johnny had been busy and had plenty of albums to work through. This was when John became John, maybe because of Cash, maybe because of the plain Jane nature of the name. For five years, work went well and he was well respected. That was the way things shook out until one of the bodies he was sent to clean up didn't seem to be quite as dead as he was led to believe.

4.

It was near Halloween, of course. Strange things like this never happen in the middle of a bright August day while you're standing in the sun with a beer and a hotdog. It's always on those short cold nights, where your breath comes in a fog and children run in front of your car dressed as characters from movies that would make them soil themselves if they'd actually watched them.

On this night, three days before the trick or treating was due to commence, John got a call, the same as usual, an anonymous one, with directions. He was in New York, planning on finishing out the year there. The caller wanted him to go to a phone booth a few blocks over. That was typical procedure too. Get a call, go to the phone box, get a few more details, and from there meet with the client or go right to the body, depending on how things were going to play out. There were always variables but John accounted for them, and the small semi-auto handgun in his jacket pocket and the old wooden handled kitchen knife jammed into his boot would help tip the odds in his favor if things went wrong, which they were wont to do. One time in Boston, he ended up with two corpses on his hands, and he was only getting paid for one of them. That's the simplest way to put it, and the simple way was how he was apt to look at things.

He answered the phone, turning away from the busy street and holding it against his shoulder. He flips out a fresh note pad and scrawls the details onto it with a 2B pencil. He didn't like pens; there was something awfully permanent about ink. He didn't like tattoos either, but that was more because of seeing his father's crudely tattooed knuckles cruising towards his own face one too many times. One knuckle said GOD' and the other one said SSON. When held together, they said *GOD'S SON* obviously. Separately they looked like half retarded gibberish. He felt they suited his dad better separate.

He found that he rarely had to answer or verify his ID, and with each of these cold calls always followed the strange tingling sensation of being watched. He supposed that everyone had their own interests to look out for, their own backs to watch. That was fine with him; money was money, regardless of who it came from or under what pretenses. He frowned as the call finished the details etched into the pad that disappeared into the same pocket as his gun. This was one of those rare jobs where he was told where and when to prepare for a body. Someone would die on Halloween night, and he had to be there to clean it up.

He didn't like these ones. When the turkey was still alive, there were too many variables. The body might not appear where it was supposed to, the mess might be greater than anticipated, and worse, the whole thing might go to shit and he could end up disposing of his employer, the only payment being the knowledge that he'd covered his own tracks. He wiped the phone with the sleeve of his jacket, getting rid of any finger prints. More out of habit than any fear, he's unlikely to ever be traced back here, but

God protects those who protect themselves. There was a woodcarving in the hall back home that said something along those lines. He grins at that. It's more of an imitation of a smile than an actual one, but it does the trick. As he steps from the booth, there's a woman waiting behind him to use it. She's on the wrong side of thirty, but then again, John will be too someday. He gives her the practiced smile and she gives him a cautious look. Her hand creeps towards her bag, on auto pilot. She knows enough about New York, men, and the world, to always be on alert. John knows that feeling well himself. It comes with the line of work.

"It's busted," he says, cocking a thumb over his shoulder.

"Is it?" she says, her hand moving away from her bag and brushing a bunch of brown curls away from her face and behind her ear. John doesn't understand people that well, which seems to make it all the easier to read them. He makes a spur of the moment decision. The frustration over the job can be tempered easily.

"Forgive me if I don't believe you," she says, after a moment, moving to push past him. He steps into her away. The hand goes into the bag.

"Come on, don't be like that," he says, stepping back, hands upraised, smiling openly. Absolute submission. "I swear on my mother's grave, it's a no-go. Let me buy you a cup of coffee and you can borrow my phone."

"I can make a call from *here*," she says, staring him down, holding out her hand for the phone. She's got him there all right. He laughs and hands her the phone. He'll play a long game on this one. He had no other plans tonight except for sanitizing his apartment and buying some supplies, but that can all wait. He's got a few days yet. She enters the number into her phone and holds it to her ear, looking John up and down as she does. He thinks she likes what she sees. He hears a gruff male voice answer and her side of the conversation only.

"Yeah, I'm fine, it went great. I'll find out in a few weeks." She pauses, giving John another appraising look. He gives her a bemused smile. The sidewalk is jammed on either side and New York is alive and filled with a million voices that

158

are oblivious to the moment the two of them are sharing, that secret knowledge passing between them, like a spark of electric.

"I'll see you in the morning. Bye." She hangs up and hands the phone back. She doesn't notice how John takes it with the sleeve of his jacket instead of his naked hand. More prints couldn't hurt.

"Thanks a bunch," she says, grinning at him.

"No problem," he says, then, trying his luck, "was that your... you know…" He gives her an awkward smile, as if to say *oh gee, how embarrassing for me.* John has never felt embarrassment.

"Oh no, I'm single. I like it that way," she steps closer, touching his arm gently. "I figure I owe you. How about that coffee? I'll pay."

"If you're paying, make it a beer."

5.

She's gone when he wakes up. That always makes it handier than having to rustle up a breakfast for them when you keep nothing but beer and industrial bottles of vinegar in your fridge. Then you have to make an excuse, and that always gives him a headache. He doesn't like to lie. Surprisingly, he's got enough at his work that he rarely has to.

He loads up his Impala with all the gear he needs, shoving it under the false bottom in the boot. On top of it, he puts a crate of beer, a few bags of potato chips, and a sleeping bag and pillow, just in case. He's got a long few days of driving ahead of him to make the destination, but he's always liked long drives. When you're chasing the horizon, you don't need to worry about anything else. Travelling from A to B was a strange limbo that he always relished since he escaped from the farm. Anyone who ever says that no man is an island has never driven cross country with nothing but a few good CDs and the purr of his engine for company.

John arrives precisely as he thought he would; about half an hour before the body is due to appear. He follows the instructions easily, seeming to have an inbuilt knowledge of

159

every road, every nook and cranny of the states. His glove compartment was stuffed with maps of North America, but it had been a long time since he'd needed to consult any of them. He rolled into New Hampshire with enough time to grab some food and set up himself up in a good vantage point near the drop off. He waited for the turkey. He had always called them that in his head, he wasn't sure why. Probably to do with the farm. A person was a turkey; a dead person was a cold turkey. They'd quit life, so it fit. He slurped a strawberry milkshake and munched on a cheeseburger. It was cold by now, but he was ravenous. He couldn't go back for more after the job. The more he was seen, the more he would be remembered.

He's in a small copse of trees near the edge of a ravine. It looked like a disused quarry, which was unusual enough in itself. His usual remit was dingy basements or high rise apartments. Usually people who would drag their victim into somewhere so secluded and abandoned wouldn't need to hide the body. He was usually hired by people in frenzy; people with blood on their hands, a dead body on the floor, and no idea what the hell to do about it. He frowned again, the cabin light in the car casting deep shadows across his furrowed brow and his blade of a nose. He didn't have much wrinkles yet, a smattering of crow's feet and a few ploughed lines on his forehead, but age was the one thing that killed everyone eventually. It was just a matter of surviving the rest of life long enough to die of it.

He had his window rolled down, the scent of the dying trees rolling up to him. He heard two distant *pop* sounds. It sounded like balloons bursting, but he knew it for the noise that a gun really makes, outside of the movies. He stepped out of his car, carrying his food with him. He leans around a tree and peers down into the darkness. There are two cars parked, headlights blazing, illuminating a rather fat guy in a big coat. John can only see him in silhouette. The fat one tucks a gun back into his pocket, and heads back towards the car. There's a slumped shape on the ground, like face down in the dry and cracked dirt. John waits for the two cars to leave, gives it half an hour exactly, and then makes his way down to the body.

He drives carefully, trying to keep quiet, but at the same time, respecting his car, not wanting to pelt the paintwork with loose stones. He gets to the clearing and parks up near the body. Glancing towards the lip of the ravine, he scans for any sign of activity. He cuts his lights and does it again, waiting for the approach of head lights or the distant shouts of drunken teenagers. A cool breeze rolls through the empty quarry, making the splits and crags in the rocks give an unearthly howl as it whistles through them. He shivers, not because of the cold. There was still something unsettling about a dead body. You never got used to it; it wasn't something you could become acclimatized to. On Halloween, as well, childhood superstition can help but creep back in. But then again the only costume he'd ever worn was his own skin.

He slips on a pair of rubber gloves and reaches under the front seat, grabbing a neatly folded body bag. Surprisingly, police were fairly lax about these. He'd had his car searched before and told them it was a dry cleaner's bag for a suit. They asked where the suit was, and he told them it was at the cleaners, before giving them a wry smile. They liked that. They laughed and let him go. They didn't find the body under the false boot.

He crouches in the dust beside the body, closing his eyes and waiting for them to adjust to the new darkness. He'd rather work by headlight, but out here, it would be more like a spotlight. How could anyone not spot him? He'd light the place up like a Jack-o-Lantern. He opens his eyes. The body is as it should be; a man, early thirties, brown hair, empty, unfocused brown eyes. He wore a suit with two bullet wounds through the jacket pocket, both at the heart, two shots for good measure. He peeled back the suit and tore a hole in the shirt with his knife. The shooter needn't have worried, there was only one entry would. Both bullets bang on target, right into the guy's heart.

John had been reading the Bible again. It felt like good karma to him to recite a little passage every time he came across a body. He tried to remind himself he wasn't a criminal, in terms of one of the Ten Commandments; he was just exploiting a loophole in them. He wasn't killing; he was just getting paid to cover it up. Another cool wind rolled through the ravine, chilling his balls and making his scalp tingle. He forgets all the Scripture he knows. Something's wrong.

"Poor bastard," he says, after a moment.

161

"I know, right?" The poor bastard replies.

6.

John was prepared for every circumstance, calm under intense pressure, and a master at keeping his true emotions hidden. Still, when the corpse spoke to him, he screamed, falling flat on his ass in the dirt, covering his vintage jeans with dust. With his scarce night vision, he watches the body slowly move to a sitting position, and turn to face him. The eyes are empty and blood lazily oozes from the exposed wound. The man regards him calmly.

"Jesus Christ!" John shouts, shuffling backwards, all professional composure forgotten.

"Not quite." The body replies, in a clipped and posh transatlantic sort of accent. "It took him three days. Seems it only took me a few minutes."

John gets to his feet, his legs threatening to give out underneath him. He tries to calm himself down but for the moment, his body is having none of it.

"You were dead. I saw it, you weren't breathing, no pulse, your eyes were..." He gestures wildly to his own eyes. "They were glass! You were dead!" In his panic, John lapses slightly from his fake and jilted *New Yawk* accent, back into his more traditional redneck lilt.

"If it's any consolation, I'm just as surprised as you are." The Dead Man says, getting to his feet. He offers John his hand. John looks at it, and then at his own, as if he's forgotten what they're both for.

John shakes, out of some built in instinct to not offend. The man grins. His skin is as pale and waxy as the moon overhead, and rather than looking dead, he just seems to be wearing an extremely effective yet subtle Halloween costume.

"It's Halloween, isn't it?" The Dead Man asks.

"Yes." John says. He tries to pull his hand away, but the grip is iron and cold, like handcuffs. The man grins.

"I guess I'll fit right in then. What's your name, son?" he says. John shakes his head in response.

"No names."

162

"Fair enough." The Dead Man replies. "Listen up; if you could be a doll and do me a favor, I'd pay you far more than those cocksuckers who hired you to get rid of my body." John doesn't ask how the man knew this. It's fairly obvious.

There's a moment of silent. The wind whips dust devils around their ankles, and The Dead Man lets go of John's hand. John zips his jacket up to his chin and shivers against the October air.

"What do you need?" John asks.

"Find out who wanted me dead," he replies, then after a moment of reflection, a grey skinned hand resting on his stubbly chin, "Oh, and find out why I'm *not actually dead.*"

"Tall order." John says.

"I agree. If you can do it by sunrise, I'll double it."

"Double what?" John says, his ears pricking up. He's been saving morsels, saving what he can, enough to quit this life. He loves it, but it's bad for your soul, he feels like every job is taking a stone away from a temple somewhere inside him. Too many stones gone, and it all comes tumbling down. Then there's not enough left of him to get into heaven. That's the only thing that scares John. That, and walking, talking corpses.

The Dead Man laughs. "You ever read The Great Gatsby?" John shakes his head.

"Of course you haven't, you're a fucking redneck. No offense."

"None taken."

"Well, this Gatsby fellow was rich as all hell, he probably wiped on hundred dollar bills." He says *hundred* the way it's meant to be said, not *hunnerd* like everyone else does. John admires that. Having never received proper education himself, he's always impressed by those who possess such clarity of speech and thought.

"I make Gatsby look like a hobo." The Dead Man says. "Help me out, and you'll never scrub blood off tiles ever again."

John gives the dead man a flat look. In a sense, every look John gives is a flat one; he just layers them with falsifications of emotion. A fake smile, a face grimace of empathy, it's all fake. His face is like a layer of icing on a cake made of feces.

"Do we have a deal, then?" The Dead Man says. "Sunrise is coming, you're not going to double your wages by standing here playing pocket billiards."

"I'm in," John says, his blue eyes giving away nothing. The Dead Man looks at him for a long moment. They look startlingly similar in that moment.

"Great," he says. They shake again.

7.

John drives, Cash turned down to the point of background noise, telling them both that *the times, they are a changin'* and John can't help but agree because there's a dead man in his passenger seat. The man has his shirt open, and is poking a long grey finger into the congealing bullet wound. It makes a sick sucking sound, like a boot stuck in the mud.

"Doesn't that hurt?" John says, curiosity overriding his usual desire for absolute silence in his own head as he drove.

"I'm dead." The Dead Man says, as if that answers it. They're away from the quarry now, heading further south. On the dash is a soggy bar mat with an address roughly scribbled on the back of it.

They head south, passing through Derry, slowing down on the main street as a kid in a white sheet sprints across the street, heading for candy. John slams on the breaks and curses out loud. A few other kids follow, hooting with laughter, carrying sacks, bags, and hollowed out lanterns filled to the brim with teeth rotting goodness. The last of the group, a straggler, is dressed as a zombie. He staggers across the road, moaning for brains, or failing that, candy. John smirks. The Dead Man snorts.

"I find that offensive," he says, gesturing towards the kid. The kid glances into the car as he passes, meeting both their eyes. He seems more afraid of John than he does of The Dead Man. They both consider this in silence as they move south yet again.

The night ticks on as they drive, the clock on the dashboard letting them know the minutes are creeping past. Cash finishes and then starts again several times, and after a while they stop for gas and a bite to eat. The Dead Man throws his burger out the window when he realizes he can't taste it. As they reach their destination, John glances again at the damp mat and notices that nagging feeling he had in his gut wasn't apprehension at driving with a dead man. It was because he recognized the name of the bar. Joe's. He couldn't put his finger on it until they pulled off the road and into the packed dirt parking lot, when he saw the ancient sign and the small, still standing tribute to Big Bill, suddenly the October night was uncharacteristically cold. The slight muggy remains of summer still ticking over as the leaves dropped dead were gone. A shiver ran through his body. He glanced at The Dead Man, who was looking at him with curiosity. It's flat and cold curiosity, not the kind of look that one man regarding another could ever give. John's hand creeps towards his gun in his jacket. A lot of fucking good that would do. Two through the heart didn't stop this guy. One through the skull might, like in those cheesy zombie flicks, but he didn't want to take that chance.

"Been here before?" The Dead Man says.

"Maybe," John replies, keeping his voice steady. "You?" The Dead Man frowns, rubbing a greying hand across his clammy forehead. He's starting to stink; John fights the urge to hang a magic tree from each of his ears.

"Everything before the bullets is becoming a bit fuzzy. Kind of feels like I'm only half here, it's like when you go to a state line, and you stand on it. One leg here. One leg there. In out, in out."

"Shake it all about." John says with an uncharacteristic smirk.

"What?"

"Nothing."

The Dead Man picks up the bar mat; turning it over in his hands like it's an ancient relic, something he barely understands anymore.

"Why would I have this? This is miles away from where I died." John offers no response. He glances at the clock. The bar is still open, but barely. It's late, past three in the morning. The lights are on but the doors are closed. A good old fashioned lock in. Halloween party on the go, maybe. They've got the perfect costumes. A veritable psychopath and a dead man walking.

165

"Maybe they grabbed you from here and drove you up to that quarry." John says, thinking out loud.

"Why would they do that?"

"Fuck knows," John says, shrugging. "I don't deal with motives, I deal with bodies."

"Charming."

John could swear he recognizes one of the cars in the lot, but that would be impossible. Well, nothing is impossible, but the better way to put it would be *highly unlikely.* So is someone rising from the dead, as a matter of fact. John leaves it. It makes his head hurt.

The Dead Man gets out of the car and stretches his legs, feigning a yawn. John can tell that he doesn't need to do either any more, but old habits die hard, even if you've died hard yourself. He gets out, locking the car. He pats his boot and his jacket pocket, checking his weapons. He checks his wallet too, and then slips his keys into his jeans pocket. He pats there once, twice, three times. The little rituals are important.

"You look like shit," John says.

"Thanks. I think I'll fit right in," The Dead Man replies, gesturing towards the porch of the bar. There's a guy dressed in a hockey mask, splattered with blood, smoking through a hole in the mask. John doesn't keep up much with popular culture so he misses the reference.

The costumed man heads back into the bar and they slip in after him. Monster Mash in full swing, a girl dressed as a vampire getting her rocks off with Dracula in the corner. Two guys in gorilla suits about to get into a fist fight over a maid. Of course, by the bar, Big Bill's seat is empty, reserved for his ghost, always. John is about to step forward, when The Dead Man holds out a cold and bony arm, holding him back.

"Look," he says, gesturing towards his chest. The bullet hole is closing over, sealing up like it's been filled with putty by a cowboy construction worker. There's probably one of those inside the bar, too.

"Great party trick," John deadpans. The Dead Man laughs.

"That hurt a little," he says, grinning. "I wonder if that means I can taste again. I fancy a bottle of beer."

The Dead Man strolls towards the bar, and John hangs back for a moment. He glances around, waiting to see if anyone recognizes him. He stands out like a sore thumb, the only one not in costume. Everyone is too caught up in the dying embers of the party. Music blares from the jukebox which John doesn't recognize, which is no surprise. He watches The Dead Man sit in Big Bill's chair. He grins like a loon at the burly blokes on either side of the stool. They're both dressed as Frankensteins, the one on the left giving it a better effort all around. John recognizes them as Bill's friends from all those years ago. One of them has gotten very fat.

The Dead Man calls the bartender over, asking for a drink. The bartender gives him a strange look. John moves closer, pulled in to the scene, as the guys on either side glance over too. Soon, the whole bar turns to see, recognition passing through the room like a ripple on the surface of the lake.

"What the hell?" John hears the bartender - dressed as a devil - say as he gets closer to the action, his hand creeping cautiously into his jacket. He glances over his shoulder. Nobody gets the jump on him anymore. The silence in the bar is complete, just like the last time John was here. Nostalgia peeks over his shoulder. Just like the good old days, before he had money, before he had work, before he had purpose. He watches The Dead Man ask for a beer and watches the bar man respond by slowly backing away towards the optics of spirits lining the back wall.

"I thought we sorted you out," the better Frankenstein says. The Dead Man turns to him, grinning, almost nervously.

"Beg your pardon?" he says. "Do I know you folks?" He turns back to the bartender. "Can I have that beer? Today, please?" John can feel tensions in the room brimming over like a pot brought to boil. He almost has a sixth sense about that kind of thing. He glances around him, slowly moving towards the door. All eyes are on The Dead Man, who seems oblivious.

"I shot him twice!" the fat Frankenstein says, falling backwards off his barstool and hitting the floor with a meaty thump. The bathroom door pushes open, and who should step out but Big Bill, in all his redneck splendor. His checkered shirt splattered with beer and blood, his cap tipped to one side, and a

167

full beard growing on his face. His skin looks suspiciously grey, like porridge, and there's a flat sheen to his eyes that John recognizes from The Dead Man. His throat has ragged scar tissue on it.

"Did you check the body?" Big Bill says, walking towards The Dead Man.

"He was *dead*," The fat Frankenstein says.

"Do you boys know anything about my predicament?" The Dead Man says, finally looking afraid. John catches on at about the same time that the walking cadaver does. The whole bar looks from Bill, to The Dead Man, and back again.

"What about the cleaner?" Bill says. "Didn't he sort it out?"

"The cleaner?" The Dead Man says his voice brightening, happy to help. "Oh, he's right over…" he turns to point at John. But John is gone; John already has the key in the ignition. He pulls out of the lot without even turning on Cash. He always puts on Cash.

Bill grabs The Dead Man by the throat. He puts two fingers to the side, feeling his pulse. The room holds its breath.

"He *is* dead." Bill says. "For Christ's sake." The two Frankensteins grab The Dead Man, dragging him kicking and screaming outside. Bill calls after them.

"Make sure he *stays* dead this time." The two nod and slam the door behind them. Bill runs a grey hand down his grey face. He takes off his cap and wipes his brow. But he's not sweating; he hasn't since John cooked his goose. He turns to address the room.

"How many fucking times do I need to tell you? This is *my* chair. This is Bill's chair." He points at the chair, points at his name engraved on the back of it.

"No one sits here but me." Bill sighs, sits down, and orders another beer than he can't smell or taste. He can't even feel the icy coldness of it, which is nothing compared to the chill of his own skin.

168

Jason Purdy is 22 years old, and from Northern Ireland. He's been writing from a very young age, mostly silly little things, short stories, novels that never got finished, and occasionally scraping together an awful comic book consisting of stick men with impossible hair. He loves reading, listening to music, and playing video games.

When he can be bothered, he enjoys going to the gym or going for a jog. He isn't bothered all that often. He reads Media Studies and Production at university and is an avid film and television fan. He's an occasional film maker with his own gear that spends too much time gathering dust, and he has a fondness for screen writing as well as novel writing. He has a roughly a thousand screenplays all over the place, circulating, hopefully making some Hollywood executive shed tears of joy, but more likely probably just being used as door stops or mug coasters.

His debut novel, Cigarette, *is out now. He completed it when he was 20 and spent the next two years on and off redrafting it between writing the two sequels and a myriad of other junk. He started writing Cigarette because he didn't want to be the kind of guy who has 'thinking of writing a book' written on his gravestone. So he started writing a book.*

Devil's Night

By Harriette Sackler

Annie Hiller stood in front of her living room window, parting the heavy drapes with an arthritic hand. Her snow white hair neatly framed a dark-complected, heavily lined face. She was a small woman, but those who knew her were not deceived by her size. She possessed strength of character that had been responsible for providing her family with its strong foundation. She was wise, loving, and solid as a rock.

The night was silent, but only for a short time, as Annie well knew. Illuminating streetlamps were a thing of the past. Most still stood, but served no purpose now. Light bulbs had been used as target practice or just were no longer functional and hadn't been replaced. There was no such thing as maintenance around here.

It was cold, the usual for late October, making her joints hurt. Mist filled the air and distorted the landscape, hiding the desolation of this part of town. Whatever residents were left made it a practice to stay inside and not venture out after dark. Truth be told, nothing ensured safety around here. It was a place of danger and hopelessness. But it hadn't always been that way. Not at all. It used to be a real neighborhood. Its small houses were well kept. Kids played in the street. Hard work led to better lives. There were jobs to be had. When a family decided to move farther out, there were others who wanted to move in. It was a good place to live and Annie and her late husband, Arthur, raised their four kids here and were happy.

Now, half the houses were deserted; that is, the ones that were still standing.

Empty lots filled with trash, the skeletons of dead cars stripped of anything worth a buck, and weeds surrounded what

171

occupied homes were left. Since the houses had no value now, owners had no choice but to abandon them and flee the city when they were able.

Strangers driving through the neighborhood would have thought this was a nightmarish painting borne of a mad artist's mind. Or the landscape of a futuristic science fiction novel of the demise of civilization. But no. This was Eastside Detroit. In 1986. On Devil's Night.

Even though the night had barely begun, Tom Hiller was weary. It seemed that the muscles supporting his six- foot frame weren't able to keep him from slumping forward, as if he carried a tremendous weight on his shoulders. His down-turned, tight-lipped mouth made him look older than his thirty-eight years.

He'd joined the department nearly sixteen years ago; following in his Dad's footsteps. He'd believed that firefighting had a noble purpose. Saving folks from accidental conflagrations resulting from faulty electrical wires or a cigarette falling from the mouth of a guy just too wiped out to keep his eyes open while he sat in his favorite chair reading the paper. Righteous stuff that came with a feeling of accomplishment. Good deeds. Service to the community.

But not anymore. Not in this place. Here all he and the others did was put out fires in abandoned buildings that'd been set by guys with too much time on their hands. It wasn't a matter of them being lazy. Christ, there were no jobs. They were frustrated and angry. They felt that they were less than men. How could you call yourself a man when you couldn't even put food on your family's table? Or keep a roof over their heads? And kids who were consigned to failed schools just stopped going to classes. For what? So they all took out their frustration and hopelessness by destroying everything that reminded them of their human condition They ripped away anything that was saleable and torched the rest. Until there was barely anything left.

Devil's Night was the worst of all. What used to be an exercise in mischief and pranks the night before Halloween was now all about arson. It used to be that kids egged houses or covered parked cars in shaving cream. But now, the sky was lit by hundreds of fires. Sirens screamed all night and into the next

172

day as battered fire engines and exhausted fire fighters made their way from one site to another. They were understaffed, poorly equipped, and badly paid. They weren't only fighting fires; they were fighting a system that didn't work. A bankrupt city. Crooked politicians had siphoned off monies that should have gone to services, the Detroit auto industry had gone bust; and the real estate market was dead. What once had been a thriving city was now the country's best example of urban failure. It was a place to escape.

Annie reached for the ringing telephone at the same time she lowered the volume on the television.

"Hello?"

"Hey, Mama just wanted to check in. Everything okay?"

"Hi Tommy. So far, so good."

"Mikey okay?"

"Yes, he went to bed about an hour ago and was sound asleep when I checked."

"Well, that's good. If all goes well, we'll be somewhere else next year at this time, Mama."

"Let's hope so, Tommy."

"Mama, are the outside lights on?"

"Yes, they are. The doors are locked, the phone is right next to me, and I'll be sitting in the living room all night"

"That's good, Mama. Well, gotta go. It's gonna be a long night. I'll check in again first chance I get."

"Tommy, you take care, you hear?"

"I will, Mama. I will."

A small figure dressed in black darted across a vacant, weed-choked lot. When he reached the rusted hulk of an abandoned car, he stopped. This was where Bobby J had told him to wait. It was freezing, and he shivered, partly from the cold, but more so, in fear and anticipation. If his Pop ever found out that he was AWOL from home or what he planned to do tonight, he wouldn't be allowed to leave the house for the rest of his life. But the chance to be one of the guys and join in the fun of Devil's Night were too strong a temptation. And, anyway, he wouldn't be gone long and would slip back into his house through the

173

bedroom window before Gram or Pop would ever know he was gone.

After all, he was twelve years old and had never done anything exciting in his whole life. Man, he was bored. He went to school each weekday and then came home and had to stay in the house, doing homework or watching TV. He wasn't allowed to hit the streets at all.

"It's just too dangerous," his Pop would tell him. "Bad things happen out there. We'll be moving to a new neighborhood before you know it and then you'll be able to spend all the time you want outside on the street. You'll have friends to hang with, movie houses, ball fields, and stores. And it'll be safe. I'm sorry it's taken so long, but I really am doing the best I can. It'll be better real soon. You'll see."

But he was just a kid and it was too hard to wait. Just once, this one time, he wanted to do something like the others. Not hurt anyone, for sure. Never do anything that bad. Just be able to say he joined in Devil's night. Just this once.

By ten that night, all hell had broken loose. Engine companies all over the city were heading from one location to another, desperately trying to contain the fires all over town. Flames shot into the sky and the smoke-filled air made it hard to breathe. Eyes watered and streaked the soot-covered faces of the firefighters. They were soaked with water and sweat. After three hours, Chief Miller gave the word that his men should head back to the station. They needed a break. They all agreed.

The first thing Tom did back at the station was peel off his rubber suit and strip down to his skivvies. He headed for the showers and was grateful for the trickle of lukewarm water that washed away the filth from his body. He again wondered why they bothered. It didn't matter one bit if all these abandoned housed and commercial propertics burned to the ground. Maybe it was better if the whole damn city was leveled. What was the downside? Why put his ass on the line for nothing?

But then he thought about Mama and his Pop. They'd worked their whole lives to provide for their four kids. They made sure the kids went to school, went to church, and did the right thing. And they'd all done good. His two sisters and brother

174

were all married with kids and they all had left Detroit for greener pastures. Then, after Pop passed, just about the time the city hit the skids, Mama watched her friends move away from their beloved neighborhood, seen the merchants she'd patronized for so many years close their shops, and, tragically, watched as the church she'd worshipped at, locked its doors.

It was a good thing when he, Sheila, and baby Mikey moved into the house. Back then, they'd had big plans to save up for a down payment on a house in the suburbs. One with a big yard, a bunch of bedrooms, and friendly neighbors. They'd wanted Mikey to go to a good school and have nice friends. Mama would come with them and continue to care for Mikey when Tom and Sheila were at work.

They socked away most of their paychecks and were just about to start house hunting when life took a tragic turn. Sheila, who'd been suffering from terrible headaches, was diagnosed with cancer. A rapidly growing tumor in her brain that quickly changed her from the laughing, loving wife and mother that she was into a shadow of herself. The treatments didn't do much of anything, but maybe, just maybe, there was a miracle out there for them. But it wasn't meant to be. In four months, she was gone. Leaving behind a husband who couldn't envision his life without her and a son too young to fully understand the loss.

He buried Sheila on a warm, sunny day in May, and the dream slipped away. Insurance hadn't covered all the expenses of those useless treatments. Bills kept coming in and their savings rapidly vanished.

"Hey, Tommy," his buddy Russell greeted him, stepping into the shower. "Shit, I'm falling on my face and we've still got hours to go. Man, there's gotta be a better way to earn a living."

"I hear ya, man." Tommy replied. "I hear ya."

"You know, Tom, my brother-in-law lives in Chicago and he's always tellin' me that the job market there is boomin'. Kate and I are givin' a lot of thought to up and leaving this hellhole and movin' on. Gotta do what's best for the family, ya know."

'I can't blame you a bit, Russ. There isn't anything left to keep you here."

"So, Tom, you gettin' close to making' the big move outta the city?" Streams of filthy water dripped off Russell's massive body as he soaped up.

"Yeah, I think so, Russ. You know, we had to start from scratch. Sheila's medical bills left us with nothing. But, I woulda done the same thing again. I woulda done anything for her. I still can't get used to the fact that she's gone. It's been really rough on Mikey, now that he understands his mom is never comin' back. And Mama has been the best. She takes care of Mikey when I'm at work and living with her really helped me out a lot. She'll move to a new house with us, not only because we need her, but because she can't stay in her house. It's just not safe. And, if ya wanna know the truth, she'll have to just abandon it, since it's not worth shit anymore. After forty-five years. Damn shame."

"Yeah, it sucks, pal." Russell said. "I'm afraid that if we don't leave here, it's goin' to break up my marriage. Kate says that with or without me, she's takin' the kids away. Even if I wanted to stick it out, I couldn't. Well, let's get some food before we head out again. It's gonna be a helluva night."

Tommy dressed, gulped down a sandwich and some strong coffee, and called home to check in.

The phone rang several times before his mom picked up. It was evident to Tommy that she'd been dozing and he really hated to wake her. But he needed to know that she and Mikey were doing okay.

"Hey, Mom. What's happening?"

"Not much, Tommy. I'm sitting here watching the news. It certainly looks as though the whole city is burning. Or what's left of it. Makes me so sad. I just hope the good Lord keeps us safe."

"Yeah, I know. I wanted to check on you and Mikey. I'll be heading out again now and won't be able to call for a while."

"I checked on Mikey about a half hour ago and he's sleeping like he usually does, buried under his covers. It' a wonder he can stay that way, with all the sirens going by."

"Well, Ma, glad we got the chance to come back to the house to shower and eat. I'll call you next time I get back to the station."

"Tommy, I'm praying the good Lord takes care of you.

"I know, Ma. I know."

Mikey stared at the burning house with both fright and fascination. He could feel the heat of the flames on his face and hear the crackle of wood as it caught fire, split, and turned to ash. At the same time, he couldn't help but think about what his pop would do if he found out that his son had been part of the Devil's Night destruction. While pop was working his butt off putting out fires, here he was with the guys setting them. But he knew it was only this once and never again.

Mikey was glad that he'd be moving out of the city soon. The guys he was with tonight were really not like him. They went to his school and lived in what used to be the neighborhood, but he knew they really weren't his friends. Setting fires was only one of the differences between them. Some of them owned guns. Others took drugs or even sold them. Mikey had never done any of these things and knew he never would. It scared the hell out of him to think that if he were caught tonight, he'd be busted and locked up.

"Hey kid, come on, we're gonna head for another house two blocks down. And we're gonna give you the chance to set the fire. That'll give ya a hard-on."

Mikey really wanted to run home, but didn't want to seem like a scared kid. So, instead, he turned to Spider and said, "Cool. That's sounds great. What are we waiting for?"

Tommy was exhausted. His crew had been going non-stop for the past five hours and there was no end in sight. They hadn't been able to take another break, since as soon as one fire was out, they were called to another. The city was a fucking inferno, the depths of hell. He wasn't alone, he knew. Every engine company in the city was fighting against the odds. Hundreds of fires had already been set and there were sure to be hundreds more before the night was over. It had reached the point where they just couldn't respond to every alarm. For lack of manpower and equipment, they now had to make choices. When they knew that a call was for a house in an occupied location, they responded. But when it was a house isolated from areas where citizens still lived, they had to let it pass. What else could they do?

Annie fitfully dozed on and off for hours. Her dreams reflected the high anxiety she felt when she was awake. Oh Lord, how she wished the morning would come. She wanted this terrible night to be over. She wanted her Tommy to come home. She wanted to tell him that it was time for them to leave their home now. If they didn't have the money together for a down payment on a house in a safe neighborhood someplace else, well, then they'd rent. Or, if need be, they could relocate to Seattle or Houston, or St. Louis, where her other children lived. Surely family would help them out.

Tonight, Annie felt a deeper sense of urgency than ever before. They'd been lucky, the good Lord has watched over them these past years. But now, something was different. A strong sense of foreboding clutched at her heart. Now. Right away. It was time for them to go.

It had been quite a night for Mikey. His guilt at being part of something so wrong was overshadowed by the excitement of seeing the flames engulfing the abandoned houses. He'd stayed out way too long and hoped that his Gram hadn't found out that he wasn't at home. There'd be hell to pay if she did.

He was just about to bid the guys goodnight, hoping they'd forget about making him torch a house himself, when Eagle, a tall, skinny fifteen-year-old, put his arm around Mikey's shoulders...

"Hey, kid, I think it's time for you to set one. It's something you'll never forget. We'll tell you what to do. It'll be a piece of cake."

Mikey felt his stomach muscles tighten. He really wanted to go home now. But he couldn't let the guys think he was afraid.

"Sounds good, Eagle. Yeah, let's get this show on the road."

They'd reached a rotting old house that looked like no one had lived there for years. The small front yard was clogged with weeds and the front porch sagged. The windows were all broken and the paint had peeled off the abandoned house. Mikey wondered how it had escaped the torch for so long.

Eagle handed Mikey a gallon can half-filled with gasoline and a box of wooden kitchen matches.

"Now, you listen to me good, kid. You go in there and look around. You'll probably need to light a match 'cause it'll be so dark inside. See if you can find any curtains left on the windows or furniture in the place. There might be old newspapers layin' around. They really go up fast. Start sprinklin' the gas around. Then the last thing you do is light a coupla matches and throw them in the gas. Then get the hell outta the place. Don't stop. Got it? We'll be waitin' here for you."

"Yeah, sounds good." Mikey said, though it really didn't sound good at all. "I'm in. See you in a few."

Mikey took a few deep breaths and walked up the rickety porch steps. The front door hung partly open on its rusty hinges and squeaked in protest as he pushed on it..

The inside of the house was pitch black since there was no light outside to filter in. He lit one of the matches and was able to see a few feet in front of him. The house was a ruined shell. Everything was gone, except for a few filthy sheets that had been left behind and now lay on the floor. In one corner of what probably had been the living room, Mikey spotted an empty liquor bottle and some discarded needles. He knew that, sometime in the past, squatters had used the house.

Mikey didn't belong here. He was sorry he had got involved in this at all. He wanted to go home. Best that he get this over with and leave. He knew that if he waited too long, he was going to throw up, or piss his pants, or worse.

The match in his hand started to burn his fingers, so he blew it out and lit another.

With his free hand, he started pouring the gas against the wall, on the floor, and over the sheets. When the can was empty, he threw it down. One more thing to do. Then he'd be through, heading for home.

Mikey pulled another match out of the box . When he struck it against the box, the hiss and flare startled him. Mikey quickly dropped it and lit another. And another. And another. They ignited the rotted floor and gas-soaked sheets right away.

As Mikey turned to head for the door as quickly as he could, his right sneaker caught on a raised floorboard and, losing his balance, he fell heavily. At first he heard, rather than felt, the loud snap as his ankle shattered. Then a crippling pain took his breath away. Before he really was aware of what had happened, Mikey was engulfed in the flames he had set. His very last thought was of his Pop.

"Oh, shit. Oh, shit. Oh, shit." Eagle paced on the cracked sidewalk as the house disappeared in the nightmarish fire. We should'na let the kid go in alone. Oh man, this is bad. He ain't comin' out.

The other boys stood in stunned silence. They'd never known of anyone who didn't get out in time. They didn't know how it could've happened. But they sure as hell knew that they'd better haul ass outta there. As the old house collapsed in on itself, they all ran off.

By the time Tommy went off duty, every bone in his body screamed with pain. As he very gingerly climbed into the driver's side of his old Ford, all he could think about was a hot shower, a big breakfast, and a soft bed. The sky was lightening on a new day, but it would take a week before the smell of smoke cleared away. Every year it seemed that the Devil's Night destruction couldn't get worse, but it always did.

Ironic that the horror of Devil's Night immediately preceded Halloween and, in most areas, children would be out in force tonight, costumed and heading door-to-door to collect the candy that would leave them with stomachaches tomorrow. But not in Eastside Detroit. It had been years since Mikey had been able to participate in the fun. Only when Tommy had driven him out to the suburbs, had his son been able to enjoy the festivities. But no more. This was the last time. Whether they were able to buy a house or rent one in a decent neighborhood, they were getting out. Right away. Mikey would be a normal kid.

Tom thought about Sheila and his heart ached. It was on nights like this that he missed her most. She was always able to see the bright side of everything. And he knew, without a doubt, that Sheila would want him to do right by their son, no matter what.

As Tommy parked the car in his driveway, he knew the first thing he would do was tell Mama and Mikey to start packing.

Annie Hiller had fought sleep as long as she could, but finally succumbed. . She wasn't able to stop terrible dreams from invading her mind as she slumped in the chair she'd occupied all night. Her heart beat so rapidly that, had she been awake, she would have feared that it would explode. Annie's face was slick with sweat. She couldn't move. Her dreams were filled with terror, more intense than she had ever experienced before. Horrible danger. Extreme pain. In her sleep, she tried to coax herself to awaken. Stop the nightmares. She knew that her grandson needed her. But, in her dream, she didn't know where he was. But how could that be? He was soundlessly sleeping in his bed, wasn't he? She couldn't help him. All she could do was scream from the very bottom of her tortured soul: *Mikey! Mikey! Mikey!*

Harriette Sackler serves as Grants Chair of the Malice Domestic Board of Directors. She is a past Agatha Award nominee for Best Short Story for "Mother Love," which was published in Chesapeake Crimes II. *In 2012, "The Factory," homage to turn of the twentieth century immigrant life, appeared in* Chesapeake Crimes-This Job is Murder. *"Thanksgiving with a Turkey," was published in* A Shaker of Margaritas: A Bad Hair Day. *Harriette's latest story, "Fishing for Justice," can be found in the newly-released anthology* Fish Nets.

Harriette is a member of Mystery Writers of America, Sisters in Crime and the Guppies.

She lives in the D.C. suburbs with her husband and their three pups and spends a great deal of time tending to her duties as Vice President of her labor of love: House with a Heart Senior Pet Sanctuary She is the very proud mom and grandmother. Visit Harriette at: www.harriettesackler.com

181

182

An Echo of Samhain
By DJ Tyrer

Paul Starling pushed his rimless spectacles up his nose so that he could better see the road ahead. It was early evening and there was a thin mist that meant visibility wasn't all that good. He was finding keeping his battered old Astra on the twisting country lanes harder than usual; the brakes felt spongy. Although he had a small personal income, the economic downturn had left it strained and even his fairly frugal habits were becoming less supportable. He would have to sell a few of his rare books, a measure he was loath to resort to, yet which was becoming ever more necessary.

The same frugal habits that had allowed him to defer his concerns over his financial state were also the reason why he didn't relish this evening. He had been invited to a Halloween dinner hosted by an old acquaintance, James Hawthorne. Hawthorne was an amateur antiquarian whose tastes leant towards the same folkloric and occult interests as Paul's, hence their regular correspondence. Although he had refused to elaborate, it seemed that Hawthorne planned to unveil some newly-acquired artifact after dinner. It struck Paul as rather too melodramatic for his tastes, which didn't really run to dinner parties, anyway. He was very much the sort of person who preferred his own company and a simple, straightforward life.

Brent Grange, his destination, was located to the west of Norwich, a lengthy drive from his home on the outskirts of Buxton. He just hoped he wouldn't get lost. It wasn't that he didn't know the way – although he had avoided installing a sat nav in the car, his excellent memory meant he could recall the general route – but he found the flat East Anglian countryside monotonous in the dark and mist and felt less than confident that he was on the right track: it would be extremely easy to miss a turning and end up miles away from the Grange.

Although he was later than he had intended, he needn't have worried about losing his way. By the large presence of cars in front of the house, it seemed that he was the last to arrive. At least he had managed to avoid being accosted for silence-filling small talk whilst waiting for his fellow guests to arrive.

Parking beside the other cars, his vehicle seeming out of place beside the large and expensive ones already there, Starling got out and headed for the front door. He didn't need to knock or ring the bell; James Hawthorne had heard the sound of the engine and come to open it himself. He stood framed in the light of the doorway, a half-smile of greeting on his lips.

"Hello, Starling. Late as usual." He was referring to Paul's tendency to be tardy in replying to correspondence.

"Hello, James. Observant as usual. Do you mind if I come in? It's chilly out here."

"Yes, come in, come in. Dinner is nearly ready, but I think you have time for a quick drink beforehand, something to warm you up. Whisky?"

"Thanks." Paul wasn't a great drinker, but he was happy to accept a little of the 'water of life' for medicinal purposes. There would doubtless be wine with the meal, but beyond that he wouldn't drink. Paul liked to keep a clear head, maintain his self-control.

"No date?"

Paul froze. He had been so busy concentrating on the drive, he had forgotten all about Arabella.

"Ah, yes, she's just coming." He turned back to the door, doing his best to block Hawthorne's view. "Arabella, darling, do come in out of the cold."

A young woman, decidedly younger than Paul's fifty years, walked into the light of the porch.

Paul's attempt to obscure Hawthorne's view was not entirely successful; he heard his acquaintance gasp as she stepped out of the misty darkness like an apparition, her incredibly-pale skin seeming almost bloodless.

"James, this is Arabella Blackstone; Arabella, this is James Hawthorne, our host."

184

"Pleased to meet you," James smiled, extending his hand. She didn't take it, but did smile and nod, saying, "And you."

Where Paul had worn his usual faded-grey suit that was a little too crumpled to be smart and James was dressed in a perfectly-tailored black suit, albeit without a tie, Arabella wore a smartly-casual charcoal pinafore dress that, whilst not quite the usual dinner outfit, looked better than her date's. Her hair was an intense black against the white of her skin and her deep-brown eyes were darkly shadowed.

"Picking up goth girls?" James joked as they went inside, whispering the comment so that she wouldn't hear. From his tone, Paul knew he was wondering what his secret was, that he found her beautiful, as well. If only he knew the truth about her; Arabella was nothing like she appeared. He was just relying on James not having abandoned his superstitious avoidance of mirrors.

They went into the drawing room where everyone was waiting. He ran his hand through his thin brown hair in an attempt to smooth it down. Tall, even with his slouched academic posture, Paul always felt as if he all eyes were upon him and hated gatherings such as this where people were well dressed and immaculately groomed. Childhood memories rose to the surface and he always felt inadequate.

"Everybody," James said as they entered, "these are Paul Starling and Arabella Blackstone." He, then, introduced the people in the room. Gesturing to a man who looked like a younger and flabbier version of himself, he said, "This is my brother, Roger." The other man in the room was Steven Mountjoy, a venture capitalist. Of the two women, one, who looked like an older version of Arabella with pale skin, dark makeup and dyed-black hair, was introduced as Lilith Adams; the other, a tall and dignified blonde, was "My wife, Annette." When she spoke, Paul could detect a hint of French accent.

Paul recognised the name Lilith Adams; she was a New Age writer. He didn't have much time for her sort of writing – too credulous – but he kept abreast of the genre nonetheless.

"Here's your drink," said James, passing him a glass. "Would Arabella like something?"

185

"No, thank you." She wouldn't be eating, either, but they would handle that when dinner was served.

"So, what is it that has brought us all here?" Paul asked. "Unless it is just to sample your cook's new recipe for pumpkin soup?" That had been in his last letter.

"Oh, Barbara's pumpkin soup is excellent, but that isn't the sole reason for this meal. I have something that I shall unveil after we have eaten. Something I think you all will find fascinating. Something... apt."

A moment later, they were interrupted by the arrival of Hawthorne's maid to inform them that dinner was ready.

"I shall not eat," Arabella informed their host discreetly.

"Oh. Are you all right?"

"A little travel sick."

"Aha, yes; I doubt Paul's car makes for a smooth ride."

"Something like that."

Dinner passed with the usual sort of small talk: the latest theories appearing in *Fortean Times*, the progress of Lilith's current manuscript on love spells, Paul's new monograph on prehistoric trackways and Mountjoy's latest business investments with which he boasted that he was turning the tide of the economic downturn.

Finally, as the maid cleared away the remains of the dessert course, their host invited them all through to the library for his announcement.

"Sit," said James as he led them in, pointing at large, comfortable-looking, green-leather armchairs arranged in a rough semi-circle. He went to the large oak desk at the far end of the library, saying, "This is what I've invited you all here to see." There was something on the desk covered by a white cloth.

He took hold of the cloth, whipped it aside with a single swift movement, then let out a scream of sheer agony as flames exploded from the cloth to engulf him, setting him ablaze. His wife screamed and there were gasps and exclamations of shock. His brother jumped out of his chair to help him, only to recoil from the fire.

James staggered backwards, shrieking. He dropped the burning cloth, but it was too late to save him. The cloth fell to the floor and scorched the parquet. James slammed back into a case

186

full of books and they began to blaze, burning brightly but swiftly.

Despite the appearance of a mild-mannered academic, Paul had faced all sorts of dangers in his life and reacted with a calm head, Arabella at his side as he seized hold of a heavy drape and tore it down before throwing it over James and forcing him to the floor, slapping at him through the drape and rolling him in an attempt to deprive the flames of oxygen.

"Douse those flames!" Paul shouted at the others.

Lilith grabbed an old-fashioned spritzer bottle from the desk and sprayed first the burning cloth and, then, the books that were burning on the shelves; Steven moved to assist by pulling other books from the shelves to prevent the flames from spreading: paper ignites easily and burns fiercely, but is rapidly consumed, meaning the removal of further material meant it was easily contained.

"Is he okay?" Roger asked, anxiously.

"I'm sorry..." said Paul. Although he had managed to put the fire out with Arabella's help, it was too late, his burns too severe: James was dead.

Annette burst into tears and her suddenly-pale brother-in-law moved to comfort her.

"What happened?" asked Steven, his voice sounding shell-shocked. "How could this happen?"

The cook and maid had arrived, attracted by the shouts and screams, but Lilith ushered them away.

"Magic," Paul said, simply.

Steven blustered for a moment, unwilling to admit the fact, but nobody present was a disbeliever, even those with little or no knowledge or experience of such things. After all, it was their shared interest in such things that had brought them together tonight, and whilst they might not have been aware that Paul was an authority in such things, they could hear the certainty in his voice.

"But, what...?" Annette asked, looking up from her tears.

"The cloth was cursed," Paul said.

"How do you know?" Roger asked, his tone suspicious.

"I didn't, not before it happened; if only I had... but, as soon as I realised what must have happened, as soon as the flames were out, I assensed it."

"A-sensed?" asked Steven.

"Assensed: astrally-sensed. I momentarily shifted my consciousness into the Near Astral where arcane energies can be observed and saw that the cloth had the residue of magic upon it. Somebody placed a curse upon that cloth, knowing that he would shortly remove it to display this..." he crossed to the desk, "...golden dagger."

"Golden dagger?" asked Steven, his voice suddenly curious.

"It's a druidic blade," Annette said. "James..." she stifled a sob. "He told me of his discovery. A genuine sacred dagger once used by druids to perform their sacrifices on Samhain millennia ago."

"Sacrifice..." muttered Steven. "Didn't they used to burn people alive? Druids, I mean. You know, the Wicker Man and all that. It fits..."

"No," replied Paul. "Well, I mean, the Druids did do that, or so Caesar said, but that was Beltain, not Samhain. I don't think there's a connection. Flames were just a convenient curse."

"But, who did?" It was Annette who asked the pertinent question. She looked at each of them in turn, wild-eyed and suspicious. "From what you said, Mr Starling, this... curse was put on the cloth a short while ago, which means it has to be somebody in the Grange."

"Well, it could have been done in advance or remotely – I will have to study it more closely – but, it would be most likely that it was done recently by somebody here."

"Who?" asked Roger, looking around pugnaciously. "Who did it? Who killed him?"

"I may be able to detect that through study. Every mage leaves a certain signature or scent upon their spells. This can be obscured or concealed, but that is difficult to do."

"How can we be certain it is not you?" Lilith interjected. "I'm not levelling an accusation, just asking a question, Mr Starling. You seem to know an awful lot about all this, but how

188

do we know we can trust you? None of us knows you, except, perhaps, by reputation."

"Fair enough. If anyone else here has the ability to verify what I say, please do. Of course, the odds are they're the killer...."

Aside from Arabella, whose face was completely unreadable, everyone else in the room exchanged worried glances, wondering who they could really trust.

"What do we do now?" Roger asked after a moment. "Do we call the police?"

"They ought to be notified," nodded Paul. "How long do you think it will take them to get here from Norwich?"

"I'd guess a minimum of twenty minutes, probably more," suggested Roger. "Assuming a car was available immediately."

"That should be enough time," said Paul after a moment's thought. "Call them; say there has been an accidental death. Don't mention murder. We don't want them rushing over mob-handed, that would only cause problems and lead to awkward questions: remember, they won't be able to catch the killer."

"Right, I – I'll make the call," agreed Roger, glad to be doing something useful.

"Steven," added Paul, "would you take the others into the drawing room, including the cook and maid? Arabella and I will look over the crime scene before the police arrive and get in the way.

The moment everyone was out of the room, Paul shut the door, turned to Arabella and asked her, "Which of them have the Gift?" Unlike him, Arabella was always sensitive to the flow of magical energy and events on the Astral, being dual-natured.

"James had no discernible Talent, so I think we can dismiss him from being responsible, a bizarre suicide." That fitted with his knowledge and observation of the man, so he nodded. "Nor does Roger, His aura also seems genuinely upset and confused over his brother's death." No matter how good the acting skills or poker face, most people had little control over the emotional secrets revealed by their aura. "Mrs Hawthorne seems to have an innate affinity for magic, but I could detect no evidence that she was conscious of it or trained. She, too, seems terribly upset over her husband's death."

"The guests?"

"Lilith has the Talent. I don't think she is very powerful, more a dabbler."

"That would fit with her love spells and her charms."

"She didn't seem too upset about his death. But, it is Steven whom I'm most suspicious of."

"Why?"

"He doesn't appear to have any magical ability, but his control over his aura is unusually strong. He has very good self-control. He could easily be your killer, masking his abilities and his feelings."

"And, what about the staff? Anything suspicious?"

"Well, I've only seen the cook briefly, when she came in here, but she seemed perfectly mundane and suitably confused and upset. There's nothing unusual about the maid, although I cannot say I was too happy to see how your aura lit up when she was serving dinner."

"Sorry; I can't help admiring her legs."

"I'm teasing! You forget, I can see your aura clearly: I'll know if ever your feelings wander..."

He was certain his aura was signalling his embarrassment clearly to her.

"So, you'd say that Steven and Lilith are our prime suspects?"

She nodded. "It's possible Roger or Annette are highly skilled and concealing their ability and their guilt, but it's unlikely. I'd definitely say it's Steven or Lilith."

Even though it wouldn't stand up in a court of law, mystical abilities could greatly reduce the time and effort required to solve a case. The only problem was that the primarily-emotional basis of the aura and similar spectral evidence made it difficult to pin down the hard facts necessary for a final conclusion. He would have to examine the cloth itself and hope that the guilty party had been unable to expunge the tell-tale traces linking them to their curse. If only they had a motivation to work with: Annette and Roger might have had something to gain in terms of inheritance or avenging some personal issue, but he could see no good reason for either of the others to have murdered him. Perhaps there was some business dealing between

Steven and James. As far as he knew, Lilith and James were as much loose acquaintances as he and James had been, less so given that he didn't think they had actually met in person before tonight. He would have to quiz the wife and brother to see what, if anything, they knew.

"The knife is disturbing," Arabella told him. "It has the power of death about it."

He had noticed that it did have an enchantment and a sense of age to it when he'd assensed the cloth, but had not really given it much attention. Now, he quickly assensed it properly and saw that she was right. There was something that he would describe as a dark stain upon the aura of the object. James was very likely right to have described it as a sacrificial dagger: although greater study would be necessary to ascertain its exact qualities, he would have guessed it drained the souls of its victims or something along those lines. He regarded such items as a reprehensible use of magic.

"I can sense it tugging at me," Arabella went on. "I don't like it..."

"I have an idea." He could understand her discomfort and he realised he could kill two birds with one stone. "Go spy on the others in the drawing room, see what you can learn, see if anyone gives anything away."

"All right," she nodded and a moment later she had vanished from sight. Arabella had already been dead when first they met, but that hadn't prevented her from doing far more than she ever had when alive. Being capable of roaming the Astral made her a very useful assistant to Paul in his investigations.

He gingerly picked the cloth up and laid it on the desk, then settled himself down in the armchair behind it. He leaned towards the cloth and allowed his mind to slip into the Ethereal, the layer of the Astral closest to the physical world, where he began to study it. He examined it for any of the threads of mystical energy that might remain of the curse. If there were any clues as to who had cast it, these would be it. But, there was nothing useful. Whoever had placed the curse had stripped away any trace of their identity. It was like a scene-of-crime officer finding the scene devoid of any expected forensic clues. It meant that whoever was behind Hawthorne's death was extremely skilled or powerful. He didn't like that.

Arabella reappeared.

"Yes?"

"Nothing useful as such, but Lilith was looking into the Ethereal. She seemed to expect someone would be watching her."

"Certainly sounds suspicious to me. I think we have our culprit." She nodded to show she agreed. "Only, we have no motive..."

"Does it really matter? We know it's her."

"Well, strongly suspect..."

"Enough to do something."

His mind wandered back to the aftermath of their host's death and what Lilith had said and he reached a decision. Arabella was right.

He strode through into the drawing room, knowing that Arabella would be close behind. He took the knife with him.

"Why did you kill him," he said, before adding, "Lilith?" The momentary lapse before she mirrored the confusion of the others in the room before he spoke her name was confirmation enough for him.

"What on earth are you on about?" she exclaimed. She was a pretty good actress, he thought.

"You know exactly what I'm talking about, Lilith. You did a good job of concealing the evidence of your crime, so good that I'd never have found out it was you if you hadn't acted so suspiciously. Well, it might've helped had you framed another. There wasn't really a wide field of candidates for killer to choose from: it was only really down to you and Steven."

"Me?" he gasped. "I hardly knew James! We had a few business dealings and he knew I was interested in the occult."

"It's all right, you don't need to deny it, we know it wasn't you," Paul reminded.

"Oh." He deflated with relief and slumped back in his chair.

"You have no proof it was me," smiled Lilith. "Besides, what could you do about it? It's not as if you could tell the police!"

"Oh, I know it's you, I have no doubts, no matter how hard you attempted to cover your crime up." He just hoped nobody would ask him to prove his case; nothing he had would stand up in the proverbial court of law. "The only question I have is: why? Why kill him? You barely knew him..."

"Yes, she did," Roger interjected. All eyes turned to him. "Her name isn't Lilith Adams, not really. It's the name she took when she got into the New Age."

"Then, who is she?"

"Lily Martin. She was at school with James; they dated."

"You mean this is all just some silly belated act of teenage revenge?"

"Silly?" snapped Lilith. "Silly? He ruined my life! He thought he could do what he wanted, the spoilt little rich boy. Perhaps, I should've been grateful to him: if it wasn't for James, I wouldn't have found the Goddess and become who I am now. But, he stole from my father. He was rich and he stole anyway. He thought he could take anything he wanted. He stole that dagger from the man who found it in France. Oh, not personally. These days, he has people to steal for him. But, he was still behind the theft.

"I was no longer powerless. He played at the occult, but I had made strides in actually using it. Finally, I could avenge my father and myself, and all the others that he had trodden underfoot over the years. He thought he could flaunt his latest acquisition in front of me. I wasn't going to take it any longer."

The room was silent when she stopped speaking, the force of her emotion having shocked them all.

Paul didn't know what to do. Roger seemed to have deflated before her words. Paul assumed that he knew what his brother had been like and found it hard not to see Lilith's actions as justice. Annette stood to denounce the woman, her voice full of hatred for the woman who had killed her husband. He felt sorry for her, but couldn't quite shake the feeling that James had got what he deserved.

Seeing his doubt in his aura, Arabella moved close to him and whispered that, "Murder is still murder even if it seems justified." He knew that she had strong views on the subject, given what had happened to her.

He ran his fingers through his hair as he tried to decide. He supposed that Arabella was right: Lilith had murdered James in cold blood and attempted to conceal her guilt. There was no justice, he decided, in what she had done. The only problem was, he had no idea what to do with her. It wasn't as if he could tell the police. Killing her was no option: that would make him as bad as her.

"The blade," whispered Arabella.

"What?"

"Use the dagger on her."

"I can't kill her!"

"No. I don't think it kills; not necessarily..."

He realised what she meant. If Arabella was right, the dagger drained the spiritual essence of its victim. If applied correctly, it would drain without killing. If he did it right, he could drain enough of her essence to render her effectively neuter in magical terms. A fitting punishment.

"I hope this doesn't hurt much," he said, stepping towards her, the golden dagger in his hand.

Lilith started to utter something, but he plunged the dagger into her shoulder before she could cast any sort of spell. She shrieked, not just from the pain of the blow, but the soul-wrenching sensation of the damage to her spirit. About thirty seconds later, she slumped back in her chair and he could see from her aura that the dagger had done what he had intended. Her magical ability would be greatly curtailed or even non-existent from now on. From the shattered expression she wore, he knew the punishment was a suitably harsh one; he just hoped that the others would understand the immensity of it.

Now, they just needed to get their stories straight for when the police arrived...

DJ Tyrer is the person behind UK small press Atlantean Publishing and has been widely published in the British and American small presses, as well as being the driving force behind The Yellow Site, *the King In Yellow wiki. His fiction has most recently appeared in* Cthulhu Haiku & Other Mythos Madness *and* Sorcery & Sanctity: A Homage to Arthur Machen, *and his novella,* The Yellow House, *and two booklets of fiction parodies have also recently been released.*

DJ's website/blog can be found at
http://djtyrer.blogspot.co.uk/

The Atlantean Publishing website can be found at
http://atlanteanpublishing.blogspot.co.uk/

The Yellow Site can be found at
http://kinginyellow.wikia.com/wiki/Have_You_Seen_The_Yellow_Sign%3F

Death of the Party
By Lance Zarimba

"When did dressing up as a witch or a vampire or a pirate become passé? Now we have to come dressed as a theme for Dan and Don's party," Nick Harper complained.

"Costumes are required," Matt Cooper said, as he pointed to the line on the bottom of the invitation. "Do you have yours picked out yet?"

"No, I have to come up with something more clever than boxes of breakfast cereal covered in blood with a knife sticking out of it." Nick picked up a knife and made stabbing motions with it before slipping it into the dish washer.

"Cereal Killer?" Matt asked.

"You got it. I'm not going in drag. Dan and Don always have a mixed party, so I don't want to be the clique gay couple, like Sonny and Cher." Nick tossed his imaginary hair back as Cher did.

"Anne won with Flo, the Progressive Insurance Lady in last year's costume contest, and Bill won the most inappropriate costume as Senator Larry Craig." Matt sat at the kitchen table with his laptop and flipped through a website of costumes.

"Bill had everyone in hysterics. He wore a refrigerator box painted like a bathroom stall, now that was clever." Nick added the gel pack to the dish washer.

"I was more amazed with him walking around all night with his pants down around his ankles, now that was even more impressive." Matt stood and shuffled around the kitchen. "Why don't you come up with a costume for me, and I'll come up with one for you."

197

"Mark was pissed at him for over a week after letting his business hang out all night long. What do you mean? You'll come up with one for me? You have a good idea, but you aren't willing to wear it? I bet it's dirty and shows a lot of skin." Nick closed and started the dish washer.

Matt just smirked.

"I look stupid," Nick complained. He looked at himself in the full length mirror. He wore his red union suit unbuttoned to show off his hairy chest. A yellow electric plug hung out the backdoor, buttoned flap with the rest of the extension cord wrapped around his waist. A black vacuum cleaner hose came out of his fly and wrapped his neck.

"You'll be the life of the party. All you have to do is add your devil horns from the Renaissance Festival and some dirt to your face and you'll be a Dirt Devil." Matt clapped his hands together as he looked over his partner's body and costume. "It would be very sexy without underwear, but …"

"No Buts, and not even my hairy one. I'm wearing a jock and a pair of briefs for modesty and then some."

"You'll be the Belle of the Ball."

"I think this may be worse than drag. So what are you going as, if I'm doing this? A French Maid? A Horny Housewife?" Nick cocked his hip as he looked at his partner.

Matt pulled out a T-shirt and shorts. He unzipped his jeans, turned his back, and stepped out of them as he bent over, showing his tight butt through his tightie whities. He stepped into the shorts and pulled them up. He adjusted himself and turned to stand in profile. A raging boner pushed against the blue nylon fabric. "I'm a Happy Camper."

"I'll say." Nick moved closer and inspected the bulge. "That's not you."

Matt smiled.

Nick pulled on the elastic waistband to find a ball on the end of a plastic device that rested on his lower abdomen to look like an erection.

"Wait until you get a real one."

"I already have one." Matt pulled his shirt off and pulled on the Camp Morning Wood T-Shirt.

"Subtle as a chainsaw." Nick adjusted his hose.

"Or as a Dirt Devil?"

"Do we have to go to Dan and Don's party? I can think of so many other things we can do at home."

"And miss *the* social event of the season. No way. I want to parade you around in all your glory and mine."

They were greeted at the door by a man dressed in the black rubber suit from *American Horror Story*. "Happy Halloween."

"Make sure you drink a lot of water with that suit," Nick warned. "We don't need you to dehydrate at the party, and watch how much alcohol you drink."

"Yes, Mom," the guy said.

"Don, is that you?" Nick stepped back and smiled. "Now I see it's you."

"Stop teasing or I'll pull on your hose," Host Don Murphy said.

"Which option did you want? Suck or blow?" Nick felt his costume for a button.

"Get in there and party. I'll find you later." Don tried to shoo them inside.

Matt slapped Nick on the butt and hurried him inside. The house was decorated with cobwebs and candles. The dining room was set up with a buffet. There was a Jack o' Lantern vomiting guacamole, a rubber bat on top of a platter of chicken wings, a smoking cauldron of punch, and meatballs that looked like eyeballs floating in a crock pot.

"The bar is downstairs," a girl dress like an iPad said.

The party had just started, but a good number of people milled around.

Nick headed over to the food table and tried the guac and chips. Matt picked up the string cheese that looked like bones. They sampled a few of the treats and decided a cold beer was calling.

"Let's head to the bar." The narrow, kitchen stairs led down to the basement. AC/DC blared louder and louder about dirty deeds as they descended. A crowd gathered around the bar, picking at peanuts, pretzels, and Chex mix as they drank.

Dan Dugan was dressed like Dracula and was mixing cocktails. "Vhat do you vant to drink?" His fangs dripped blood on his pale chin.

"Blue Moons," Matt said.

"Vith an orange or vithout?"

"With a big juicy piece."

"But I can't fit it in your bottle." Dan twisted the caps open and handed the cold bottles over. "Great costumes. Nick, we could use you in the morning after the party."

"I want to be used during the party."

"I can arrange that." Dracula pointed out the walk-out patio door. "Hot tub is ready for anyone who wants."

"Costumes and hot tubs don't mix well." Nick took a drink of his cold beer.

"Ve'll see," Dan flashed his fangs. "Thanks for coming to the party, will find you guys later. Go get something to eat; we have so much food upstairs. And the backyard is decked out too, by the hot tub, in case you need some fresh air or a hot dip."

"I didn't bring my Speedo," Matt said.

"Hot tub is a Speedo free zone."

"Even better," Nick said.

"Just don't plug in out there. We don't want anyone lighting up. Zip, Zap," he pretended to being electrocuted.

"That's for Frankenstein," Nick said.

"He's around here somewhere." Dan flapped his cape around and saw more people coming down the stairs. "If you see Bill around, send him over. We're missing a few pricey things since he house-sat for us. We haven't found where he put them, yet."

"We'll send him your way as soon as we see him," Nick said.

A new couple drew near and Dan turned to see what they wanted to drink.

Nick and Matt slipped away and scanned the crowd for anyone they knew. They clinked their bottles and headed back upstairs for food.

After eating a heaping plate of treats, Nick and Matt headed outside to cool off from the body heat that filled the house. All the lights burned, and the guests milled around in hot costumes.

"I'm even hot in these shorts and T-shirt." Matt wiped sweat away from his brow.

"With that raging hard on in your pants, who wouldn't be hot?" Nick unbuttoned another button on his chest and ran his fingers through the mass of wet hair between his pecs.

No one was outside in the backyard, but orange lights winked and blinked in the dark. The hot tub bubbled with the lid on. A few pairs of red eyes blinked on and off throughout the backyard.

"Dan and Don have put a lot of work into this party, and each year it gets bigger and bigger." Matt set his beer down on the hot tub lid.

"Why would you run the jets if the tub is closed?" Nick asked.

"Maybe to keep the heat in?"

"You would love to have a hot tub at home wouldn't you?" Nick came to stand next to him and touched his shoulder.

"Oh yes. I love to soak and relax, and what could be better than to be able to spend time in hot water with you?" Matt rubbed the wet cover of the hot tub, almost caressing it as a lover.

"You can open it and look inside. I'm sure you can even jump in, hard on and all. I think my gym bag is in the car with my sweats."

Matt opened the latch and pushed half of the lid up. "That's funny, they must have put food coloring to make it red, to make it look like a bubbling tub of blood."

A pale hand bobbed up, and as Matt reached for it, a head broke the red surface. But this head they knew: it was Bill's. Not in his Senator Craig's costume, but in a Speedo and with a butcher knife sticking out of his chest.

Nick reached into his union suit and pulled his cell phone out of his jock. He pressed 911.

The patio door slid open and vampire Dan came out with his cape wide open. "Do you vant to soak in the vat of ..." but before the word blood never escaped his mouth as he feel to his knees with a gasp. "Oh my God. Bill. Is he ..."

Nick saw the interest of several people at the bar, as Dan dropped to his knees. He hurried to block their exit to join them at the crime scene. "Everything is okay, but you need to stay inside."

A siren sounded in the distance.

Matt helped Dan return to the house, even paler than before. He grabbed onto the patio door frame to stabilize him. Dan entered the house and found an empty seat and sat down.

Ivana and Donald Trump (Skip and Brenda Harrison) leaned forward and asked, "Are you okay? Was something in the hot tub?"

Dan swallowed hard and closed his eyes. "Someone," escaped from his mouth.

Brenda gasped. "Who?"

"Bill," was all he could say.

Nick didn't wait to hear more; he headed back to Matt and noticed red and blue flashing lights in front of the house. The flashes reflected off the neighbors' houses.

"I bet Don has no clue what's going on," Matt said.

Two officers made their way through the house and exited the patio door. They approached cautiously.

"I'm Nick. I called 911." He raised his hands to show he was unarmed and stepped back.

Matt did the same and stood next to him.

The police looked into the hot tub. Officer Burdick turned and asked, "Have you touched anything?"

"I opened the hot tub lid to look inside, and that's when we discovered Bill," Matt said.

"So you know the victim?" Burdick pulled out a notebook.

"He's a friend of ours," Nick said.

"Did he have any enemies?" He flipped open his notebook and wrote something inside.

Matt and Nick looked at each other and shook their heads. "Not that I know of," Nick said.

"How long have you been at the party?"

Nick pulled his cell phone out of his jock, and felt his face burn when realized how that must have looked. "We've been here over an hour."

A crime scene team arrived and started taking pictures of the hot tub and the surrounding area.

"So, all you touched was the lid?" Burdick asked.

"As soon as we opened the hot tub, we saw the red water. The next thing, Bill's hand came out of the water and then his head. That's when I called 911." Nick watched as they shone lights over the dead grass.

"Was the hot tub running?"

"We thought that was strange, but figured it was to help the water warm."

Burdick stared at the men, wrote something down in his notebook, and headed back to the hot tub.

"Can we re-join the party?" Nick called to his back.

"Just don't leave until we talk to you guys again, and don't say anything about what you saw until we're all done, please."

"Will do." Nick crossed his arms over his chest; the cool night had finally chilled him. He noticed the goose bumps all over Matt's arms and legs.

Brenda and Skip rushed to the door as they approached. "Is Bill..?"

Nick nodded.

Brenda turned into her husband's arms and cried. She taught with Bill at the high school and always enjoyed working with him.

Skip tried to comfort her.

Dan stood up and grabbed Nick's arm. "Did he suffer?"

"I'm not sure, but it looked like it was quick."

"Did he drown? But why was the water red?" Dan asked.

Nick looked at Matt, unsure of what to say. "I'm not sure we can say anything until the investigation is done. Burdick asked us to say nothing."

"Do you think…" Dan's voice trailed off. A worried look came into his eyes. It looked like he was going to bolt upstairs to check on Don.

"Were you or Don upset with Bill?" Nick asked.

There was a flurry of activity at the top of the stairs as Don raced down in his rubber suit. He had pulled the hood off, and his face was flushed, hard to tell if it was from the full body

203

rubber or the police. He rushed into Dan's arms. "I can't believe it. Who would do such a thing?"

"I'm sure the police will figure it out." Dan tried to calm his partner.

"Did you have a chance to talk to him? Before?" Don asked.

Dan rubbed Don's back as he held him. "I didn't."

Don tensed, but he didn't let go.

Matt nudged Nick and pointed upstairs. Nick went up the steps and walked through the kitchen. As they entered the living room, they saw an officer stationed at the front door to bar anyone who tried to leave.

The crowd upstairs didn't seem to be aware of the body in the backyard. They continued to eat and talk.

Nick had lost his appetite, and Matt just scanned the crowd. "Have you seen Mark yet? I wonder if he knows."

Mark was Bill's partner of five years. They had a rocky relationship, but always managed to keep moving forward in their relationship.

The bathroom door opened and Mark stepped out. He wore a Tarzan leopard skin outfit. One of his muscular shoulders was bare, still deeply tan from the summer. A groomed layer of hair covered his pecs and thinned down his chest. His eyes were red as he wiped away his tears. A rope was tied around his waist and his leopard skin skirt was very short. His long, hairy legs rippled with muscles as he approached Matt and Nick.

Nick wondered what he wore underneath such a short costume.

Matt smiled at him as he read his partner's mind.

"Who would want to hurt Bill?" Mark asked. He gasped and started to cry again.

The other guests in the kitchen left, not wanting to be in the same room with all of that emotion.

Nick hugged Mark. "I'm so sorry."

"Did you find him? Did he suffer?" Mark asked looking deep into his eyes.

Matt stepped forward and joined the hug. "I doubt he felt a thing."

They held each other until Mark stopped crying, and they released him.

Nick looked around the kitchen and saw the butcher knife was missing from the knife rack. There was a small smudge of something on the wooden block. As he stepped closer, Nick realized it was blood.

Matt caught Nick's gaze and tensed as he saw the spot. He turned Mark away from the knives and wondered if they should tell Burdick, or let him figure it out for himself.

"Mark do you think you should go upstairs and lie down? I'm sure the police are going to be a while, so this will be a long night before anyone goes home." Nick caressed Mark's back as he tried to soothe his friend.

Mark's body jerked as he inhaled deeply with violent gasps. He had stopped crying, but his body shook.

"I think we should go find you a blanket to keep you warm and prevent you from going into shock." Nick guided him to the stairs going up and gently pushed him forward.

Mark started to protest, but he turned and headed up the steps.

The three men headed to Dan and Don's bedroom and found a soft fleece at the foot of their bed. Nick wrapped it around Mark and hugged him tight.

Mark sat down on the foot of the bed and shook.

"Do you want to be alone? Or do you want us to stay with you?" Matt asked.

Mark curled up into a ball on the bed.

Nick touched his hip and felt a hard bump. "If you need us, call us on your cell phone." He tapped the phone and kissed the top of his head.

Matt bent over and kissed him too and walked over to the bedside table and turned on a light.

Nick turned off the overhead light and the room descended from a harsh white light into a warm glow.

As Nick closed the door, leaving it open just a slant, Matt saw a light coming from a room at the other end of the hallway. They walked down to see what was happening in that room. A woman dressed like a gypsy dealt Tarot cards for a sailor in a very tight white uniform. Her long blood red nails peeled one card off the table at a time and flipped them over.

"I see a long time of loneliness and isolation, but soon a blond will stumble into your life and stir things up. This will seem like chaos and led into a crazy time for you, but weather the storm. True happiness will emerge as the two of you get into sync." She flinched.

As she looked up at the doorway, Matt and Nick stood there. Her eye lashes flickered as her sculpted nailed hand rose to her brow and rubbed across the center of her forehead. Her face contorted into a grimace. Her other hand rose and pointed a blood red nail at them. "You have seen death, and it is following you. You need to beware for one so close will bring you death." Her eyes rolled back into her head, and she slumped over in her seat.

Matt nudged Nick. "Way to go Nick, you really know how to kill a party."

The gypsy's audience turned to stare at them. Many familiar faces looked stunned, uncertain of what they had just witnessed. Was it a Halloween prank? Or had they heard about the hot tub?

Nick figured with the flashing police lights and the house being in lockdown, they all knew what was going on.

Ron and Dave leaned away from them as they looked back at the gypsy.

She slowly shook her head and blinked her eyes. "Sorry, I don't know what..." she looked up and saw Matt and Nick. "Stay close to each other and watch each other's back tonight."

The sailor rose from his seat, his tight pants hugging his butt. He slipped over to a corner, unsure of what he had just seen.

"Who is next?" the woman asked. She looked into Nick's eyes, daring him to sit down.

Nick stepped back into the hallway.

Her gaze went to Matt.

Matt held up his hands and backed away. "That was uncomfortable," he whispered to Nick.

Nick bumped into Jay Christensen when he turned to go downstairs. "Sorry, Jay, I hope I didn't hurt you. How have you been?"

Jay was drunk. He was flying high and feeling no pain. "Hey dudes, how's it hanging? Rad party." His Teenage Mutant Ninja Turtle costume was twisted and wrinkled.

"What have you been up to?" Matt asked as he high-fived Jay.

"Man, I lost my new job and lookin' again. If you have any leads, let me know, man."

Nick nodded, knowing that Jay was out of control and would have a hard time finding another job in marketing or anywhere.

"Have you seen Ball-Breaker Brenda and her dog Skip? I'm sure; he's on a short leash tonight. Bad dog, bad dog." Jay's voice was very loud.

Matt guided him into the guest room and asked, "What happened?"

"BBB was supposed to be out of town visiting her Mom, but came home early and caught Skip in bed with Bill. Doggie style. Awkward." He made the sound of a whip cracking and laughed. "I'm sure his ass was grass after that. Her BBF banging her hubby, bad dog. Maybe in time she'll put him down."

Nick looked at Matt.

"Hey guys, you got any?" He held out his hand and sniffed.

"Sorry dude, fresh out," Nick said.

"Nick, I thought you used something to help you write all those stories." He tapped the side of his nose.

"That stuff stops my ideas, so I just rely on the gray cells." Nick shook his head slowly.

Jay turned to Matt. "How about you, Mr. Jock Strap? He's too good for that stuff, but I'm sure with you training those pro footballers, you've seen your share of the party favors the boys use."

"I try not to play with my work like that, Jay. Easiest way to get punted out of the field and end up with no field goal," Matt said.

"All right dudes, great seeing ya, well, get pucked up and party on. My glass is empty and I need a refill." He raised his red cup and staggered to the steps.

Nick reached out for him once as he almost tripped, but Jay caught the railing and slid down the railing.

"Poor guy," Matt said.

There was a loud thump, and Jay tumbled down the rest of the stairs.

Matt looked at Nick before running down to check on Jay.

Nick followed close behind, but Jay wasn't in the kitchen. He motioned to the basement, when they heard his voice say, "I'm fine, I'm fine, just get me another beer and I'd be better."

Nick turned to Matt. "You made me come to this, remember?"

"I know, I know," Matt apologized.

Nick gasped and pointed at the knife block on the kitchen counter.

"What?" Burdick asked, as he entered the kitchen.

"There's another knife missing."

There was a space were the smaller version of the butcher knife had been.

"How long ago was that?" Burdick stepped closer to the knives as if scanning for fingerprints. He saw the blood smudge and pointed at that.

"It was there before," Matt said.

"Why didn't you guys come and find me?" he demanded.

"Bill's partner, Mark came downstairs and looked like he was going into shock, so we got him a blanket and put him into bed."

"How long ago was that?" Burdick asked.

"We stopped by the fortune teller room and came down here. That's when we ran into you." Matt looked at the knife rack.

"How long?" Burdick pressed.

"Fifteen minutes?" Nick guessed.

Burdick rolled his eyes. "Have you overheard anything? Did you find out anything?"

Matt and Nick looked at each other. Matt nodded, and Nick started, "Bill hasn't been the most faithful of men. Mark suspected he was cheating on him."

Burdick wrote in his book.

Matt leaned forward. "Bill house-sat for Dan and Don, and they found a few things missing, some very expensive things."

"Such as?"

Dan entered the kitchen and bit his lower lip. "A digital camera, a laptop, a brand new Blu-Ray player, an expensive watch, and two rings, so far."

"Could they have been misplaced?" Burdick asked. "Have you filed a report?"

"I was supposed to ask him about that tonight, but I never had the chance to catch him alone." Dan shook his head.

"Someone did," Burdick said.

"Well, it wasn't me." Dan's vampire make-up was sweating off and his face flushed red underneath.

"Could Don have spoken with him?" Nick asked.

"He told me he hadn't seen him yet," Dan said. He pulled his vampire teeth out and shoved them into his pocket. "How soon will this be over?"

Burdick pursed his lips and closed his notebook. "We'll try to hurry, but we want to question everyone before they leave. How many did you invite to the party?"

"A lot," Dan said and went to find Don.

"Anyone else or anything else?" Burdick asked before he put the notebook away.

"Including gossip?" Nick asked.

"I'll take it all," Burdick opened his book.

"Seems like his co-worker Brenda may have caught Bill in bed with her husband, but that is all a rumor."

"Brenda and Skip Harrison, the teacher and her lawyer husband?"

"Yes."

"You run with a wild crowd." Burdick looked them. "Do you guys have anything to admit about Bill? He sure seems to have gotten around."

"He's a friend of a friend, but we don't know him that well. He teaches at the high school and has been dating Mark for five years." Nick looked at his partner; his look asked if he knew more.

Matt shook his head. "I hardly talked to Bill. He was always too busy to talk to me."

"Anything else? You guys have been most helpful." Burdick closed his notebook.

"Is this our interview, and we can go after this?" Nick asked.

Burdick smiled, but it didn't reach his eyes. "I have a lot more to ask, but it's just not your turn yet. I was looking for Mark."

"He's upstairs in the master bedroom." Nick pointed up.

Burdick nodded and ascended the steps.

"Do you feel like we're prime suspects?" Matt asked, as soon as Burdick was out of hearing range.

"I do," Nick agreed.

Sweat ran down Matt's forehead. "I could use some fresh air, how about you?"

"Sure, I'll go outside with you. I could use a change of scenery."

The kitchen door was open to the deck, so they stepped out that door instead of going into the basement to get out.

The smell of a cigarette greeted them as they started down the deck steps to the backyard.

Brenda and Skip huddled in a dark corner. Brenda puffed on a cigarette, making the tip glow red. Skip coughed and waved his hand in front of his face. She blew the smoke into his face.

The crime scene team had removed Bill from the hot tub, and it looked like he was in a body bag on a gurney. The ambulance crews pushed the gurney across the back yard to the sidewalk where Matt and Nick stood.

They stepped back onto the stairs to let them pass.

The small wheels bumped along the broken concrete walkway.

The other policemen packed up their gear and headed back into the house.

Matt and Nick waited for them to enter, before they moved over and joined Brenda and Skip.

"How awful," Brenda said, as she took another long drag on her cigarette.

"Did the police find anything else?" Nick asked.

210

"They have been searching everywhere and bagging a lot of things." Skip said. He looked down into his drink, watching the liquid swirl around the glass.

"I wonder what they were looking for," Nick said.

"I'm sure they were looking for something that fell off the killer's costume when he stabbed Bill."

Silence hung in the air, but Nick finally broke it, "How did you know Bill was stabbed?"

"That… that policeman asked if anyone saw someone with a butcher's knife…"

Skip touched her on the shoulder as he moved closer to her. "Maybe we should head inside, dear."

"Burdick never mentioned anything about a knife," Matt said.

Brenda dropped her cigarette and ground it out. Her hand disappeared inside the slit in her Ivana Trump dress. She swung around with a carving knife and lurched at Matt.

Nick pulled the vacuum hose out of his fly and grabbed onto both ends. He flipped it over his head and whipped it forward just as if he was going to jump rope. The black hose flew up and over his head and over Brenda.

Matt fell back, knocking Skip to the ground.

Skip struggled to free himself as Brenda's scream rose in the back yard.

The black plastic hose flipped over Brenda's head and caught her around her waist, slowing her progress toward Matt. She slashed wildly with the knife, blindly trying to hit anything in her way.

Nick pulled back with all of his might and caught her, almost lifting her off the ground.

Brenda spun around once she realized she was caught. The tension on the vacuum hose lessened, as she rushed at Nick, her arm raised above her head. The knife sliced downward with a flash.

"Nick!" Matt shouted.

Nick ran around Brenda, wrapping the hose around her, trying to catch her arm before she slashed him with the knife.

"Freeze," Burdick yelled, as he exited the patio door. His gun was drawn and ready. Slowly he stepped out of the patio door as the party goers watched in horror. "Brenda, stop!"

Skip tried to stop him, but Matt wrapped his arms around his skinny frame. "Don't make this any worse," he said into the lawyer's ear.

Skip stopped struggling and said, "Please, Brenda."

Brenda lashed out one more time.

Nick twisted the hose and caught her wrist.

Brenda paused as she looked at her husband and then at the gun. She slowly relaxed her fingers and let go of the knife. It fell to the patio and clattered on the bricks.

Burdick holstered his gun and reached behind him to get his handcuffs. He quickly secured them around Brenda's wrist.

She hung her head in shame.

Burdick looked over at Nick and Matt. "Thanks for all your help. Sorry for ruining the party." He turned his attention to his prisoner. "Brenda and Skip Harrison, you have the right to remain silent …"

"Next year, I'm not going to Dan and Don's party." Nick tossed the black hose and electric cord into the back seat of the car. His back flap had opened up, and it was a cool seat that he sat on. He jumped a little from the shock.

"I should've told you that the flap was open, but I was enjoying the view too much."

Nick glared at him.

"And I'll admit it now: we don't have to go to their Halloween party next year."

"Yeah. Thank God." Nick rubbed his eyes and stopped, slowly he turned to Matt. "And why is that?"

"Because I agreed we'd host next year." Matt cringed as he put the car into drive.

"There could be another Halloween murder. The night's not over, yet." Nick said as he reached into the backseat for his vacuum cleaner hose.

Lance Zarimba is an occupational therapist working in Minneapolis, MN. He lives in a haunted house that the man who invented Old Dutch potato chips built. It is only natural, since he grew up watching Dark Shadows *in the Upper Peninsula of Michigan, and he enjoys all of the classic monster movies. He also loves mysteries and collects books. His nephew, Matthew, helped him come up with the idea for* Oh No, My Best Friend is a Zombie, Oh No, Our Best Friend is a Vampire, *and* Oh No, My Brother is Frankenstein's Monster. *He has a mystery,* Vacation Therapy *and over 100 short stories. His short stories can be found in* Mayhem in the Midlands, *Pat Dennis'* Who Died in Here? 25 mystery stories of crimes and bathrooms, *Jay Hartman's* The Killer Wore Cranberry *and* Moon Shot: Murder and Mayhem on the Edge of Space, *Anne Frasier's* Deadly Treats, *and Jeani Rector's* Shadow Masters. *He can be reached at LanceZarimba@yahoo.com .*

www.ingramcontent.com/pod-product-compliance
Lightning Source LLC
Chambersburg PA
CBHW020946180626
46814CB00003B/951